SHADOW REALM

the beginning

Jody Brady

BRADYREALMS

Copyright © 2020 by Jody Brady. All Rights Reserved

All rights reserved. No part of this book may be reproduced in any form or by any electronic or mechanical means, including information storage and retrieval systems, without permission in writing from the author except in the case of brief quotations embodied in critical articles and reviews.

This book is a work of fiction. Names, characters, places, and incidents are a product of the author's imagination. Any resemblance to actual persons, living or dead, is entirely coincidental.

Cover pictures taken from the public domain at www.unsplash.com

Printed in the United States of America

First printing December 2020
Revised 2023
Bradyrealms
The Justice Project

Millers Creek, NC

ISBN 9798583720262

CHAPTER ONE

Death rides at night, even in the torrential rainfall outside. I lay in a darkened cave, cold and frightened, seeking shelter from the violent storm. As the storm grew stronger, vicious lightning strikes crashed against the cold, barren mountain peaks with increased intensity, illuminating the night with brilliant flashes of energy. Thunder reverberated across the canyon walls. Sheets of rain marched in successive waves, like an army assaulting the mountain.

The wind drove the water deeper within my shelter, forcing me back into the blackness that was my cavern of fear. But as ferocious as the storm was, it was not the primary cause of my distress, for out in the darkness, death rode. Sahat traveled across the land by night, searching for those trapped in this land of shadows.

Evil reigned supreme in this land over those like me who did not know the Light of the world. I lived in a land of shadows and illusions, filled with traps and hidden dangers, roving bands of outlaws, and the ever-present Sahat.

Links of death chained me. As time went by, new links appeared, making it ever more challenging to overcome and survive. The links directly resulted from an ancient curse that had befallen my race. There were times when I no longer wished to endure, but deep within me, in my dormant spirit, there was a will to fight, to escape this land and its terrors somehow, to find the Light the legends spoke of that could reverse the curse of death upon me. I had two chains across my shoulders that were a heavy burden, but I still survived.

I pulled a filthy blanket close around me. I watched as the rain slowed and the lightning faded to the west. As the noise of the falling rain receded, I faintly heard someone out in the darkness running through the trees below the cave entrance. The person scrambled along the rocky shore of the river below my hiding place, traveling closer as I waited in the dark shadows. As the person came close, the echo of a distant horn call pierced through the thick pine forest across the river like a nightmare. The Sahat had located their prey.

"Please! Someone help me!"

It was a woman's voice; she undoubtedly knew what the horn meant as I did. I heard her struggle through the thickets on the steep slope above the river. I imagined she was trying desperately to find a place of sanctuary, a place where the evil soldiers could not locate her. Several times, I heard her fall. Her cries for help were unanswered and grew in desperation and terror. Then, the horsemen rode closer along the rocky shoreline.

I lay frozen in my cave, frightened and ashamed. Finally, she climbed out of the rocky gorge through the laurel and into the open forest below the cave entrance.

Shadows floated in the darkness. I heard her desperation and fatigue as she collapsed not thirty feet from the entrance. I finally saw her as she crawled through the mud with her last bit of strength toward my hiding place. I could have helped her. I should have assisted her, but I did not. I lay under my filthy blanket against the cold, damp walls of the cave of my fears, hoping that the Sahat would not find me.

Outside, the rain suddenly ceased, and the wind blew harder, pushing the weakening clouds away and revealing openings where scattered stars blinked from behind the veil of darkness. The full moon appeared briefly, ducking in and out from behind the retreating clouds, intermittently illuminating the darkness outside the cave. Water ran everywhere, leftover from the recent downpour, dripping from hidden crevices in the rocky walls.

The woman collapsed face down in the mud within a few feet of the cave opening where I lay hidden. A mounted horseman appeared from the side of the cave door, and another pushed his way through the undergrowth from which the girl had struggled.

The two shrouded figures were armored soldiers dressed in black and riding black horses. They wore helmets, revealing only their piercing crimson eyes through tiny slits. Their eyes illuminated the darkness with an eerie red glow wherever they looked. Both carried a shield with a striking red dragon emblazoned on the front in their left hand and a double-edged axe in their right. Their horses glared with the same evil, piercing red eyes. The horses pranced and snorted as the two soldiers herded the woman into the open area at the cave entrance.

The woman's will was broken, her sobbing cries echoing against the cave walls.

With the creak of leather and rattling of chain mail, one of the soldiers dismounted and walked toward the woman on her knees in the mud, who had cowered away from him. The second Sahat remained on his horse, his piercing eyes scanning the surroundings.

He looked into the cave.

I lay perfectly still near the back of the cave. My heart raced with fear. I dared not move and give my position away. Twin beams of red light penetrated the darkness of the cave. He seemed to look directly at me. I hoped to appear as one of the rocks. I lay still as he continued to scan the cave and then looked directly at me again, although he did not seem to see me, and then I knew that he did see me! I was too frightened to move as he edged his great horse toward me and entered the cave, stopping just inside the opening.

"Ah, it appears we have another fugitive hiding in the cave," he remarked, and the other and the girl looked into the cave.

What was I to do? I had no place to run, no way of escape.

"Is his time come?" the first asked.

"No," answered the mounted one, "He is weak but still has life in him."

The soldier laughed scornfully, "He is no threat. He cowers in the darkness, too terrified to move, even as one of his own pleads for help." The soldier looked again at me, "You're pathetic. You know that?"

The mounted Sahat turned his horse away, dismissing me. He dismounted and walked over to the first soldier who stood over the woman. I lay there trembling, my heart pounding, sweat dripping from my face. I had to get rid of these chains! I had to find the people of the Light to save myself. I looked back at the horrible scene unfolding before me and then turned away. I could do nothing.

"Look what we have here," the first soldier said.

"A pretty young wench," the second commented as the other grabbed the girl by her long, matted hair and pulled her up until she stood between them.

"Please don't! Please don't," the girl cried, "Please give me another chance! Allow me more time. I am sure that my chains will be removed. I have a small bit of the Light."

She reached under her torn shirt and pulled out a tiny glimmer of light tied to a small leather thong, holding it up toward her assailants with both hands, pleading for mercy.

I could not believe what I was seeing! I had heard stories of the Light but never thought I would see it. Many said it had the power to remove the chains of death and free us from this dreadful place. Maybe there was hope for the girl after all. Both soldiers quickly looked away.

"No!" the first shouted, knocking it out of her hands.

The girl struggled desperately away from the soldier's grasp, reaching out for the Light as it fell down the steep ravine and into the river below and disappeared in the murky water.

She began to cry miserably then, knowing that all was lost. The second soldier angrily ripped the chain from her and then tore her dress away as well, revealing her naked body to the glow of the full moon that had finally commanded the night sky with the retreat of the stormy weather.

From across the river, another horse slowly walked along the trail through the thick underbrush underneath the giant hemlock and birch. The horse splashed through the water and picked its way closer to the cave, and then suddenly, the rider was in the opening at the cave entrance.

The rider dressed in black but, unlike the soldiers, did not appear to wear the chain mail and had no visible weapons. He wore a black leather shirt and trousers with high-riding boots. A hooded cape fastened around his neck by a large golden brooch, encrusted with rubies in the sign of the red dragon. When he dismounted, the two soldiers knelt before him, pulling the girl down with them as well.

"My lord," they both said in unison. The first continued as they stood up again, leaving the girl on her knees between them, "This is the girl who we have been searching for these past few days, the one said to have the Light, although what good it has done her, I do not know."

"Outstanding," their leader said surprisingly gently, "You have done well. Can you give me the Light, for it must be destroyed?"

"My lord," the second one lied, "the girl must have hidden it before we captured her. It is not with her now, as you can see."

He reached down, grabbed her hair, and yanked her back to her feet to show his master that she did not possess the Light. At first, the leader was angered, but then he calmed down.

"That is most unfortunate. I was hoping to ensure that whatever portion of the Light was taken could be destroyed so that no one would come upon it again, but no matter."

He turned to the girl as the two Sahat backed to their horses standing nearby. "Don't worry, my child. You are finally going to be free from this place."

He caressed her cheek and wiped the tears from her eyes, calming her down. I lay in my cave and watched in shock. What was going on?

"But the Light is gone," she whimpered. I never had a chance to understand its power, but it was a beautiful thing." She paused and began to cry softly again. "I have nothing now but emptiness," she whispered.

The man walked around her, suddenly stopped, and stared directly into the cave.

"There is another?" he asked.

One of the soldiers stepped forward, "Yes, my lord, a fugitive hides in the cave. He is a deplorable creature, pitiful. He could have helped the girl but did not."

I began to tremble again as the leader entered the cave and stopped inside the doorway. Outside, I could only see a shadow standing against the moon's light.

"Is it true, then, you could have helped and did not?" he asked into the darkness, but I did not answer him.   "Fugitive, you will answer me!" he commanded. "Show yourself so I can see the coward who would not help one of his kind."

I stood then, knowing that I could do nothing else, my heart pounding, and seeing me, the man laughed. "They were right. You are a pitiful creature. Tell me, boy, what is your name?"

"Jonathan," I managed to answer through my fear.

"Well, Jonathan, the coward of the cave, your time is not yet, but you will have to live the rest of your pathetic existence with the memory of what you have seen tonight."

I saw his face when he stepped back into the moon's light. His eyes were dark. He sported curly black hair and a thick mustache. A jagged scar ran down his cheek. He turned, dismissing me as the soldiers had done earlier, and returned to the girl.

He laughed again, and his dark eyes turned into the same fiery red of the dragon emblem, and the girl screamed. Fire shot forward from the darkness, covering her body, and she disappeared. Still, her terrified screams continued, fading into an abyss until only the river's gurgling and the rainwater dripping remained.

Without another word, the soldiers mounted the waiting horses and rode off into the night. With relief, I realized that I would not be taken on at least this night.

I lay in the darkness and began to cry. I had watched another person like me die and had done nothing to help her. With more clarity than ever, I knew that if I could not remove the chains that bound me, I would soon be destroyed, a person without hope.

It was early morning when the night was at its darkest and coldest; just before the hint of a new day began to glow far off against the eastern horizon, I slowly and cautiously crawled out from my hiding place. I walked through the brush to the river below, the previous night's images still fresh in my mind. A girl had died here, a person lost forever, and there was no evidence present of what had happened.

I was deeply troubled by what I had seen. Why had the Light not saved her? For my entire existence, I had heard that the Light of this world, if possessed by a person, would win that person freedom from the chains of death. I had seen a tiny sliver of the Light for the first time just as the soldiers had knocked it from her. It had fallen somewhere along the creek, and the best time to search for Light is the darkest time of the night. I searched for some time along the riverbank, each passing moment bringing me closer to the dawn of a new day. Although I did not understand why the Light had not helped the girl, the Light intrigued me. She thought the Light was her only hope, but it had done nothing.

I looked slowly along the rocky shoreline and reflected on what had happened. I lived in a land full of beauty and dread, life and death, a land of horror and loneliness, depression and pain. I was trapped by the chains of death around my shoulders. Somewhere, or so the stories told, was a place where all people were free and happy with no worries of the Sahat or of starvation, depression, loneliness, and suffering.

Searching near a rotting log, I saw a glimmer of Light shining out from the dark, murky water. The Light seemed to dance along the water as I reached down to pick it up by the leather band that had secured it around the waist of the girl. It was small, about the size of the end of my little finger, but very beautiful. The Light glowed with an intense heat, yet it did not burn my hands. It had no tangible substance that I could feel. When I first saw it lying in the water, I imagined it would feel like a small pebble or piece of metal, but I could not feel it.

The Light felt cool to the touch, but my flesh could not determine its substance. The Light encompassed everything that I had ever dreamed of. Love, peace, happiness, life; everything pure and good was bottled up in that tiny sliver of white light. Now I understood why I had heard so much about the Light and those who understood its power. This Light was the source of my freedom, but I had to find out how it should be used. I did not know how much time was left for me before my soul was lost forever, but whatever time I had, I would learn more about the Light.

I carefully placed the Light in my small pouch, attached to an old leather belt around my waist. The sun emerged with a great burst of bright orange, painting the lingering clouds with shades of pink and violet, and the darkness immediately disappeared. That is what happens every time darkness encounters light, I thought as I walked along the shoreline. For the first time in my entire existence, I had hope for the future.

CHAPTER TWO

My name is Jonathan. I have lived in this land my entire life. I am from the deep forest of Basar against the western mountains. The Forests of Basar are ancient stands of pine mixed with equally old stands of oak and hickory growing on the steep slopes and craggy hills above the plains of Apistia. Many fugitives live in the forest because of the broken terrain and hidden valleys that offer shelter and sanctuary from the Sahat. We live in caves, rocky outcrops, or large hollow trees, any place where shelter can be found. My diet is simple: fruits, nuts, and berries gathered from the forest mixed with certain roots and, if lucky, an occasional rabbit or small mammal that I manage to trap with one of my snares.

I have two complete chains around my shoulders, one being molded in the last year alone by my master, who does not know how I suffer or doesn't care. The chains hang over my left shoulder and then diagonally across my back and chest to my waist. They are a constant irritation, although I have worn them since childhood and have learned to deal with them the best that I can.

There was a time before the curse of mankind's rebellion when my race was free, but after man's weakness rebelled against the creator, the chains of death appeared. I am alone, but I have a feeling deep within that says I should not be, that I am incomplete.

I tried to dismiss what I had seen the previous night but could not. The image of the girl disappearing in the flame haunted my memories. I knew that if I could not turn the process around soon, I, too, would be overburdened by the chains, and the Sahat would overtake me. If I could not find the secret to the Light, I would suffer the fate of that poor, wretched girl. I will never forget the desperation in her eyes and the brokenness of her spirit.

But this morning, as the sun continued to rise in the eastern sky, I had renewed hope. Invariably, the morning brings hope because the terrors of another night are over.

The trail I followed led me along the edge of the great forest of Basar. The ridge was heavily timbered and barely passable except at a few trails. After crossing the gap, the trail descended to the opposite side of the hill until it finally reached the edge of the great savanna, where the trail forked. One trail proceeded along the forest's edge to a small fishing village called Soma. The main trail continued across the grassland toward the rising sun to a vast walled city called Hedone along the mighty Pleonexia River. It was to this city that I traveled.

I continued along the river trail, walking steadily through the day, always watching for trouble. I usually traveled alone, only occasionally with others. I carried a bit of food but decided it should be saved. Sooner or later, I would come across something along the trail, and in mid-afternoon, I did.

I walked to a bend in the river where the trail left the river for a short distance, climbing the slope to the top of a low ridge that followed the ridge top for several miles before it descended back down to the riverbank. Along this trail, the water flowed through a deep gorge with high canyon walls above both shores, preventing anyone from following the river along the shoreline. I spotted a small area covered with mountain blueberries along the ridge-top trail.

I collected as many berries as possible in my small knapsack and ate until I was full. It was a good lunch. The berries were ripe and very sweet. Forcing myself to leave the meadow, I continued on my way.

Occasionally, I saw a bird or two, and once, I thought I saw a bear way off through the forest. I hurried on down the trail, leaving him behind. I walked for the entire day, resting for only short periods. I needed to find a place of shelter before the sunset. The Sahat would reappear as soon as the sun melted away, and I did not want to get caught out in the open. I knew of a small cave along the trail used by such as me.

As the late afternoon sun descended, I realized it would be a close-run thing on whether I would make the cave before darkness embraced the day. I began to run along the trail.

The deep gorge below disappeared in the shadows of the night, but I knew I was getting closer. The trail dropped quickly back down to the river. Overhead, a few scattered stars revealed themselves in the fading light. The cave was coming into my view up ahead by the trail. I slowed to a walk, cautiously approaching the opening, which lay dark and empty before me. Another night of fitful sleep in a damp, cold cave, at least I had found shelter.

I lay under my torn blanket, huddled against the cave's back wall, trying to hold in as much heat under the blanket as possible. I needed sleep, but it was beginning to rain again outside, and my body shook with the damp chill. It was then that I remembered the Light.

Careful to keep the blanket over me, I reached into my pouch and brought out the tiny sliver of light that had become my hope. It shimmered a rich, translucent white. As I held the Light in my hands, it warmed, which was a great comfort, and soon I fell asleep.

I woke up suddenly in the early morning hours. I had slept better than on any night I could remember. The Light was still in my hand, the leather band wrapped around my wrist, still glowing and producing a small amount of heat that warmed my hands. I carefully placed the Light back into the pouch and rolled up my blanket.

I walked to the cave opening with the bedroll across my shoulder and peered outside. The rain had stopped. Traveling in the dark could be risky, but I had renewed hope.

The clouds had left in the night, revealing a vast, star-filled sky. The full moon shone brightly upon the rain-drenched land. Water dripped off the trees and shrubs, cascaded over rocky ledges, and plummeted through the stream channel to a small waterfall.

Slowly, the night gave way to morning. The moon and stars fought valiantly to keep control of the sky, but the sun was too intense for them. One by one, the stars disappeared until only the moon and a few brighter stars remained. They finally surrendered to the light as the sun's wondrous beauty rose above the trees, a golden ball of warmth and hope.

I had made it through another night.

I climbed a rocky trail that ascended through a cathedral of tall, stately pines. A thick bed of needles made walking easy, and my sore feet appreciated the softness. The pungent aroma of pine was thick, and I breathed deeply, the air refreshing and clean. Several of the dead trees harbored large woodland birds. An eagle circled above, gliding gracefully across the early morning sky.

The lower areas in the valleys below lay shrouded in mist, but even the fog slowly retreated from the sun's strengthening rays as the light penetrated the moisture in the morning air. The eagle circled over me in the sky above, among the few fiery red wisps of clouds. Smaller birds fluttered among the trees, and somewhere in the distance, a bobwhite called. A second bird answered closer among the pines along the trail ahead. The two continued calling each other, searching, drawing ever closer.

I continued through the open pine forest until the trail reached the mountain gap and descended to the other side.

There was a place just as the trail lowered under the crest of the hill where I saw faint glimpses of the great plains in the valley below. Although the plains below looked relatively close, it was late afternoon before I finally reached the forest's edge. Before I reached the great expanse of the plains of man's soul, the savanna of Apistia was barren of trees except at scattered springs and along the rivers that meandered across its expanse.

The gurgling sound of running water revealed a stream along the trail at the forest's edge. I refreshed my thirst from the cold, clear water and filled my canteen.

I left the trail and walked along the edge of the forest for close to a mile in search of a great oak tree where I knew shelter could be found. I had used it several times as I traveled to Hedone for the yearly census.

The tree was ancient, with a trunk over six feet and thick branches reaching eighty feet. At about twenty feet, the massive trunk forked into four limbs, each larger than any surrounding forest tree. These, in turn, branched upward into hundreds of smaller limbs covered with thick foliage. On one side of the trunk, facing the great savanna, a blackened fire scar looked out over the great expanse. Over the years, the scar had rotted away, creating a large hole at the tree's base that extended upward to the fork. The tree stood silently where it had always been, unchanged since my last visit almost a year before.

I took a small stick and poked around inside the opening. After satisfying myself that there was nothing in the hole, I reached into the opening and pulled on a small rope, and a rope ladder rolled down from the limbs above. I climbed up the ladder into the thick canopy among the four limbs to a small wooden structure with a floor, three walls, and a roof. The fourth side was covered with heavy burlap. I lay my pouch on the floor and climbed back down the ladder, reached into the fire scar, pulled on the rope again, and the ladder disappeared back up into the foliage.

Looking at the sun, I figured I only had about an hour of daylight left. I began searching for food nearby. After a while, I found a thicket of ripe blackberries along the forest's edge and picked what few were left. I also saw a gnarled old apple tree, hanging full of small apples, with the ground below covered. A swarm of flies and small, yellow bees fed on the apples on the ground, and the place smelled of the decay of rotting fruit. I filled the burlap sack with the apples, concentrating on the ones that were not ripe so that they would keep longer.

The fruit tasted sweet, but I needed meat, so finding a small game trail, I placed a couple of my snares, and with just a few minutes remaining of another day, I carefully made my way back to the tree. I climbed back into the small tree house, pulling the ladder behind me just as the sun melted away behind the barren plains. I ate blackberries and one apple. Hopefully, in the morning, my snares would yield a rabbit. I anticipated the wondrous aroma of a rabbit cooking over an open fire.

From where I sat, I peered through a slit in the burlap door and saw the plains below. Soon, the horsemen would tread heavily over me as I hid in the tree.

CHAPTER THREE

Crickets sang in the darkness, and the leaves rustled softly. I sat at the edge of my small shelter, my feet dangling over the edge. The past days' travel had worn me out and had lacerated my feet in several places. My leather shoes were shredded.

The chains chafed at my shoulder, and I worked to try to position them more comfortably. With increasing sadness, I noticed another link had been added to the second chain, making it the third this past month. I stared angrily at the chains as I pulled to no avail to remove them.

I stretched, causing a few of my neighbors to move about in the limbs above. Just before the sun disappeared, a flock of passenger pigeons had settled into my tree with a great flutter of activity. It took some time for the birds to settle back down. A few flapped and fluttered around me, upset at me for waking them from their peaceful sleep.

If only I could have peace. I lay down, knowing that even in my despair, my body needed rest. As before, the small Light offered warmth and encouragement after pulling it from the pouch.

I awakened suddenly in the early morning hours. I lay very still, my eyes open, yet it was so dark in the shelter that I could see nothing. I did not move and made no noise. Something had awakened me, but I did not know what. All was quiet, and then I heard a muffled sound below the tree. Listening carefully and allowing my eyes to adjust to the darkness, I located the opening in the door to my shelter. As I eased my body into a sitting position, I reached over and pulled up the burlap curtain slightly and peered out into the night, which was lighter because of the moon. I bent over just enough to see down to the tree's base.

Someone was under the tree! The pale moon gave me light enough to make out a shadowy figure. Someone dismounted from a horse, which meant it was a Sahat, for I had never seen anyone else with a horse outside the cities. The creak of leather and metal broke the stillness of the night as the rider walked a little distance from the horse.

The horse stomped and snorted impatiently, its red eyes glowing in the darkness. The soldier returned to his horse and led him to the edge of the forest to the small stream, where I heard the horse drinking from the water. A few minutes later, several others arrived, and they, too, dismounted, allowing their mounts to drink as well.

My heart beat hard as I sat in the dark, listening to the warriors' low voices talking among themselves and the crunch of the dry, dead leaves as they stretched their legs. After a few minutes, they mounted and trotted out into the open moonlight, where I saw five shadowy figures. They waited there facing the open prairie, their red eyes scanning the grassland with beams of scarlet light.

I heard more horses galloping out in the darkness a few minutes later.

And dogs! A fugitive's worst nightmare! Vicious, bloodthirsty hounds that feasted on stricken souls, tearing and maiming with jagged teeth. They had no power to kill, but their poison ate at the spirits of men. In this realm, death was often slow, agonizing, and hopeless.

The grassland lay before me, washed in the ghostly pale light of a full moon. Pale, red lights flashed, searching the rolling hills. I counted five people running, three close and two further back. The dogs howled lustfully somewhere out in the eerie landscape. At first, I did not see the hounds, and then the tall grass moved behind the last two fugitives, bending and growing closer.

A black shadow pounced from the tall grass, and then several more, and the last fugitive disappeared; a second later, another one, their terrified screams haunting. The barking ceased, replaced by the sickening growls as the horses galloped past the two that had fallen.

The soldiers below stirred, and one stood up in his stirrups. Pale light washed the horizon, and the soldiers beneath me spread out.

I glimpsed other horsemen following behind the dogs. I could have warned them, but what good would it do? Fear of the Sahat kept me from doing so. So, I watched as the three fugitives ran unexpectedly into the waiting soldiers, only yards away from the shelter of the thick forest.

They stopped, panting heavily from their wild run across the grasslands, looking for a way to escape. The horsemen crowded them as the dogs nipped at their legs, herding them together until they stood back-to-back before the dark soldiers.

I knew that it was the end when three other horsemen reigned in their mounts across from the ones under the tree, one of which was the dark leader that had vanquished the poor girl back at the cave. He had known that I was close then. Would he know now?

He walked his great horse within a few feet of the three fugitives and called the dogs back. The dogs immediately trotted off behind the horses and sat side by side.

One of the three fugitives was a woman. All three carried what appeared to be a sword and a small shield. How could this be? I thought. There was no place to obtain weapons such as those carried by the fugitives. Only the soldiers had weapons.

One soldier said, "You signed the contract. You and the other two belong to me now. We made a deal, and it is your time." He continued to circle the three as they stood still slowly. I watched, amazed, for I had never seen a confrontation like this before.

He continued, "Why do you wish to break the contract? The ruler of this realm promised you riches beyond your very dreams."

"Lies!" one of the fugitives interrupted, "Everything that was promised to us was lies. We have now found the truth."

"No!" the leader countered, "you have made a grave error in judgment. The Overlord of the Realm is the only way to life. If you do not abide by the contract and come with us, then you will be killed here, and your souls will be left to rot in this barren land. Your time has come. Your master is near death."

The leader backed his mount up to where the dogs sat in the grass, allowing the soldiers to close the circle around the three fugitives.

Once again, I was to witness the death by fire of three more of my kind. The darkness faded, giving way to the pale gray of morning. I could see the fugitives below more clearly. The soldiers looked the same as before, but the fugitives appeared different than I had ever witnessed. Although dressed in simple clothing, I could see no chains. They must have been hidden under their cloaks.

One of the fugitives stepped up, and from under his cloak, he pulled a sword, pointing it toward the leader, "You have lied to us long enough, Krino. We do not have to listen and obey any longer. We lived most of our lives in terror because of the contract forced upon us by our master, but now we realize that we have control of our destiny. We were enslaved, but now we are free!"

He pulled back his shirt, revealing a bare chest, "See, I have no chains. You have no rights to us now because we have been set free from the chains of this world."

"No! You will not talk of such things in my presence. You are not free, but live an illusion," the leader called Krino countered.

"We wish no reward from you," the woman interrupted, "for you offer no reward; you only offer death."

"Yes, I offer death only because you have broken the contract. Even with your pitiful weapons, the soldiers will kill you." Krino waved his hand, "Your time has come. You have chosen death. So be it."

"No, we have chosen life," one of the fugitives said, and they all brandished swords to defend themselves.

Krino spoke to his soldiers as he turned his horse to ride away, "Kill them and feed their bodies to the wolves of the plains of sin."

As one, the soldiers charged the three, and to my amazement, the fugitives did not run but stood their ground and fought back with shields and a double-edged sword. This defense surprised the soldiers, and they held back, their horses stomping impatiently.

The soldiers hesitated momentarily and then rode into the three, welding their great battle axes. The horsemen pushed the three apart, isolating them. The woman dodged and thrust her sword into the flanks of one horse, which screamed in pain, blood splashing across its shoulder and over the woman. She blocked a vicious blow with her shield, which knocked her to the ground under the feet of the wounded horse. She quickly stood up, only to be knocked down again by a second horseman who swung an axe against her with a massive strength that struck her shield and glanced off her shoulder. She continued to struggle, although weakened by the blow. One of the others stood close beside her and blocked another blow that would most likely have killed her.

The three swords glowed with a bright white light that illuminated the morning in contrast to the fiery red sparks of the axes. I only saw dark figures like shadows in the heavy dust with brilliant flashes of white and crimson lights as the weapons hit.

Metal against metal, horses snorted, men shouted, and great dust clouds rose from the earth, caused by the mighty horsemen.

I saw the woman again as another horseman pushed his mount against her, and I watched as a great red axe struck her. She fell to her knees then, dropping her sword. With the last bit of strength left within her, she flung the axe back at her assailant, but it clamored harmlessly to the ground. She reached for her fallen sword and fell face down into the dust.

The man who had first spoken so bravely before stood over the fallen woman and slashed his sword into the front legs of her assailant's horse. A sudden burst of red flame shot forward as the soldier fell from the wounded horse, but not before he had struck a mortal blow against the brave man, knocking him down next to the woman.

Only one fugitive stood now. The other two lay across each other at his feet.

The soldiers backed away. The lone fugitive stood over his fallen comrades, panting heavily. He held the shield in his left hand, badly damaged with a shattered arm, and his blood-stained sword in his right hand. The two others were not dead, as I had first thought. They moaned, and the man began to stir, turning to assist the woman who bled heavily from the wounds to her shoulder and chest. She would not be alive for long, I thought, and then they would be burned by fire, even after fighting so courageously.

One of the Sahat spoke, "You fight bravely."

"We have something to fight for," the standing fugitive answered.

"And what would that be?" the Sahat asked.

"Eternal life" was the answer.

"You have no life but what we allow. It is your time now. You will soon be enslaved forever," the Sahat countered scornfully.

The two on the ground helped each other to their knees, the man holding up the woman.

"Yes, we are fully aware that our time has come, but we are no longer afraid."

The man smiled as a bright light suddenly engulfed all three of them. The Sahat stared in disbelief, and one of the horses panicked, rearing up and throwing his rider to the ground. The other horses backed away as the riders shielded their eyes from the intense light. Although I had to shield my eyes, I continued to watch what was happening.

Instead of three figures in the light, there now appeared to be four!

Thinking my eyes were playing tricks on me, I squinted and blinked to clear my vision. Still, there they were: four beings together in that wild light. Suddenly, the light vanished, and the three fugitives were gone.

The soldiers stared at the empty ground before them, only the dead horse and soldier's body remaining. The rider thrown from his horse remounted as the sun emerged over the distant horizon. They did not say a word but turned their horses toward the open plain, leaving the body of their fallen comrade where he lay.

I stared at the bodies lying beneath my tree. Who were the three runaways who had dared fight against the Sahat? How did they get weapons? And most importantly, what had happened to them in the light? Who was the fourth figure in the white flames? There had been three, and suddenly, another man taller than the three appeared. I needed to take a closer look.

I frantically pulled at the rope ladder to force it down with nervous hands, but it would not budge. Looking out the open door into the foliage above, I noticed the ladder tangled in the limbs. I leaned outward to grasp it, but it was beyond my reach. Tentatively, I crawled out onto the limb and reached again. Suddenly, the limb gave way. I had crawled out too far and panicked. I lunged back for the safety of the door. It was too late. I knew I was going to fall, and I grasped wildly around me as I heard the sickening, final crack as the limb broke free. I fell over backward, hitting my head, and all was dark.

CHAPTER FOUR

I ran through a dark land. All around me, others were running as well. Behind me, great horses galloped. I felt the hot breath as the horses closed in behind me. I could not run fast enough to escape. The chains were too heavy, dragging the ground and pulling me down. One by one, screaming in pain, those around me engulfed in flames as the dark horsemen of death overtook them on the plains of sin. I stumbled and fell over into a darkened pit as a great black, death horse lunged over me. I had slipped into a pit of despair and realized no hope any longer existed.

Then I climbed a mountain, trying to reach safety at the summit above, but the hill was too steep, the path too narrow. All around me were people like me, climbing as I for the ridgeline above. Warriors stood beneath us in the valley below. We were out of reach of their weapons and were struggling desperately to escape as they began to climb toward us. Still, our chains weighed us down. Others around me, their chains of death too heavy to bear, fell to their bloody deaths on the rocky ledges below, but I kept climbing slowly. Just a few more feet, and I would make it to the top of the mountain. To my horror, I realized too late that soldiers were standing above me as well, and I was climbing into a trap. I reached the summit, just to be pushed off the other side of the ridge and fall into the valley of death below.

Through the haze, I glimpsed the sun. A slight breeze stirred, blowing the leaves across my face. I lay in the tall grass on my back under the heavy limb of the tree. The rope ladder now hung down, reaching just inches from the ground, dangling back and forth. I fought to regain full consciousness. What had happened to me? Looking around me, I saw the broken limb and remembered. I had fallen from the tree and must have passed out. Thankfully, the lingering memories of my dreams receded from where they had come from.

Sitting up caused a wave of nauseating pain through my head. I felt the back of my head and pulled back a hand covered in blood. My ankle hurt as well. The ankle was swollen and throbbing. I saw that it was severely sprained or, worse yet, maybe even broken. Glancing up at the sun, I knew that I had been unconscious for at least half of the day. I had lost precious time, and with my injury, there was no way that I could make my second shelter by nightfall.

With a wounded ankle, my chances of survival were slim. Also, if I made it to the city, I could not find work to support myself if I was crippled. My ankle was swollen, and I could not walk. I needed to see something in which to fashion a crutch. The cold waters of the stream were nearby, so I dragged myself through the grass toward the edge of the forest.

Along the edge of a small pine grove was a tangle of fallen trees killed by insects. I found a strong limb that could serve as a crude crutch here. Using the branch, I pulled myself upright, careful not to put any weight on the ankle. I haltingly made my way through the brush to the creek near the place of my snare. The creek meandered along the forest's edge for several hundred feet until it turned at an upheaval of broken rock and entered the dark understory of laurel.

I lowered my ankle into the cold water and was immediately rewarded as the cold numbed the pain. I knew that I was in trouble. This was no place to be crippled. I needed to allow some time to heal, but I did not know how much time.

I had to journey to the city for the required census. Each year, the fugitives in the land had to travel to Hedone along the river Pleonexia to be counted, and I had never missed one. It was said that great terror awaited those who missed the census, and I did not wish to suffer any more than I already did.

As I sat by the stream, my wounded ankle immersed in the frigid waters, a great anguish overcame me. How much more could I take in this land of no hope? As in my dreams, I indeed had fallen into a pit of despair. It would be so easy to end my life here by the stream, but deep inside of me, there was a small glimmer of hope. I had seen great mysteries over the past few days. Reaching my belt, I realized I had not been wearing the pouch that held the Light when I had fallen; it was still up in the tree house. It had given me comfort before. Maybe it would again.

With several sticks and a few strips of torn cloth from my shirt, I splinted my ankle and, taking the crutch, slowly made my way back to the tree. I checked the snares, finding one unlucky rabbit. I set the snare up again, and holding tightly to the rabbit, I hobbled back to the tree, exhausted by the time I reached its shade. I slumped down against the trunk, my head throbbing with pain. The nagging pain of an empty stomach reminded me that it had been a while since I had eaten. I wanted to build a fire and cook the rabbit, but I did not have the strength. The rabbit lay beside me.

Overhead, large, black birds circled, and with horror, I realized that they were vultures. Undoubtedly, they sensed my weakness and were waiting for me to die or grow so weak that I could not defend myself from their attack. One of the great beasts landed nearby. Finding a rock, I threw it at the bird. It jumped back but did not fly away. Another bird landed behind the first.

With the fear of being eaten alive, I frantically pulled myself up the ladder, trying to reach the safety of the tree house. The pain in my head blurred my vision and caused me to become sick. I desperately needed to reach the shelter, and with my last strength, I managed to grasp the ledge and pull myself back through the burlap door, where I passed out on the wooden floor.

I woke up in the middle of the night with a severe headache. Fighting through the blur of troubled sleep, I again had to think very carefully to understand what had happened to me fully. My bedroll and small pack lay piled against the back of the shelter. The door to the shelter was open. The rabbit lay in the opposite corner, as were my pouch and crutch. Peering out the door into the moonlit night, I saw no birds but heard them. They were roosting for the night in the tree, which meant that in the morning, they would be waiting for me. I closed the burlap door and fell back to sleep.

A great flurry of wings woke me in a panic. I quickly rose, and immediately, the sickening dizziness blurred my vision. My head and ankle both throbbed with pain, but with closer inspection, I noticed that the swelling in my ankle had subsided somewhat from what it had been the day before.

The great vultures had flown away, or so it seemed. I opened the door and looked outside, confirming the birds were gone. From my vantage point, I realized why they had appeared the day before. Below in the grass lay the grizzly remains of the Sahat and his horse, picked clean by the vultures.

I dragged the pouch to me and reached inside. I pulled out the tiny sliver of Light. The Light glowed in my hands, warm and comforting, which gave me some hope even though I did not understand anything about it. Legends had spoken that if we found the Light of this world, our chains of death would be removed, but I did not know how to do this. With renewed strength, I knew I would need to recover and make my way to the city. Maybe I could find the answers in the great city by the river Pleonexia.

I climbed down the tree carefully. Although my head and ankle still hurt, I felt better than the day before, although I was famished. I gathered wood and built a small fire, starting with a bit of flint and steel, a rich man's possession in this world.

I roasted the rabbit and added some apples; I ate better than in weeks. After finishing the meal, I returned to the stream, where I washed myself in the cold water and filled my canteen. During the night, the snare had captured another rabbit, larger than the one before, and my spirits rose.

For the next two days, I rested by the tree. My ankle mended nicely, and my strength returned. The snares had netted two more rabbits and a grouse, and I ate well. I also found wild potatoes and onions and simmered stew in the small pot I carried.

Once, on the second day, I watched hidden in the thick brush as a band of fugitives traveled by. Later that same night, another band of Sahat rode quickly past in the dark. The longer I stayed, the harder it would be for me to reach the city on time. Although my ankle was tender to the touch and I could not put any weight on it, if I were careful, I could walk.

The morning was unseasonably warm as I regretfully left my shelter. With a pack full of potatoes, onions, and fruit on my back, the pouch around my waist, and my walking stick to assist me, I set out again across the plains. No sooner than I began to leave, I spotted a shiny object in the tall grass next to the soldier's remains. A blood-stained knife lay in the matted grass. I quickly picked up the weapon and placed it in my pouch, for any weapon was a great treasure in this land. With a knife and a strong staff, I could fashion a spear and kill a larger game. With renewed hope, I once again started my journey.

As far as I could see, yellow grass swayed ever so slightly in the breeze, an endless rolling sea that stretched to the horizon. The heat waves shimmered along the horizon, earth and sky merging, almost melting together in a cloudless haze, trying to hide the faint outline of a distant mountain range that danced behind the veil. Although exhausted by the heat and endless walking, I continued to find shelter before nightfall.

Somewhere ahead, an oasis hid behind the rolling hills, a place of rest and shelter. Although water was there among the trees, most likely, people would be there as well, and I was apprehensive of meeting anyone out here on the plains. In the city, there were strict laws that even protected fugitives like me, but there were no laws out here.

Soon, I knew I should see the scattered trees around the water. I saw them through the haze, dancing upon the sun's heat waves across the yellow grass. The trees vanished and then reappeared. As I walked toward the dancing trees, they seemed to back away until they finally began to take shape. I could make out individual trees and branches; eventually, I saw the glimmering water of a small pond behind them.

But that was not all I saw, for around the water, interspersed among the ancient oaks, stood many tents of all sizes and colors. Had they been there before, or was I imagining this? Indeed, the bright red, blue, and orange tents would have stood out like a beacon against the yellow grass. I continued onward more slowly. I needed the water, but I was wary of strangers. I was apprehensive of what lay before me.

The year before, when I had stopped at this same oasis, there had only been a couple of weary travelers like me, but now there were over two dozen tents positioned among the shade of the trees. Most were small, but two were over a hundred feet long and were connected, the larger tent striped red and blue. I saw two armed men at the doorway to the large tent. They each wore a bronze breastplate and helmet and carried a lance. A sword was slung over their backs, and they had a bronze shield, the front painted red with a golden star.

I lay down in the tall grass just behind the crest of the ridge overlooking the valley. As badly as I needed the water, I did not want to be found by the people below me. Across the pond from the tents was a corral with perhaps thirty horses. I spotted two young men walking among them. I also saw men and women walking among the tents. Some were cooking over open fires. Others were washing clothes at the water's edge. Children played among the oaks, laughing.

Although the people appeared friendly, they were strangers, and strangers could be enemies. I needed water and rest but was worried about entering the camp. Maybe I could wait until night and sneak into the camp for water. The aroma from the cooking floated upward to me on the soft breeze, and I realized I was again hungry.

"Well. Look what we have here".

Startled, I quickly rolled over to face two bronze warriors, their lances pointing at my throat, their armored chests shining brightly against the sun. One of the two flipped up the visor on his helmet with the gloved hand, revealing blue eyes and a heavy blonde mustache.

"What is your name?" he demanded.

"Jonathan," I managed to stammer.

"What is your business here?" he asked.

"I am thirsty. I have traveled from the forest of Basar, and I still have far to go to reach Hedone for the census."

The second one removed his helmet, revealing thick, curly black hair, dark eyes, and a black mustache. They both remained vigilant, their spears trapping me to the ground. The dark one remarked to the first without taking his eyes from me, "It looks as if we have found a fugitive."

The blond asked, "Are you a fugitive, Jonathan of Basar?"

"Yes," I answered.

The dark-haired man reached out his hand to me. At first, I did not take the hand, untrusting of all strangers, but something in his eyes told me that everything would be all right. I grabbed the hand, and he pulled me up as the other handed me my stuff.

"You may stay with us tonight, wary fugitive, and do not worry of the Sahat. They are no threat to us. We are no longer fugitives but children of Halom. The Light has set us free."

The two guards assisted me down the slope to the grove of trees, and one pointed to the cooking fires, "Welcome Jonathan of Basar to our home."

I followed them into the encampment as several of the children gathered around to follow.

CHAPTER FIVE

The grand citadel had been carved out of the mesa countless ages before by untold creatures not of this world using unknown powers of darkness. Massive towers and battlements stood out against the face of the granite walls of the mesa that rose over a hundred feet above the valley floor. The only entrance to the citadel was colossal iron gates that faced the western sky, protected by an intricate series of round towers and ramparts that extended over a thousand feet out into the grasslands.

To reach the inner gate on the mesa's wall, a traveler had to first pass through three smaller gates after passing through a maze of corridors and dead ends. A hundred archers always guarded the maze from their positions along the battlements. A company of black knights guarded the inner gate, and sentries manned the outer ring of towers to warn of approaching visitors.

Above the inner gate carved out of the rock walls, a balcony commanded the approach where each morning, the rising sun would shine across the balcony as if originating from within. A blinding light would illuminate the entire keep below as the sun rose. The light would move slowly across the keep as the day progressed until the sun set across the grassland. Then, a brilliant flash of light would streak across the maze below and into the balcony as if the sun had vanished within. All who approached the castle marveled at this mystery.

Hundreds of other balconies and battlements dotted the face of the mountain. In a few places, stone stairways connected the different levels, and in three areas near the entrance, these steps reached the mountain's summit. Across the summit, dark forests guarded scattered wooden shelters interspersed with bright yellow grasslands. At times, great herds of black horses galloped along the edge of the cliff, thundering across the mesa, their mighty hooves beating into the rich soil, at times raising clouds of dust that caught the wind and drifted across the sky over the prairie below. This was the training ground of the Sahat.

Behind the balconies and battlements, the mountain extended a great catacomb of thousands of rooms and corridors, dark chambers, deadly prison cells, massive dining halls, meeting rooms, storehouses, and kitchens. The master of the castle alone knew the complex labyrinth entirely. His subjects only knew of the areas where they were required to be, where they lived and worked so that if the master wished, he could forever imprison them with no hope of escape.

A single dirt road crossed the barren valley floor from the west and entered the outside gate between the two round towers. Banners of crimson and gold lined the ramparts between the gates above the maze, their canvas fluttering in the soft breeze. From one of the towers at the first gate, three sentries scanned the horizon for any sign of life out across the Plains of Sin.

The largest of the three reflected on the group of Sahat, who had entered through the gate the day before as he climbed the ladder to his perch high above the outer gate. They had been four in number, riding tired mounts, themselves weakened by a hard night's travel. Two were visibly wounded, one very seriously by the look of him. The sentry had later heard that their leader had been killed and beheaded by a warrior in silver armor. Although the riders claimed victory because the warriors were no longer alive in the realm, all knew they had failed to capture their prey and destroy them by fire as required. The Light had been found again in the land, first among a group in the city of Hedone that had somehow escaped capture and then out on the plains near the forest, where the Light itself had been lost when the fugitive had been destroyed before she had embraced its power.

A small dust cloud appeared across the plains, shimmering in the morning heat.

"Riders approaching," one of the sentries announced.

The large watchman peered through his telescope for a closer look. A party of four knights traveled side by side along the road, their red plumes blowing in the wind. They rode white horses and wore full body armor, not the chain mail worn by the Sahat and knights of Kratos, but plated armor of polished bronze. A painted dark green lion was emblazoned on their breastplates and shields, the shields fastened to the front flanks of their horses against their saddles. Each wore a black cloak attached to a red brooch shaped like a star. Their helmets hid their faces from view.

"It appears to be Archon Planos's warriors," he told the watchman, who had backed away from the telescope to let his superior look.

"One of them may be Archon Planos, although it is always hard to be sure. Give the challenge and open the outer gate. I will go down and guide them through the maze," the captain ordered.

"Archers to ready!" the watchman called out, and suddenly, the walls above the maze between the gates swarmed with archers.

Another order was given, and a company of knights formed ranks behind the second gate. The gate defenders took their jobs very seriously. Failure to protect the gate from an assault meant death, and no matter who came, they always responded in the same manner.

The captain was pleased with his men's quick response as he climbed back to where his horse waited. He mounted and rode to the outside gate that slowly opened before him, one of the heavy gears whining loudly for a second. It needed servicing again, the captain thought. Above, the watchman challenged, "Stop and announce yourself."

A strong voice answered outside the opening gate: "I introduce to you Archon Planos, ruler over the hills of Halom."

The four horsemen stopped abreast of each other, all looking the same, their faces covered by their bronze helmets. The horses stomped impatiently as they waited for the gates to open. The captain rode his horse through the gate, pulling his mount to one side of the four horsemen. In his past encounters with this race, he had never learned to trust them, for they never appeared to be what they indeed were.

The one closest to the captain pointed to the archers above, "You show a sign of force to allies?" he asked.

"All who approach these gates receive the same reception. I am here to ensure that you are truly who you claim to be," the captain answered.

"Very well."

The four riders began to transform. The captain expected this and was not surprised, but he could hear disbelief gasps from the above walls. Two became more prominent, revealing curly black hair that grew from beneath their helmets. A third appeared to grow smaller until a woman sat on her horse before the captain, her armor shaped to conform to her feminine body. The woman pulled off her helmet, shaking loose, beautiful black hair that cascaded over her shoulders until its locks settled across her back, touching the horse's flanks. She had a lovely face, deep green eyes, and a devilish, lusty smile.

Only one did not change. This one stepped his horse forward, allowing the two larger warriors to move to either side of him. The woman trotted her horse up to the captain, positioning herself between him and the other three, her thigh touching his.

"Captain, my name is Zanah. This is Archon Planos, as you can now see. We have traveled far to meet in council with the Master. Will you kindly show us through the maze to meet him?"

The captain thought she was indeed a remarkable woman but also a deadly one. He backed away from her. He had never trusted her kind but knew that the Master put much faith in them. The captain had seen them transform into many beings, but only the Master knew their true form. He cleared his throat, addressing Archon Planos directly to avert his eyes from those of the woman.

"My Lord, the Master is meeting with others currently. I will lead you to your chambers and see that you are well-fed and rested from your journey. The council will meet in the morning. Please, follow me."

The captain turned and rode back through the gate. Zanah fell in beside him, again pushing herself so close that their thighs touched.

"Will you see I am well rested, Captain?" she asked seductively.

The captain would have responded in another time and place, but not here and not with this woman. Archon Planos and the others followed. Behind them, the gate began to close. Overhead, an order was given, and the archers vanished from sight as the interior gate began to open.

CHAPTER SIX

There were many more tents around the oasis than I had first seen. The guards escorted me through the village toward the largest tent in the middle of the encampment. The dark-haired one assisted me after noticing that I walked with a limp. My ankle was sore and swollen again. Children played among the trees, falling in behind us as we passed by, their wide eyes curious of the stranger in their midst. The small village was alive with people.

I had never seen people who appeared to be as happy as these. Even in the city where food and wealth were plentiful to those who lived there, I had not seen such as these people around me now. In the Forest of Basar, there were no places where fugitives gathered and lived. We were always alone, fighting to stay alive. There was no laughter, no happiness. Even the glorious beauty of the rugged mountains, dark forests, and flower-covered meadows did not overcome the continuing depression that plagued me as I traveled. But here, I saw joyful families for the first time. I saw people who were not afraid.

The two guards led me through the last row of tents to the larger one in the center as a gang of children followed. An armed guard stood by the door to the tent.

"We have a fugitive from the Forest of Basar who seeks safety. Is Captain Connelly in his quarters?" one of my escorts asked.

The guard answered that the captain was inside and turned to enter the door, but an older man emerged from behind the canvas before he could.

The two sentries bowed slightly. "Sir, this is Jonathan, a fugitive from the forest traveling to Hedone for the census. He's been injured and needs food and shelter."

Captain Connelly looked at me with large black eyes. Long red hair and a graying, reddish beard covered much of his face. Across the side of his left cheek, a scar began under his eye and disappeared beneath the beard. His spirit had been gravely wounded in the past. He was a distinguished man who was a natural leader of men, and I stood a little straighter in front of him as he glanced down at my injured leg, noticing my rudimentary crutch and simple belongings.

"You have hurt yourself, young man. I will grant your request," he smiled a warm, compassionate smile, "You will have the rest that you need, and no worries. You are not a fugitive here. You are safe now. Come with me. I will have my daughter prepare a place for you. You will sleep in my tent."

I entered the tent behind Captain Connelly and followed him into the outer room.

In the outer room, three curtained doors led to other sections. From the inside, I saw the wooden poles that formed the skeleton and supported the heavy fabric. Although sturdy enough to withstand the heaviest winds, the tents could be dismantled quickly and transported on the wagons parked next to the corral. It appeared to me that these people were nomads. I had heard of the race that constantly traveled across the Plains of Sin.

Over to one side of the room sat a small wooden desk and chair with an oil lamp, paper, ink, quill, and what appeared to be leather-bound books across the desktop. Books were something that I rarely saw, and I had never held one. I had heard tales that great mysteries lay hidden in the thick pages protected by the leather, but only if you could understand the writing. I could not read, so the mysteries remained locked up to me. I believed that only the evil one possessed this type of knowledge. They controlled this information, but it appeared that others could obtain such information as well.

"Jonathan, you wait here," the captain motioned for me to sit on the second chair across from the desk.

He walked over to the desk, closed one of the books, and placed it in a leather bag. "I have a business to attend to. We have gathered many goats, and I intend to sell them to a merchant traveling to Hedone in the morning. My daughter will ensure you eat and have a place to sleep for the night."

"Thank you, sir. I greatly appreciate your kindness," I answered as I sat down, placing my bedroll, pack, and crutch on the floor beside me.

With not a word more, he left me there to my thoughts. I was tired and hungry, and my ankle hurt from the past two travel days. My chains had torn the skin across my back and shoulder, and I was sweaty and dirty. Wrinkling my nose at my stench, I realized I most needed a bath.

Undoubtedly thinking the same thing, the captain entered the room again, "I have made arrangements for you to bathe, and your wounds will be treated as well."

Who would have thought just days before, when I first found the Light that had given me warmth and peace in a cold and harsh world, that I would be treated so kindly today? Indeed, the Light, whatever it was, offered hope.

By nature, I was curious; although tired, I could not help but wonder what lay hidden in the books on the desk. I leaned over to the desk and touched the first book. The smooth-grained leather felt warm to my fingertips as I caressed the cover. I looked around the room quickly, carefully flipping through the heavy pages. They were filled with markings that meant nothing to me. Pictures of a red star and a cross were on several pages, but I could not read all the symbols. In the city, I had seen people record their market transactions on parchment using ink and quill, but I never actually saw the figures they had written.

I longed to understand what those symbols told me and how the Light worked. Hopefully, this group of people could help me to understand. After all, they appeared not to wear the chains of death. I turned to the book's last page and saw a colored drawing of a red dragon standing on a cross, holding a star in his claws. The hideous dragon stood amid a great battlefield, surrounded by the mangled, bloodied bodies of warriors who all wore the symbol of the cross. The depiction was a horrid spectacle of savagery and murder in sharp contrast to everything peaceful in the camp around me. The red dragon resembled those I had seen earlier on the shields of the Sahat.

The more I looked at the picture, the greater it held on my psyche. I could not pull away from its savage beauty. The dragon came alive in my spirit, and although frightened by its wickedness, I could not look away. I continued to gaze deeper into the mystery of the picture before me. The dragon's green eyes shone like two emeralds, and then, as I watched, the monster slowly turned his head from the picture on the book's page to stare directly into my eyes. It pulled me deeper into the trance.

Suddenly, a surge of heat shot forward from the pouch on my belt that held the Light. Brilliant shafts of blue light shot forward, and the dragon receded into the page, its image blurred. It startled me so that I jumped back from the book, released from the trance of evil. I dropped the heavy book back on the desk as the blue light disappeared.

"I hate that picture. I wish my father would remove it from the book, but he keeps it there as a reminder of what can happen," a feminine voice said from behind, further breaking the spell with which the bloody image had bound me.

I turned and almost fell from my chair, startled and ashamed.

"I'm sorry. I should not have been so nosy," I stammered while regaining my balance.

Before me stood the most gorgeous woman I had ever seen; she was just a few inches over five feet tall. Long, raven black hair adorned her head, unruly tassels partially covering her dark green eyes. She had sun-kissed cheeks and bronzed skin. She wore a simple dress with a dark green sash around her thin waist that matched the color of her eyes. A sprinkling of small white flowers adorned her brow. She smelled of lavender and wildflowers, and suddenly, I was fully aware of my disheveled appearance and stench and promptly looked down to the floor. I had never seen such a beautiful creature in my life.

"That's okay," she spoke softly with the slow accent of the southern plains, "But my father does not allow anyone but his most trusted warriors to read from most of his books. Even I do not have his permission, but I confess, this book I have read." she patted the closed book with her finger and continued, "If you wish, I will ask my father if you may read from its pages as well."

Embarrassed, I answered, "That would not be necessary. I cannot understand the symbols. I have never seen the inside of a book."

"Oh, I'm sorry," her voice was kind and sympathetic. I can remember as a small child when I was in chains, but there is hope. You will see."

Her warm smile and bright eyes captured me, but then I blushed and glanced back down to the floor. I must have been a sight to her with my torn and filthy clothes and unwashed body.

"I am very sorry. I have not introduced myself. My name is Lillian, daughter of Captain Connelly," she said as she bowed gracefully.

"I am... I am Jonathan," I managed to answer.

She smiled again.

"My father has asked me to ensure you are fed and have a place to sleep. Can I help with your things?"

She noticed my makeshift crutch and my splinted ankle, "Oh my. You have been injured. Let me help."

Lillian reached for my crutch, but I would not allow her to assist me. I quickly grabbed the crutch with one hand and the burlap pack with the other. I had never been in the presence of such a wonderful creature as the girl standing before me, and I was deeply embarrassed by my appearance.

"I fell from a tree." I could think of nothing else to say.

She pulled the tent flap open for me and held my arm as we walked out together. She smelled of sweet rose blossoms in the spring.

I followed her through the exit and entered a large dining room with a long wooden table and high-back chairs for a dozen diners. Across the dining room, another door led out to a courtyard where several older women were busy cooking. To the right, a corridor led into the shadows, with rooms on both sides of the hallway. Lillian led me through the dining room, past the table, and into the courtyard, surrounded by the tent's canvas walls, a collection of many smaller tents connected.

In the far corner of the courtyard, a woman poured heated water from a pot into a large tub. After filling the tub, she pulled a dividing screen from the wall, stretched it in front of it, and walked away.

"You may take a bath here. I will call for you when our dinner is ready," Lillian advised.

She handed me clean clothes from a chest nearby, "These belonged to one of the herders, but he needs them no longer."

I looked at her questioningly. "He was lost upon the trail several weeks ago and never returned," she answered. They look to be your size."

I pulled the screen around me and disrobed. A drying towel of soft, warm cloth lay folded beside the tub. On top of the towel sat a large block of fragrant herbed soap, its edges sharp. It appeared fresh cut from a larger piece.

Although I had washed my tattered clothes and myself in the forest's cold mountain waters, I had never bathed in hot water with soap. I carefully entered the steamy water, which immediately began to relax my weary muscles, especially my ankle, which still hurt and was slightly swollen.

Taking the heavily scented soap, I cleansed the filth from my body and chains. The skin where the chains continually chafed was raw, sore, and, at times, bloody and infected. The soap soothed my wounds, and the more I washed, the more I realized that it had therapeutic properties because the scars disappeared, and the inflammation in my ankle lessened.

Beyond the screen, the women around the cooking fire whispered among themselves. The meal appeared complete because I heard them carrying the food into the adjacent dining room, leaving me alone in the courtyard.

Regretfully, I rushed with my bath. I was famished, and the water quickly turned black as I washed days of grime from me. I stepped out of the tub, clean and rejuvenated. I had never felt so good. I was amazed to see my wounds around the chains were gone. I dressed hurriedly in the outfit that Lillian had given me, which consisted of a loose pair of gray pants and a white shirt with a tie string halfway down the front, both made of cotton, and a new pair of sandals.

After dressing, I walked out from the bathing area to where I had placed my belongings and noticed with alarm that they had vanished. I frantically searched the now-empty courtyard for the pouch, bedroll, and pack, but they were nowhere to be found.

"You must be hungry," Lillian interrupted my search.

"Yes, I am, but first, I must locate my pack. I thought I left it here in the courtyard."

"I took them to your room," she answered. "Let me show you, and then we'll eat. "

My room was one of the first in the corridor. My belongings lay on the floor next to the door. Leaving everything else, I grabbed the pouch and rope belt. Then I secured the pouch around my waist with the belt and tucked in my new shirt. Satisfied that the Light was secure inside, I returned to the dining room full of people, including Captain Connelly, Lillian, and others I had not seen before.

A variety of food covered the table. A large roast dominated the center, surrounded by potatoes, onions, cheese, loaves of baked bread, and a wide variety of fruit.

As the others sat, I stood there staring at the food. Lillian looked up at me and smiled, motioning to the empty seat beside her. I limped over to the chair and sat next to the girl.

"Good, good young man," the captain spoke, "A bath has done you well. Now enjoy our rich bounty, and afterward, we will talk of your travels and the things that you have seen."

"Thank you, Captain. I owe you my life," I said sincerely and began to eat.

CHAPTER SEVEN

Deep within the darkened catacombs, underneath the vast cliff bastion of the dragon, was a grand banquet hall with high stone walls covered with tapestries showing scenes of historic battles of ages gone by. Each picture represented the personal battles of thousands of souls who had been defeated by the forces of the castle's master. Each day, an unseen hand created new depictions as fugitives were taken from the realm by fire. A series of torches illuminated the great hall, casting flickering shadows as the warriors began to enter the room.

A large oak table dominated the center of the room, surrounded by high-backed chairs, each adorned with a multicolored shield. The Archons, or rulers of the realm, sat around the table as their servants stood behind them along the wall. The castle servants, all fugitives promised freedom from their chains, placed trays of food and drink in front of each of the warriors and stood nervously close by. They were vigilant for any sign that their services were needed, knowing that a lashing would be their reward if they were not prompt.

The warriors consumed large quantities of food and wine with great lust for more, shouting and laughing as they did so as the servants busily ran from one to another. The kitchen staff brought more food to the buffets along one wall, and plates were refilled as the warriors continued eating.

At the appointed time, the master of the keep, who sat at the head of the table opposite the door to the kitchen, stood up, and the others abruptly became quiet. On cue, the servants and the warrior's heralds left the room and closed the door behind them.

All stared at the Master, who stood silently at the head of the table, nursing his goblet of wine, pondering the previous discussions before the meal.

"Time is short," he started, "We must step up our patrols. More fugitives will travel to the census, and many can no longer run."

Archon Krino stood up then. The Council was the only time anyone could disagree with the Master without fear, and even at this table, few held the Master's trust enough to do so. "Master, some of the fugitives no longer run. A few weapons have been among them, and I lost a warrior several days ago."

"Weapons in the hands of fugitives? How do they fight with their chains?" asked Archon Sarkinos, Ruler of Hedone, a tall, blond warrior with blue eyes.

He was slender and handsome face that stood out from the other warriors. He dressed like a dandy with multicolored robes of fine silk, gold earrings, and necklaces and wore no armor. He armed himself only with a knife, distasteful of more barbarian weapons that threatened his sense of dress and style. His most effective weapon was the lust for the pleasures of life that he gave freely to all who called Hedone their home.

"The Sahat caught up to a band of them near the great forest, which had no chains and were armed with the swords of the Bene Elohim. They fought but had not been trained to use their weapons properly," answered Krino.

"Swords of the Light!" shouted Athemitos of Soma, a bearded warrior who specialized in pursuing the young, taking great satisfaction in the blood of the innocent, especially the unborn, "This cannot be. There has been no Bene Elohim in this realm for years."

"Apparently, my bearded friend," Archon Sarkinos spoke softly, as was his custom, "They must be present if their weapons have been found."

"What Archon Krino has said is true," countered the Master, "Several fugitives have been found with small pieces of the Light, but they were destroyed before they could use its power. That means that somewhere hiding in the realm is either a Bene Elohim or a fugitive that is an Apostolos Or."

The Master referred to a person who could spread the Light through the realm. The title literally meant one sent forth to give the Light.

"The last Apostolos Or left the realm for Soteria years ago when their citadel was captured. His family still lives in Hedone, but they are no harm. They are weak and powerless. They enjoy the riches too much to follow the Light as they did before," Archon Sarkinos added.

"Sarkinos, if that is true, then there must be a Bene Elohim somewhere that has exposed the Light to the fugitives searching for another leader," the Master responded.

"What are we to do?" asked Krino, "If the fugitives are armed with the swords of Light, they will soon learn to fight. As they gain strength, more of the Bene Elohim will come."

"You are a coward, Krino!" Athemitos shouted across the table. "If we strike at the young, they will never learn to fight. You have lost your desire for the blood of the innocent."

Krino drew his sword, "I am no coward, Athemitos, simply because I do not prey on the young like you. Have you ever faced the devoted that were no longer fugitives? They are brave warriors. Have you crossed blades with the Saterians or the Bene Elohim? Well, I have and have the mark to prove it." He pulled the hair from his face to show the scar across his cheek. "If the Bene Elohim are among us again and the fugitives are armed, they will be a formidable enemy, especially if they have a leader among them."

"Sit down, Krino," the Master ordered, "Sheath your weapon. You too, Athemitos. You both have your assignments. Athemitos is to destroy the young, and Krino is to battle the devoted if they appear. Both of you have done well. Athemitos, if you destroy the young, Krino and the others will have less to fight."

The Master walked over to the corner table and refilled his golden goblet.

"The blood of the lost," he said and drank. "For years, we have ruled this land, capturing many souls for the Overlord. We have turned many others into our servants. Although we were victorious in our last battle with the Saterians, our forces were greatly weakened. Since then, we have been able to separate and destroy rebellious factions because of their inability to join in union with each other," he laughed, "In fact, there were times when the fugitives fought each other so much that we had little to do. But one thing is clear. If the fugitives are free of their chains and armed, they will be a force to reckon with. If they become unified, their strength increases because the Bene Elohim will begin appearing in ever-greater numbers. If the Light appears and the Apostolos Or is found, we will be hard-pressed to hold this realm."

The Master slammed both fists on the table and leaned over the goblet.

"This is unacceptable. We will not allow them, cannot allow them to become unified!"

"How will we stop them?" Archon Krino asked, "You know that we cannot fight the Light if the fugitives are united if they understand and believe the power that the Light gives them. We have seen the presence of the Light these past few weeks. The Sahat have gone to intercept those who have been given the Light. So far, we have been lucky. Those the Sahat have caught with the Light did not know its true power and continued to believe that they were still bound in the chains of death."

"The key to keeping them from believing and unifying is confusion. We will continue earnestly seeking the fugitives. We will continue our reign of fear over them but deceive them into accepting a counterfeit. Then, even though the Light may appear in increasing numbers, they will not be able to utilize its power, which is why Archon Planos has been summoned," the Master said and sat down.

All eyes turned to Planos and Zanah, who sat next to him and had remained silent throughout the conversation.

"And what do you propose?" Archon Krino asked.

Archon Planos spoke very little, using Zanah as his spokeswoman. She stood, as was the custom. Zanah relished this position because she was keenly aware of the reaction her presence had on the men around her. After all, in her present form, she was a gorgeous woman.

"Gentlemen, as the Master has said, the fugitives are weak if they do not understand that when the Light appears, they have power over their master. We must continue to confuse them, break down any unification, and destroy anyone capable of leadership. In addition to what you are doing in pursuing the lost ones and destroying the young, we must lead astray those who have acquired the Light."

She began to walk around the room, stopping behind each of the men and placing her hands on their shoulders. Her presence was intoxicating, as she well knew; therefore, she was determined to use her seduction to her advantage, even here. She continued as she slowly walked around each of the warriors.

"We will deceive by producing a counterfeit that promises freedom, but in the end only leads to death. If the Bene Elohim appear, we will discredit them in the eyes of our subjects, thus reducing their power and ability to assist any fugitive that may have the Light."

She stopped behind Athemitos, rubbing her slender fingers through his curly hair. Leaning over his shoulder, she brushed her cheek against his beard while looking at each of the others with her mesmerizing green eyes.

"We will lead astray by enticements and seduction," she spoke softly and kissed Athemitos lightly.

She then stepped behind the tall Archon Sarkinos, ruler over Hedone with its greed and mercilessness, and massaged his shoulders, playing with one of his earrings of gold, "We will take those who have found the Light and through charms and enticements, force them to trade the Light for the lust of the flesh. Then, my brave and beautiful, mighty, and strong warriors of the realm, the resistance will crumble before it ever starts, and the Bene Elohim will not arrive in numbers enough to make a difference."

With these words, the seductress returned to her seat and sat down. Her provocative voice and presence had taken the warriors, except for the Master.

Archon Planos spoke, breaking the trance after Zanah had sat back down beside him.

"It is a great honor to assist these great warriors in ridding this realm of the Light once and for all,"

"To victory!" shouted the Master.

"To victory!' shouted all the warriors.

And with these words, the Council ended for the evening to be resumed the next day, as more plans would be made.

CHAPTER EIGHT

A narrow trail twisted up the weathered slopes of the mountain toward a distant pinnacle shrouded in the fog of ignorance and disbelief. At first, the trail meandered through the shadowy pines along the lower ledges before ascending into a barren, treeless landscape of broken rock and narrow ledges. At this point, the trail crisscrossed the rocky incline, weaving its way through a tortured landscape, only wide enough for those who traveled the trace to toil up the slopes in a single file. There were a few places where the trail widened or was sheltered from the incredible vastness of open space below by a ledge of broken granite, but for most of its length, there was nothing below the trail but an empty void into the shadowed valley.

Along the trail, fugitives labored upward, forced on by those pressing from below in the forest. I stood at a distance, staring wonderfully at the towering mountain, the peaks reaching into the cloak of the heavy fog with broken fingers of stone. The people pushed forever upward along the twisting, treacherous trail, carrying their belongings on their backs, fugitives searching for a new home, the hopeless searching for hope.

To my dismay, I saw many plummet from the trail along the upper slopes, descending into the darkness with agonizing screams of pain. At times, they fell individually, and at other times, the ones above fell into groups below, sending numerous fugitives to their deaths all at once. None on the lower slopes seemed to perceive the death above and kept climbing even though they could not see above them. Sometimes, the stronger would help the weak, but this was rare. Most of the fugitives were only concerned with their trail and ascent, and they did not see the carnage around them until it was too late.

I screamed to them to warn them but to no avail. And suddenly, I stood on the trail myself, trapped on the ledge high on the mountain just below the thick fog that hid the upper peaks from view. I tried to turn to go back down the hill to the shelter within the pine forest on the lower shoulders of the range, but the fugitives climbing below me pressed me forward. The trail was so narrow that I could barely place one foot before the other.

Below, a tumbling of broken rock slanted down the slope for fifty feet before ending at the great void. The weight of my chains was a great encumbrance as I climbed upward. My hands were raw and bloody from the broken rock. As I climbed, I left a trail of blood mixed in with the dried blood left on the stones from those that had gone up before me. I grew weaker as the sun's heat bore down upon me. All around me, fugitives like me walked steadily upward, caught in this dreadful trap of death and affliction.

Why was I on the trail? Where were we heading? " To the summit, " someone said. " To freedom above, " someone else suggested. But no one knew for sure. We could all see those above us climbing closer to the rocky precipice masked in the fog. If they could make it, so could we. With renewed hope and strength, I pushed onward.

Suddenly, a child on the trail above lost her footing and fell among the rocky ledges. For a moment, she hung desperately to the ledge before slipping into the void of shadows as I watched, helpless to save her. Another time, a heavy, bearded man lost his balance and fell back down the trail toward me. I stepped back against the jagged rocks, fearful that the man would push me from the trail. He grabbed those below to try to stop his fall, pushing them off the trail until he finally disappeared over the cliff.

We kept pushing upward toward the summit. The trail became even more treacherous as we entered the fog, but we were within sight of the summit and gained hope. Others ahead of us climbed the last section of the trail to the ridge top. I could see them now as they reached the summit at last, and several turned to help those below before disappearing over the ridgeline. I urgently climbed the previous section and finally made it to the summit only to find, to my horror, that I had climbed the mountain only to take a step to supposed safety across the ridge to fall to my death into the great blackness of hopelessness.

I awakened abruptly, my heart pounding, sweaty and frightened. Disoriented, I sat up in my bed in the room's darkness. Where was I? And then, with relief, I knew it had only been a dream. I was safe in my room in the tent of the family of Captain Connelly among friends. Even in this place of comfort and safety, my nightmares attacked me while I slept. The nightmares were more frequent now, frightening, real.

A gentle breeze stirred faintly through the room from the open window near the bed; all was quiet except for the willows' rustling in the breeze. Outside, a sliver of the moon and stars filled the dark sky. I could no longer sleep. I was afraid to sleep for fear that the nightmares would return to haunt me.

I stood up and walked over to a small table from the window in the opposite corner of the room, where an assortment of fruit lay in a wooden bowl. Taking a handful of fresh strawberries, I walked back over to the window and peered outside to look at the beautiful night sky and reflect on what had happened to me.

A few days before, I had been crippled and starving, all alone on an endless prairie without hope. And now, after meeting these people, I am safe and beginning to heal. Captain Connelly had offered me a place of refuge until I was well enough to continue my journey to Hedone. I shuddered at the thought of leaving this place to travel again across the barren plains to the city, but I knew that I could only stay a few weeks before I would have to leave.

And then there was the girl Lillian, the most beautiful creature I had ever seen with her long hair and brilliant green eyes.

I had met others at the dinner table, including Lillian's older brother Jason and two cousins, Thaddeus and Enoch, all three powerfully built men who were somewhat older than I. The captain's older sister, whom everyone called Aunt Ruthy, had sat beside me, insisting that I eat even after eating far more than my stomach was used to. She was a jolly, short, round lady who loved to talk. She also had two daughters living with the family, Christie and Catherine, who were dark-headed teenage twins. The girls were as shy as their mother was talkative.

While eating, I asked Lillian where her mother, as well as Ruth's husband, were and learned that they had both been killed many years before. I regretted asking such a question that had brought back bad memories and caused even Aunt Ruthy to become melancholy for a time. I was embarrassed and ashamed of my forwardness, and all was quiet momentarily. Captain Connelly broke the awkwardness by proposing a dinner-ending toast to "Those who have gone before," as he stated it, and the dinner was over.

As I stood looking out the window into the great expanse of time and space, I wondered again how I could be free of my chains and live a life that those in this small band of nomads lived. These people had found a way but had not shared anything with me so far. They had only said that the Sahat did not bother them, and they were free of their chains.

Tomorrow, I would ask. I needed to know. All my life, in the Forest of Basar, I had heard stories of the power of the Light that would take away our chains of death and free us from this bondage so that our spirits would be free and we would no longer be slaves to our masters in the other realm. I had a portion of the Light now, but how to use it, I did not know. Maybe it was not the Light spoken of, but only a stone or crystal.

In the darkness, I found my pouch, carefully removed the Light from its hiding place, and placed it in my open hand. How could this free me of my chains and break the bondage of my spirit? It had not saved the girl, even though she placed great hope in it. It had not destroyed the Sahat, although they appeared frightened in its presence. How could it help me more than just providing warmth and a glimmer of light in a darkened, cold cavern?

I rolled the Light around in my hand, amazed that it had no substance that I could feel, even though I could move it with my finger, and it gave off a soothing warmth to the skin. It began to grow in warmth and even in size as I investigated its image, even though when I pulled it from the pouch, it appeared smaller than when I had first found it. As I gazed into its wonder, the larger it became, the more mesmerized I was by its translucent white-blue light, which glowed like a small candle in an otherwise darkened realm of shadows.

Approaching horses broke the spell, and with chronic fear, I fully expected to see the Sahat entering the camp. I quickly placed the Light back into the pouch. Although the room became dark once more, there was lingering warmth around me from its presence.

Peering out the window toward the corral, I was greatly relieved to see that there was no Sahat, only three hooded riders who dismounted with the assistance of the attendants who guarded the inner camp throughout the night. One of the attendants escorted the shadowy figures to a large striped tent near the captain's outer office and immediately returned to his station near the corral.

There was a lot that I wished to know about these people and this place, but now I finished the remaining strawberries and returned to my bed. The Light had soothed my mind, and I was again sleepy, no longer fearing the nightmare that had awakened me. The last I heard before drifting back to sleep were the sounds of other riders entering the camp and whispered conversations near my window.

"Is he the one?"

"Possibly, but we are not sure. In any event, we shall initiate the ceremony of the chains, and it will no longer matter."

"Very good; we'll leave in the morning then."

Was that the captain's voice? In the fog of sleep, I could not tell.

CHAPTER NINE

Thick, long black hair rested across the shoulders of the tall warrior, a small portion of it braided, as was the custom with his race called the Bene Elohim. He wore loose-fitting, soft leather pants and a cotton shirt overlaid with braided chain mail. Around his waist, he wore a wide black belt with a silver buckle that held a pair of knives in leather sheaths covered with embroidered beadwork. He wore black riding boots and hardened leather leggings that protected his knees and lower legs. A purple overcoat attached around his neck by a silver brooch emblazoned with eagle wings draped over his shoulders. Under the cloak, a double-edged short sword was connected to a sling across his chest, only the pearl handle above his left shoulder.

The warrior stood silently, gazing intently across the prairie, while his horse stood just behind him. The horse walked up closer and nudged him playfully. The warrior patted his long-time companion as both continued to look over the land of shadows. The horse was a broad-shouldered, black stallion, solid and proud, although tired from the last few days of travel. He bore a leather saddle with a bed roll, canteens, and saddlebags across his back. A shield was fastened to the front left of the saddle, covering her flank, and a broadsword lay across the right, along with a crossbow and quiver of arrows.

Together, rider and horse viewed a territory that no one had seen of their clan for many years, where the enemy reigned supreme, a place of darkened shadows and a land of illusions. Although a remnant still existed in the land, thousands of fugitives roamed the realm, lost without hope unless someone could lead them to the truth, which was why the warrior had been summoned to the realm weeks before.

It was time to invade the Shadow Realm with the True Light.

Although a formidable adversary with countless victories behind him, the warrior was only one. He would have to stay hidden until the faithful mobilized, working clandestinely at first. The faithful were the true power behind his strength; they were too few and scattered now. They must first be unified.

He knew that the Sahat would soon appear with the coming of night, and although he did not fear them, his orders were to remain unseen until the appointed time. There was a leader to be found in the realm, a leader that would take the role of the Apostolos Or, one that would usher in a new invasion of the Spirit of the Light in a darkened world of eternal shadows.

The horse nuzzled the man, pushing him back into the shelter of the trees.

"Yes, my friend, we are at war again. Let's find a place to rest our weary bodies. We will begin our search tomorrow, but tonight, we will sleep."

The warrior led his horse deeper into the forest, following a stream until he found a large cave to offer shelter for him and his horse. Leading the horse into the cave, he stripped off the gear and brushed his mount thoroughly, soothing his tired muscles. The warrior climbed down the trail to a small woodland opening filled with lush grass. Taking his sword, he cut the grass until he had gathered enough and carried it back to the cave, laying it on the cave floor.

"Here you go, boy. You have ridden hard these past few days. Rest yourself and eat well."

The horse nodded approvingly and began to eat as the warrior went out to collect wood for a small fire.

Tonight, he would have a warm fire and would eat well. Earlier, he had killed a rabbit and began to prepare it to roast over the fire. Outside, the wind blew, stirring the fire and whispering a ghostly moan through the cave.

The warrior looked up and around him, noticing that his horse had stopped eating and was also listening, lifting his head slightly to smell the breeze. Outside the cave was complete darkness, the only light being the small fire that cast shadows against the cave walls and illuminated the entranceway slightly. The cave continued to moan as the wind pushed its life through the tunneled rock, opening behind the main outer room of the cavern as if the stones themselves were alive.

The warrior covered the cave's entrance to block the wind and hide his fire. The moaning stopped. As he finished cooking the rabbit, the horse lowered his head to continue eating the grass. By the time he had eaten, his companion had fallen asleep, full of the lush grass. Smiling, the warrior wondered how the horse could doze on three legs. He unrolled his bedroll and lay down with his saddle as a pillow.

Outside in the darkness, he thought he heard a faint scream. Somewhere, far off in the night, another fugitive was lost forever. He lay his head down with great sorrow, knowing all could be lost if his mission failed.

CHAPTER TEN

The sun woke me up, its warm caress brushing my face. I had slept better than I ever remembered, even after having the dream of the night before. The pungent aroma of bacon cooking over an open fire drifted through the open window. Outside the tent walls, the nomads bustled about; dogs barked, and children played. There appeared to be a significant amount of work outside, and I was curious to see what was happening.

I stood up, stretched, and shuffled with the help of the crutch over to the washbasin. My ankle was stiff from the night of inactivity, and I gingerly flexed it as I leaned against the washbasin. Whatever was in the soap I had used the first day to bathe was continuing to heal my leg and the many cuts and abrasions caused by the chains. I poured water into the basin, splashed the cold water across my face, washed myself, and dressed. Taking my trusty crutch, I limped over to the door.

Lillian met me just outside the door to my room.

"Good morning, Jonathan; I trust you slept well?" she asked.

"Yes, I did. Tell me, what is all the commotion outside?"

"I was coming to wake you. The council has met, and we are moving the encampment to another location earlier than expected. You need to gather your things and follow me."

I only had my pouch, pack, and bedroll, so it didn't take long to gather my belongings, and I followed her through the maze of corridors to the main exit from the tents.

With excellent efficiency, the nomads broke down their homes and packed everything in the wagons parked nearby, each wagon pulled by a team of four horses. They were beginning to take down the string of tents belonging to the captain, so we walked a distance away, and Lillian showed me where to stow away my gear. I kept the pouch with me.

"You must be hungry." Lillian led me to a nearby willow tree where her aunt cleaned up from the breakfast. She placed a plate full of bacon, eggs, and a mug of hot coffee in my hands and ordered me to eat by the tree. I offered to assist with the packing, but both women refused, saying that I was a guest and was in no shape to help with my broken ankle. No sooner than I finished my breakfast, Aunt Ruthy hurried up and took the dishes from me; she hurriedly washed them in a basin of water next to the fire and packed them away, complaining about moving in such a hurry.

The entire camp was loaded up in no time, and I found myself sitting on one of the wagons behind the most enormous four horses I had ever observed. Lillian sat alongside me with the reins, controlling those dreadful beasts in her tiny hands. How could someone as petite as Lillian control such giant devils as before us? I wondered as we waited for all the wagons to line up for the journey to start.

No one had questioned the order to move. The council had met, and the decision had been made the night before. I thought of the riders I had seen the night before and wondered where they had gone. The sizeable striped tent they had entered had been loaded on one of the wagons near the back of the caravan and driven by one of the sentries.

There appeared to be forty to fifty wagons in single file, lined up behind us over the small hill past the willows and out of sight behind the ridge. A dozen sentries on horseback fanned out in front of us, and many more were scattered along the flanks and rear. Captain Connelly rode the entire length of the wagon train to ensure that all were ready before returning to the front of the line and stopping next to our wagon.

"Jonathan, my boy. I hope that you are ready for the journey of a lifetime. The council has stated that you may stay with us if you wish. When we reach our destination at Halom, we will assist you with those worrisome chains," He winked at Lillian, "Daughter, you give this lad an easy travel."

Off he rode to the front of the line and commanded the caravan to begin its journey.

The wagons rolled forward with a sudden lurch that caught me off guard because of a swift lash from Lillian's whip across the rear of the horses. With increasing anticipation, I looked over my shoulder to see the grand procession behind us, a single line of wagons across the open grassland, all moving together like a living, breathing organism. I did not know where we were going, but I understood it had to be better than my original destination. Could it be possible? Could I avoid the census and stay with these nomads?

I looked at Lillian, who smiled at me with those beautiful green eyes and sun-kissed face, "Did you hear that, Jonathan? The council has decided to allow you to stay with us. Soon, you will be like us, and your chains will be gone!"

We traveled along a narrow wagon trail that ascended a series of low hills, over which the captain and the forward scouts had disappeared earlier. I considered the dream from the night before, in which I had been climbing a mountain toward an unknown promise of hope only to fall into the abyss on the other side. I quickly dismissed the dream when we reached the top of the hill, and I could see far-off mountains and a bright new future. Maybe I had finally found peace and a home.

We settled down then, the initial excitement of the journey over. The arduous, dusty trail lay ahead of us, and I soon found riding on a wooden buckboard over a rocky trail uncomfortable. Lillian could handle the horses very well, and as the day wore on, we began to talk. I was surprised when she told me that she was eighteen years old. When she asked my age, I shrugged and told her I had no clue of my age, although I considered myself older than eighteen.

Her family had long ago lived in the trading city of Hedone, a great walled city ruled over by Archon Sarkinos, a greedy and ruthless tyrant who lived a life of luxury in a castle overlooking the cliffs on the river Pleonexia. He was a dandy dressed in silk and furs and was forever surrounded by female bodyguards. I had only seen him at a distance while in the great city for the census as he traveled through the city. The people of Hedone all lived a life of luxury if they stayed in the town. They traded with the nomads and with caravans from Soma, and some said from other realms across the ocean and used the fugitives who came each year as slave labor.

When a fugitive entered the city for the census, a link of chains could be removed, but he would have to work for several months and then be thrown outside the walls, usually without food, to wander again. At times, Archon Sarkinos would grant citizenship to a fugitive, and he could live within the walls, but the chains were not removed. They were decorated as part of the clothing worn and, by some form of magic, were no longer a burden. I did not understand this, nor did Lillian.

Lillian lived in the city as a child until her father led the family away in search of a new life. That had been a time before Archon Sarkinos when several factions controlled sections of the city. She could only remember wearing the chains as a small child while living in the city, in contrast to my memories of forever having the chains around me, although as a child, they were fewer in number.

Although the healing bath had helped to close the open wounds caused by the chains, I noticed as we continued to travel over the dusty trail through the yellow grass of an endless prairie the chains were again beginning to rub open wounds into my shoulders with every turn of the wheel.

I pulled at the chains of death to reposition them in a more comfortable way when Lillian, who must have been watching me, commented, "It won't be long until you will be set free of your chains forever. My father will make the necessary arrangements when we reach our destination."

I thought, " Hope of all hope, " as I gazed into her green eyes. "Where, pray tell, are we going? The prairie seems to go off into eternity."

"Each year, as the summer season begins, we travel to the higher steppes near the great mountains of Halom, where the air is fresh, and the grass is sweet for our herds. Halom has endless groves of ancient oaks and rivers of clear and cold water filled with trout. We spend the summer and the fall there each year."

"If the place is so beautiful, why don't you always stay there? Build homes and raise your goats and cattle there."

"We are a nomadic people, a small clan among many scattered across the land. When my father left the city, as did many others many years ago with its great walls and stone houses, crowded streets, and filth, he vowed never to live in such a place as that again. I can barely remember living in a small house near the city gate as a child. Those were not good memories, Jonathan. But now, we are free to go where we want, when we want. We raise our herds, hunt from the land, and trade with the city dwellers. The council protects us, and we are free of the chains of death."

"Do you remember your mother?" I asked and immediately regretted the question, remembering how the family had reacted several nights before.

Lillian stared past me with saddened eyes that, in time, sparkled with a hatred of something past, "I barely remember my mother. She left us, abandoned us in the city. That is all I know."

"I'm sorry for asking," I apologized, "I did not mean to cause sadness. I don't remember either of my parents. You are fortunate to have a father and family around you. I have been alone my entire life, even as the smallest child."

Lillian turned, looking deep into my eyes with sympathy.

"How did you survive as a child? What happened to your parents?" she asked.

"I never knew what happened to my parents. My earliest memories are of a great city and fires that burned through the night. I think I was only four or five, and I remember being cold. There was a woman. She had long hair and smelled of wood smoke, you know, the smell of hickory burning in the campfires."

The wagon jumped suddenly as the front wheel rolled over a rock, and Lillian steadied the horses as I tried to remember more. However, I could only vaguely remember the woman who had picked me up outside the city walls and carried me into the forest.

"I think she must have been a fugitive because she took me to the great forests of Basar, and for a while, she cared for me the best she could. But then, one night, she left the cave we were sleeping in and never returned. I remember the horns blowing. After that, I traveled through the forest until, one day, a band of warriors trapped me in a tree. I thought that I was hidden, but they saw me and cut the tree down with me in it. I was taken to the city where I was told I must return there yearly for the required census that all fugitives must do. I have been doing that since, hoping the city dwellers would one day allow me to stay."

I looked down at my feet, closing my eyes as I told my story. I had never told anyone before, but something about Lillian and her family allowed me to trust them. I had received very little kindness from anyone except the woman. I realized then that I could not even remember her name.

With a sudden fling of her hair, Lillian turned. "Such a sad story, Jonathan. It must have been so difficult. But that is behind you now. Father has power with the Council. He can help you. Oh, look! I see trees ahead, and the day is almost over. Indeed, my father will camp us by those trees tonight. "

I also saw the trees ahead, a small ribbon of dark green against the eternal yellow of the Plains of Sin called Apistia. In this country, trees meant water and a place to camp for the night. I was ready for rest. The day's journey had stiffened my joints, and my ankle throbbed again from the constant jolting of the wagon. I was also hungry. Although we had stopped to rest briefly earlier in the day, the captain had pushed us hard so that we could reach the oasis before nightfall. Now, as we traveled toward the distant ribbon of greenery that marked the location of water, I was glad that we had continued as we had done during the day.

Smelling the water, the horses suddenly quickened their pace, and it was difficult for Lillian to hold them back. To one side, the herds of goats, sheep, and cattle pushed harder toward the water, and the young herdsmen continued to drive them forward. The sentries rode ahead as scouts to ensure the campsite was safe, wary of roving bandits that forever crisscrossed the plains, robbing and pillaging those who were weaker.

Jason and Thaddeus, assisting the herdsmen, galloped up to our wagon and reined in as Lillian forced the unwilling horses to stop on a slight rise overlooking the trees that sheltered a glistening pond. We awaited the all-clear sign from the scouts searching below.

"So, Jonathan of Basar," Jason said, grinning as he restrained his impatient horse, "I see you have survived my sister's driving."

"I do just fine, Jason," Lillian responded.

"You have improved over last year," commented Thaddeus.

"I am a little sore from the ride, but I'm alive," I added as the scouts gave the sign, and we proceeded down the gentle slope to the water below.

CHAPTER ELEVEN

We pulled the wagons into a circle, end to end, around the pond along the outer rim of trees. While some unhitched the horses, others began to build the cooking fires for the night, gathering wood from the grove of trees. A windstorm or tornado most likely caused many downed trees and limbs.

After allowing the herds to water, the animals were driven into a corral built years before. The work had been quickly attended to by the herdsmen, whose job was to always look after the herd, even when in camp. I was amazed at the efficiency with which the nomads worked, feeling useless as I leaned against a tree near the wagons.

Captain Connelly directed the sentries to stand watch along the rise of hills outside the trees that entirely ringed the pond. The sentries stood watch where they could see the surrounding countryside and still be visible from the camp. They worked four-hour shifts, with eight sentries watching at any time.

After assuring himself that the camp was secure for the night, I watched as the captain settled down under one of the trees to smoke a pipe and rest until dinner, which was already being prepared by each of the women of the different families that were a part of the clan. This was a cheerful, secure place, and I could not believe I was here. Only a few days before, I had been alone with a broken ankle, in desperate need of food, shelter, and rest. Now, I was among friends.

Taking my crutch, I hobbled over to the fire, where Aunt Ruth busily prepared the evening meal with her daughters Cristina and Catherine. Lillian was not prone to the feminine arts of cooking and sewing, unlike her cousins. She preferred the horses, herds, and the hunt to her aunt's disdain. Even now, as the ladies were preparing supper, I noticed Lillian by the corral, herding the team of horses into the fence with the others and closing the gate. She wrangled horses better than most of the herdsmen.

"Oh, my boy, you must be tuckered," exclaimed Aunt Ruth. Here, sit by the fire and rest your legs. Cristina, take the boy some food and water. " And off she went to take the Captain his supper, who still sat by the tree smoking his pipe.

Lillian finally finished with the horses, and after preparing a plate for herself, she walked over and sat next to me. Her presence always made me nervous, unlike the other girls younger than me, but I liked her near me. We gathered around the fire for the evening meal, and seeing this, the captain also came over to give the customary dinner toast.

"To those who have gone before."

We all began to eat, and I was hungry, but like always, the women had prepared plenty. After dinner, we talked long into the night. Captain Connelly was a great storyteller, and I sat by the fire among the children like a small child, spellbound by his tales. Many children from across the camp and many adults were there, listening to him recount stories of great kingdoms and battles, hidden treasures, and far-off lands.

The captain knew a great deal about the land, and I wanted to find the time to show him the Light, but I did not feel comfortable doing so for some reason. All my life, I had heard the stories about the Light that would take the chains of death away, but these people seemed not to have ever heard of such a thing. And yet, they were all free of their chains. Maybe the legends of the forest were just that, legends. But here in this place, for the first time, I was among people who were not bound by the chains and did not fear the Sahat.

With great hands, the captain pulled me to my feet, saying, "Tonight, I give you Jonathan of Basar."

To my embarrassment, he introduced me to the camp as " a fugitive who wears the chains of death. But when we reach Halom, we will meet with the council, which has decided to rid him of his chains, and if he so chooses, he can stay with us."

As everyone watched, he looked directly into my eyes, "What say you, Jonathan of Basar? Will you stay with us and rid yourself of these chains?"

I could say nothing but only nod, and he gave me a great hug as the crowd applauded. Originating from my pouch, a sudden burst of frozen energy shot through my chest and shoulders and just as quickly disappeared. Connelly didn't seem to feel it, for he patted me twice on the back and let me go, but for a moment, as we stood there, I looked into his eyes and thought I saw fear or maybe confusion. He returned to the tree and gathered the children around him to tell his stories again. I sat back down by the tree.

"Jonathan, are you okay?" Lillian asked.

"Yes, I'm tired and overly excited about losing these chains. I have always dreamed of a time when I would be free. Lillian, you and your family are wonderful people. I have lived a life of death and hopelessness, but now, for the first time in my life, I have hope."

I repositioned the chains as we talked. They tore at my flesh, rubbing eternal scars across my soul. While doing so, I noticed that another link had been added, which had caused new wounds to fester. Lillian saw the bleeding open wound as well, the blood staining my shirt.

"Let me get something for that," she said and ran over to her wagon, returning a short time later with a small leather bag. Pulling my shirt off, I revealed raw and bloody wounds from the new link added while I ate dinner just moments before.

Lillian applied a soothing, healing ointment to the wound before covering the open sore with bandages, "There you are. That should heal the wound during the night. Soon, you will be free of the chains, I promise."

I pulled my shirt back on and settled back against the tree. Captain Connelly had finished his story, and the children were returning to their camps for the night.

"I prepared you a bed under the wagon, Jonathan if you wish to sleep," Lillian offered.

"Could we stay here a bit longer? I enjoy your company and would like to know more about eliminating these chains. Have you ever helped others like me?"

"Yes, we have added several fugitives to our clan this past year. Each time, the Council will meet and decide whether the fugitive should be freed."

"How do they make that decision? Many fugitives like me wish to be free. Why can't all be freed from their chains? Only death awaits us."

"I do not know for sure. My father says the council knows the heart. If your heart is pure, then you can be free. There are many evil fugitives, and we do not wish them to join our clan. We are a happy people. We travel across the land and go wherever we wish."

I remembered my encounters with bands of fugitives who preyed on the weak.

"I was once attacked by fugitives who left me for dead and took all that I owned. So, I know firsthand about the evil ones."

"Oh my! Jonathan, what happened?" she asked, scooting closer to me in anticipation of my answer.

"I was on the trail from Basar to Hedone. I owned a bow then and had three arrows that I had made myself. I had just killed a turkey, which was a rare thing, before owning the bow and decided to build a fire and cook it. They must have smelled the meat cooking or seen the smoke. I remember one running out from the trees toward me, and then someone struck me from behind, knocking me down into the fire. I rolled over to escape the fire, and another jumped on me, holding me down. They took everything: the turkey, bedroll, food, and bow and arrows. I was left with nothing but the clothes on my back and a few apples falling from the pack as they left."

"But how did you live after that? How did you get food?" Lillian asked.

"Like I always have. One day at a time. I search the woods for food, trade for supplies in the city using emeralds that I dig from the river when I find them, and travel to the census once a year." I shrugged. It was the only life that I had ever known until now.

It was getting late. Many of the clan had already retired for the night, but a few remained by the small, scattered fires. It turned out to be a beautiful night, covered by a sky full of stars, with a new moon and very dark. A cool breeze blew the slightest scent of wood smoke from the fires across us. Out in the darkness, crickets sang their song. Somewhere, an owl hooted, and then further off, coyotes yelped in unison, their song lonely and somehow depressing. I stretched my wounded leg, rubbing the ankle while looking back into Lillian's shadowed face.

"Is your father on the council?" I asked.

"No, the council comes and goes as they wish. They stay in the large striped tent when they are with us. Otherwise, they live in Halom under the cliffs of Crystalline. They usually visit us only at night and remain in their tent during the day. Very few of us have ever seen them in person. I have only seen them as they rode in at night and would not recognize them if I saw them in the day. That is one thing that I forgot to tell you. No one is to go near their tent when we are in the encampment at night. The council is very secretive, and only the clan's leaders, such as my father, know who they are. They look after us. They are the reason that we are free. They have allowed us to defend ourselves and travel anywhere within the plain as far as the forest and the sea."

I thought about the shadowy figures from the night before. They must have been members of the council.

"Lillian, this is all new to me. I have lived the life of a fugitive all of my life. A life without hope, but I have always heard of stories of the power of the Light that can take my chains away. Have you ever heard such stories?"

"No, only the Council can remove our chains. Look around you. We do not wear the chains of death and have never seen this Light you are talking of."

I repositioned my leg nervously. The healing potion began to relax the muscles around the new wound across my shoulder.

"I have seen many strange things these past few weeks. Before I started my journey from the forest to the city of Hedone for the census, I had only heard the stories. But in the last few weeks, I have seen wondrous things."

I hesitated as I looked into her eyes, the flickering light from the nearby fire dancing playfully across her dark hair and face. She brushed back a stray lock of hair from her face, hooked it behind her ear, and turned her head, waiting for me to continue. I did not know why I was telling her, but I had to tell someone. I had to learn more about what I had seen. Things were happening very fast, and as I talked, I felt the increasing warmth of the Light within the pouch around my waist. I could not discount its hold over me.

"I hid in a cave during a storm as the Sahat searched for their prey. A woman was captured near the cave entrance, and I watched as she was killed. She had the Light. The riders appeared frightened of it and threw it in the river, where I later found it."

"It did the girl no good, Jonathan. They killed her anyway." Lillian commented pointedly.

"I know, but when I saw it for a moment before it was lost in the water, its beauty captured my spirit. It may not truly have the power to remove my chains, but it is a remarkable light, the most beautiful thing I have ever seen."

Lillian's eyes sparkled with interest. She pulled her thick hair from her face again with both hands and began rolling it behind her head, braiding it into one long rope to keep it from her face.

"Do you still have it? I would love to see it."

I watched as she continued working with her unruly hair, rose to her knees, and scooted closer to me. I stared for a moment, her presence intoxicating to me, before reaching into my pouch and carefully removing the Light from its hiding place, holding it by the leather band, and placing it in my left hand. The Light was very small, illuminating only my hand. As I looked into its energy, it became warmer and grew, producing shimmering blue-white light that spread out slowly, pushing back the darkness around my hand and then my arm.

Lillian settled back down next to me, finally satisfied with the placement of her hair.

"It's beautiful. I have never seen such a beautiful gem in my life!" Lillian exclaimed in wonderment. "No wonder you have kept it. It must be worth a small fortune. Jonathan, I'm sure many merchants in Hedone would pay dearly for such as this if you ever needed to sell it. Even if it did not remove the chains as your legends said, it is still worth keeping."

She raised her hand almost to the point where the boundary of light extended from my hand. The truly remarkable thing about the Light is its ability to consume all the darkness within its influence. Still, there was always a definite boundary between the expanse of the Light and the darkness around it. One was either totally in the dark or totally in the light. There was no middle ground, no iridescent shadows of half-light, no degrees of intensity like that which occur from the flickering light produced by the campfire or from a torch.

"Yes, but be careful. It has no substance that I can feel. You can only pick it up by the band. Every time I try to touch it, it melts away or moves."

I poked at the Light to show her, and it moved away from my finger, causing us to laugh. It was as if the Light was a living, breathing organism.

"It is not a jewel, then?" she asked.

"It is more beautiful than any gem, but it is not one. It may appear to be one, but it is not hard. It has no physical substance to it. It is only light."

I lifted my hand toward her, and the Light grew in intensity, illuminating her hands and arms as if it were rewarding us for our interest in it. She also reached out to touch it, captivated by its wonder, as was I.

"Jonathan, it is truly a beautiful light, but it is growing so bright that it hurts my eyes."

Lillian shielded her eyes with her other hand and looked down. For a moment, the Light suddenly illuminated her entire body. I gasped.

The young woman with brilliant green eyes, flowing raven black hair, and bronzed skin, transformed before my eyes as the Light surrounded her. I saw a gray, hollowed face with vacant, dead eyes and diseased, wrinkled skin. Her hair was matted and torn, and heavy chains crossed over her breasts. Her clothing was torn and stained from the dried blood of her many wounds caused by the continued chafing of the metal chains. In horror, I pulled back from her and dropped the Light, which immediately lost its brilliance and returned to its small form. The apparition that I had briefly seen before me disappeared. Lillian sat there, still shielding her eyes.

What had happened? I wondered. Was my mind playing tricks? Were the nightmares that plagued my sleep like a disease now invading my thoughts as well, or was it the Light?

"You, okay?" Lillian asked, looking up at me. You look as if you have seen a ghost."

I reached down and quickly retrieved the dimming Light from the sandy ground and placed it back into the pouch, "Yes, but I am tired and startled as well by the light's brilliance."

"It is getting late, and it appears that most everyone else has already gone to bed," she said, standing up and taking my hand, which was still trembling. I'll show you your bed."

I needed to sleep.

CHAPTER TWELVE

The warrior finally picked up the trail of his prey near the forest's edge near a large oak, a hidden shelter built among the foliage. The fugitive had stayed there several days, having killed and eaten rabbits on at least two occasions, and from the sign, he must have been injured. The warrior also noticed the bones of a headless man and a horse. He only stayed a few minutes by the tree, ensuring he confirmed his prey's direction.

"He travels across the plains," he commented to his patiently nearby horse, "most likely for the census."

Mounting up, he followed the trail of a lone fugitive, who now walked with a cane and traveled very slowly by the number of points along the way where he had rested in the tall grass.

For the better part of a day, he rode across the yellow grasslands, seeing no sign of life, ever wary of a passing enemy patrol, until he topped a low rise and saw the green ribbon of trees against the horizon that marked the location of water. He reined in his horse some distance from the tree line, and, taking his telescope, he carefully scanned the trees for any sign of life. Satisfied that no one was near the water, he placed the telescope back into its sheath and spurred his horse onward. He rode quietly down to the water's edge and allowed the horse to drink as he dismounted. He took a drink himself and refilled his canteens.

All around, the grass was matted, and there were several fire pits and a corral across the pond built from the narrow poles of young aspen that grew in a thick grove nearby. He pulled his glove from his hand and, kneeling by one of the pits, sifted through the ashes. They were still warm. Standing, he dusted off his hand and replaced the glove. Whoever had been here had left this very day. Had the encampment found the fugitive before they left, or was he still hiding among the trees or within the tall grass? He had been wounded and possibly had a broken leg. Therefore, he would have been desperate for water and food by the time he had reached the oasis. But was he desperate enough to enter the camp? The warrior scanned the surrounding hills, looking for any sign that the fugitive was still there.

He mounted his horse and trotted back up to the low rise. The fugitive had been following a walking trail thousands of fugitives had used over the years. There had been many footprints along the trail, but only one showed evidence of walking with a limp and the presence of a walking stick. Sitting atop the horse, he noticed a place where the grass had been matted down as if someone had been crawling up the hill.

Of course, the fugitive must have known that a large band of nomads occupied the oasis, and he had crawled carefully to a vantage point from where he could look over the camp. The warrior dismounted and carefully inspected the site. Two other men, considerably larger than the fugitive, had walked up to the hiding place from behind, and all three had descended the hill to the camp.

"Well, my friend," he said to his horse, "we are getting close. Undoubtedly, he has joined the nomads."

He remounted and located the trail leaving the camp, which was not hard to find. As far out across the grassland as one could see, parallel ribbons of tracks led off into the horizon, a wagon road. The herds had traveled parallel to the wagons. The warrior was several hours behind them or at least no more than a day behind, and he knew that he did not have much time, but he also understood that the nomads never traveled at night, and he should quickly gain on them. He allowed his horse to set a steady gallop and followed the trail off to the north.

The sun's location against the horizon convinced him he had a few hours of daylight. He would surely come across their encampment if he rode through the night. He rode along the trail for a short distance and then decided to leave the road and ride across the area where the herds had been driven to mask his trail.

He traveled for the remainder of the afternoon, seeing no sign of life anywhere among the endless plains. And then the red-tailed hawk appeared overhead, circling high among the wisp of clouds that drifted lazily across the deep blue sky. The bird flew overhead for half an hour before it finally peeled off and descended over the low ridgeline to the west. The warrior didn't notice when the bird had eventually left him.

As darkness approached, he descended upon several goats on the trail. Reining in his horse, he sat for a moment studying the country around him as he drank from his canteen. The horse lowered his head and grazed among the grass, favoring the light blue flowers that grew over the grass.

The goats were most likely part of the herds he had been following. That meant that sooner or later, a herdsman would return to gather any strays, so he turned his horse and rode quickly toward the east and away from the trail, crossing a broken country of rock and shorter, sparser grass to detour the trail and stay out of sight of any herdsmen.

Over the next ridge, he thought he saw the thin trails of several clouds of smoke that most likely marked the evening nomad camp. From his limited knowledge of this portion of the realm, he remembered an oasis near the rocky hills that would make a secure camp for the travelers. He continued to ride through the rocks, more slowly now and carefully. The smoke blew lazily up from behind the ridge, and he continued to ride through the rocks until he found a place where he could safely approach the camp without being seen by the sentries.

If he could determine where the sentries were located, he could find a place along the ridge to spy on the camp and locate the fugitive among them.

Overhead in the darkening sky, the hawk reappeared and flew a few wide circles, unknown to the lone warrior, as he slowly approached the outer perimeter of the nomad camp. The hawk circled several times and then dropped behind the ridgeline to the west, where several knights waited.

Their leader, the Captain of the Guard, had been ordered several days before by Archon Krino to search for evidence that an interloper had invaded the land. The Master had spies throughout the realm, one of which had crossed the path of a strange warrior of an unknown race, and word had quickly reached the castle that the new warrior had appeared. The hawk flew down rapidly among the band of knights and, with a flutter of wings, gracefully landed on the outstretched gloved arm of its master.

"It appears that you have found someone, my friend," the knight spoke softly to his bird. "Lead us to him," he ordered, and with this command, the great bird again soared high above as the knights galloped across the plains below in pursuit.

The warrior finally reached a point among the rock outcrops where he could get a better sight of the smoke and their origin, several cooking fires with a line of wagons around them, circled end to end. The nomads were in the process of settling down for the night. He only had a few moments before darkness and wished to get a closer look within the encampment but knew that there would be sentries nearby whom he wanted to avoid. A small stream flowed down the hill to his left, lined with a thicket of alders and occasional sycamores.

He backed his horse closer to the stream, away from the rocks, and dismounted. He pulled down on the reigns, forcing the horse to lie in the tall grass.

"Stay here, boy," he patted him, knowing he would stay until he came back or whistled for him.

Taking his telescope, crossbow, and quiver of arrows, he carefully crawled up through the grass to the summit overlooking the camp. From this point, he saw the entire camp and, through the telescope, spied the inhabitants, looking for the fugitive.

Across the pond, horses grazed on the lush grass within a corral. Cattle and goats filled another corral across the camp. People busily prepared the camp for the night, and the warrior saw no sentries. A small band of armored warriors circled an older, bearded man near one of the wagons. The man looked familiar. The bearded man appeared to be giving the men orders. In pairs, the warriors left the circle of wagons, two walking in his direction. They were the sentries, the warrior thought.

He only had a few moments, so taking one more last look around the camp, he quietly backed down the hill to where his horse lay hidden in the grass and rode back down to the stream. He followed the water upstream toward the camp to a small grove of aspen that spilled over the ridge at a gap where the stream flowed through. Hopefully, he could use the thickets as cover and infiltrate the camp through the stream under the cover of darkness.

Overhead, a hawk circled and quickly flew away, unnoticed by the warrior who was intent on calculating a safe passage over the gap in the hills to the camp on the other side.

Crickets sang among the alders, and laughter from the camp floated in the light breeze now and again, but otherwise, there was no sound. The warrior left his horse near the stream and climbed the hill near the gap, stopping midway up in the grass. He caught a brief glimpse of one of the sentries walking the ridgeline, exposed against the night sky. Watching the sentry, he began to understand the pattern.

People are creatures of habit; if one could understand the habit, one could take advantage of it. Counting the time when one sentry was hidden from view by the crest of the hill, he would have a few moments to quickly pass over the gap and into the camp near the wagons where, hopefully, he could lay in wait and watch for the fugitive.

He had to get a closer look and somehow contact the fugitive who had a portion of the Light without the nomads knowing he was among them. The nomads would pose a severe threat because of their hatred of his race, and he was now the only one in a land filled with enemies. But hopefully, with time, that would change, and others of his kind could enter the realm after he contacted the chosen one. He was used to working alone. It sharpened his senses because he only had himself and his horse.

Behind him, his horse stirred among the grass. Something must have caused him to move, the warrior thought. The sentry was out of sight and hopefully did not hear anything.

The warrior turned to look back down the hill to the stream. Something wasn't right. The crickets had stopped their nightly chorus along the stream, which was suddenly deadly quiet. Even his horse no longer made a sound. Something slowly moved among the darkened shadows beneath the alders.

Turning ever so slightly so as not to give away his position, higher above the stream among the tall grass, he focused on the area below his horse. At times, in the break of thick vegetation, he saw the moon's reflection on the water in the stream as it happily, unknowingly traveled along its eternal course among smoothed stones toward a distant ocean. If someone were moving toward his horse, he would have to pass the opening and cast a shadow over the water.

The warrior watched the water intently as he carefully removed one of the arrows from his quiver and placed it on the ground next to him, pushing the point down into the soft soil. He then placed another arrow on the crossbow and pulled the bow back to the cocked position, the whole time watching the break in the vegetation for any sign that someone was close.

A cloud covered the moon, and the night had become even darker. He heard no sound and saw nothing, but every sense told him that an enemy was close. He reasoned that it could not be the Sahat because, at night, their red eyes cast an eerie glow that frightened the fugitives and illuminated the darkness with beams of red wherever they looked. Although it could be a nomad from the camp, it was improbable. After dark, they stayed within their encampment, protected by their sentries.

The cloud moved on, and he saw the reflection on the water again. He waited, perfectly still, watching the spot and listening intently. Suddenly, the horse jerked his head up and pulled against the rope that held him. The warrior knew the horse was smart, but he worried that if he freed herself, the horse may approach him and give away his position.

The horse most likely could smell them, the one upwind anyway. Who were they? Fugitive bandits in search of food or weapons? Most likely not. They usually traveled in groups and rarely at night for fear of the Sahat. That left only the knights of Kratos, and upon this realization that those in the darkness could be of this race, the warrior swore. Maybe his presence had been noticed, and the knights had been sent in search of him. Or it could have been just a coincidence.

In any case, if the knights of Kratos were near, he was in trouble and would have to contact the fugitive somehow and escape with greater haste than he had first anticipated. He thought one problem at a time as he stared at the break in the foliage, keeping his ears tuned to the horse and the second person approaching from the other direction.

The horse finally pulled free of the slip knot and, trailing the rope behind him, trotted a short distance, his ears forward and alert, his mighty head reaching high, searching the night air with strong nostrils. The warrior thought the knights had to know now that he was hiding nearby and must crouch somewhere among the shadows, listening and watching for him as he did for them.

The horse pranced one way and then another, then with a sudden jump, he turned and trotted upstream. With a sudden shock of concern, the warrior realized they were after his horse. With his horse captured or killed, he would be easy prey when morning came. He had to do something and do it quickly! If they captured his horse, he was done for. On the other hand, if he exposed himself to save the horse, others hiding nearby could attack him from behind.

    The horse suddenly reared up, clawing the air with his front hooves as a darkened figure emerged from the brush, grabbing the rope. Another passed by the opening in the foliage, casting a brief shadow on the moonlit water. The warrior took quick aim and fired his weapon, immediately grabbing for the second arrow embedded in the ground next to him. He reloaded as he stood from his hidden position. He shouted a command to his horse that had escaped the outstretched arms of the first shadowy figure, tearing away from the assailant; the animal galloped across the grass on an intersecting course with the warrior running now, scanning the area below.

    A sentry challenged from high above on the ridge, and he knew they would soon come to search the area as well. He had to catch up to the horse and escape into the night. The fugitive would have to wait.

    He heard the uncanny screech of a hawk, and with the flutter of wings, a great bird suddenly dropped out of the darkness above, raking his sharp nails across the warrior's shoulders and, with surprising strength, knocking him down. He quickly rolled over and regained his footing as a dark knight rose from the grass below him, wielding a massive double-edged broadsword. The warrior soon fired his second arrow, but the missile glanced off the thick armored shoulder and sailed into the darkness toward the sentries above.

CHAPTER THIRTEEN

I lay under the wagon, troubled by the horrid, ghostly figure I had seen in the translucent light. My mind must have been playing tricks on me. How could such a beautiful creature as Lillian turn into the specter I had briefly seen? What type of enchantment did the Light possess that would change someone as it had done? What kind of evil? But how could something that had given me hope be evil? My mind was filled with imagery of everything I had seen, but there were few answers. I wanted to sleep, to forget the images, but I feared sleep because of the nightmares.

The camp was quiet. The cooking fires burned low, some only gleaming red coals, others flickering lights as individual logs continued to burn. A soft breeze blew with a slight chill. Crickets along the edge of the pond sang, as did an occasional frog.

A challenge by one of the sentries on the hill above my wagon broke the silence, and I heard people running. Captain Connelly emerged from his wagon, a sword in hand, as other men emerged from various wagons around the camp. I quickly crawled from under the wagon and noticed the sisters and Lillian peeking inside their wagon.

"What's up?" Cristina asked as Jason rose from the other wagon, a short sword in hand.

"Stay in the wagons, girls," he ordered, "There is danger afoot tonight."

But as usual, Lillian did not heed his warning and climbed from the wagon in her long nightgown and bare feet. She held a short dagger.

"Oh, Jason, You're too melodramatic."

What type of girl I had befriended who appeared to fear nothing, I thought. Wildly different than myself, I reasoned, who feared everything.

The sentries searched along the ridge. Someone threw a large bundle of branches on the fire, which immediately blazed up and illuminated the camp, casting shadows across the night as men ran from their wagons to the camp's perimeter. One of the sentries ran down from the hill. He passed by the fire, and I noticed he carried an arrow.

"What have you found, Theos?' called Connelly.

The sentry gave Connelly the arrow as many of the band converged on them to witness what had been found. The Captain closely inspected the arrow, noticing the markings that he had seen once before long ago.

"The arrow of a Bene Elohim!" he gasped, breaking it with disgust and throwing it into the fire, "Theos, take another with you on our fastest horses and ride ahead to Halom. Alert the Council that a Bene Elohim has been located in the realm. We are still several days journey from the safety of Halom, but if you ride hard, you should make it in a day."

The sentry turned and ran to the corral as Connelly stared off into the darkness. For the first time, I saw pure hatred in his eyes. Who were the Bene Elohim, and what had they done to cause such anger in this man? He turned quickly, almost knocking me down. As if he had heard my questioning thoughts, he answered me, "Those are the ones who killed my wife long ago. If their evil and intolerance are in the realm, we must hunt them down and destroy them."

He walked past me, shouting orders for the sentries and other men to search the area carefully around the camp. If the Bene Elohim was nearby, he wanted him captured.

"Take the torches and search carefully, but beware because they are a treacherous lot. Jason gathered the camp and set guards among the wagons and the corrals. We will constantly watch through the night, and at first light, we will move out."

The whole camp suddenly sprang into action as they prepared for battle in case an attack came, and once again, I felt useless, empty-handed, and weak. Then I remembered the knife I had with me, the one I had found by the tree house.

I quickly grabbed the pouch, belted it around me, pulled the knife from the bag, and pushed it deep into the belt around my waist. Lillian noticed the weapon, and I felt strength for the first time, knowing she had also seen me prepare for battle. If she only knew the great fear that filled my soul, I thought, but for once in my life, I would push that fear aside and take a stand.

The fight between the warrior and the knights of Kratos continued in the darkness. A knight swung the sword downward as the warrior sheathed the crossbow and drew his golden sword from the scabbard across his back, dodging the heavy blow—the sentries above searched among the ridges.

Another dark knight rose as the warrior struck a glancing blow across the chest of the first knight just as his horse galloped by, knocking the second knight to the ground. The warrior quickly pulled himself up and mounted his horse, but a third knight blocked his path, reaching for the reins. The warrior slashed down, the sword crashing against the knight's broadsword, showering with bright, fiery sparks, and the horse reared and turned, knocking this knight to the ground as well. Gaining control, the warrior turned the horse toward the open prairie to escape.

Back in the camp, a sentry shouted a warning and pointed toward a horseman riding past the fire's light. Captain Connelly mounted his horse, and several others carrying torches rode after the horseman, who had escaped through the gap near the stream.

In the darkness below the ridge, the knights of Kratos quickly mounted their horses, standing among the aspen to pursue as the hawk circled overhead.

"Hold!" commanded their Captain, whom the first arrow had wounded. He swore to himself as he pulled the arrow from his thigh and quickly packed the wound to stop the bleeding.

"The nomads are chasing him. We are to remain unseen to them. Archon Planos would be greatly upset if he knew we were so far out on the plains near his territory. Kevin, follow the chase from a distance and ensure the Bene Elohim is captured. If they fail, we will pursue him again after the nomads have left. If I am correct, they are on their yearly migration to the hills of Halom for the summer."

The knight Kevin saluted and galloped off after the retreating nomads, whose flickering torches danced in the darkness as they rode in pursuit of the lone Bene Elohim.

The captain shook his head in disbelief, studying the arrow that had wounded him closely. It had the markings of a Bene Elohim. The captain, a son of an alcoholic who had beat him and his mother in the name of the Light that the Bene Elohim upheld, had been recruited by Archon Krino as a youth. He had vowed that he would do everything in his power to drive out those who rebelled against the Master of the realm and had risen through the ranks to become a Captain among the

Knights of Kratos, a man noted for his determination and loyalty to the Master.

This lone warrior had been a wary opponent. They had failed to capture him even though they outnumbered him five to one, but it had been a close-run thing. The trap had almost worked. If the nomads did not capture the warrior, he would be more careful next time.

He grimaced at the pain caused by the arrow that he held in his hand. As a child, those who professed to have the Light had caused pain to him as well. The Light that was supposed to offer hope only offered pain as it had done on this night. As a reminder, he placed the arrow in the saddlebag and mounted his horse as his men waited.

"You okay, Patrick?" asked a bearded knight named Peter, the only one who had ever called him by his first name. He was a trusted friend and the only one among his men who had been with him since his quest began.

"I'll be alright."

"What do you think? It has been a while since a Bene Elohim has been seen in the land." Peter asked as he tore a bit of dried beef with his teeth and gave his friend a piece.

"I don't know, but if the nomads capture him, we'll ride back and let Krino know. Something's going on, that's for sure."

Patrick accepted the beef and waited, reflecting on what was happening. There had been changes. Sahat had returned reporting armed resistance, and now they had verified that a Bene Elohim was in the realm. If there was one, then more were sure to come.

Repressed memories long forgotten began to invade Patrick's subconscious. Dreams of shadowing warriors, piercing lights, and chained bodies haunted his dreams at night. Now, the arrow of the Bene Elohim had wounded him, and even now, he could feel a strange yearning for an unknown or perhaps forgotten presence. His leg ached, but the bandages held tightly, and the wound had not been too deep.

The nomads had crossed ahead of the Bene Elohom, and although his horse was fast and powerful, he was also tired from the hard ride across the plains. The warrior had been careful not to be seen, but apparently, someone had come upon his trail. In any event, he knew that he was in danger of being captured, and suddenly, with an assurance from deep within, he understood that being caught by the nomads had been the plan all along. He reined in his horse and dismounted. He tied the crossbow to the saddle.

"Run, boy, as fast as you can, but stay close. I will call you when the time comes."

The Bene Elohim smacked the horse across the flank, and he ran off into the darkness, leaving him standing to face the oncoming nomads. The warrior drew his sword and turned to face the nomads closing in, a dozen riders carrying torches that illuminated the night and cast dancing shadows across the prairie. He did not wish to harm them; after all, they were partly why he was in the realm, to begin with, but he did want to ensure that his horse had time to run to safety. Overhead, the hawk soared in the darkness, and Kevin pulled up behind a low earth swell to watch from a distance.

A horseman rode up upon the warrior, surprised that he was no longer running but had dismounted and stood in front of him, sword in hand. The Bene Elohim knocked him from the saddle with the sword's flat side, and the rider fell hard to the ground as the startled horse galloped on by. A second and third rider approached, and then a dozen sentries quickly surrounded him.

The one who had fallen was severely shaken and moaned with pain from a broken arm as he stood up to retrieve his horse, which stood off at a distance. The torch he had carried lay in the grass, burning brightly and setting the grass on fire, but because of the rains the week before, the fire only smoldered and produced more smoke than fire.

Seeing that his horse had escaped across the open prairie, the Bene Elohim dropped his sword and raised his hands in surrender. Captain Connelly pushed through the sentries and dismounted in front of him. He held a short sword and placed the tip against the Bene Elohim's throat.

Captain Connelly announced to the sentries around him, "Gentlemen, we have here in front of us, Malak of Christendom. You sure are a long way from home, Malak."

Connelly sheathed his sword, and without looking away from the Bene Elohim, he reached down and picked up Malak's sword, holding it in his hand and examining it closely. It was a fine weapon, razor sharp and fashioned from the strongest steel with a pearl handle.

"I vowed that the next time that I saw you, I would kill you. I would tear out your heart and watch while you died, but I have changed. The hatred for you is still strong, but I control it now."

Malak spoke for the first time, "It was her choice, Connelly. You know it was your wife's choice. She chose the way to live by the power of the Light, a choice you could have taken that would have saved your entire family. I did not kill her."

"Enough of your lies! You killed dear Sarah with the words of seduction, your fanciful dreams. Look around you. We have been freed of our chains. The way that Sarah chose led to a life of slavery. She chose the Light that you preach more than her own family, and it cost her life. But I chose the way of life. We are free to roam the plains, marry, and raise our families. We are protected from the Sahat, and the Council protects us from your kind. I will not kill you, but I will take you to the Council for them to decide your fate."

Connelly motioned to one of the sentries, who hit Malak hard across the back of his head, knocking him to the ground. They then bound his feet and arms and placed him across one of the horses. Kevin waited until they were out of sight over the low rise of grassland and then turned back to report what he had seen.

Malak's horse raced across the prairie until he could run no more, knowing that he had to remain free and ready to come to Malak's assistance when needed. She stopped beneath the comforting arms of a lone oak tree to rest and wait until morning, when he would follow the nomads as they continued their journey. Wherever the master went, he would follow and take him to safety when the time was right. But now he was tired, worn down by the constant travel of the past few days. An unseen hand caressed him as he rested, and strength flowed back into his weary muscles. He slept the night away, hidden beneath the overshadowing embrace of the ancient oak with its protective limbs.

CHAPTER FOURTEEN

We stood by the wagons, waiting expectantly, watching the shadows around us for any sign of an attack. The sentries that had remained on the perimeter after the horsemen had left gathered back at the camp to add their strength to those of us who guarded the wagons. I felt the same sickening feeling I had experienced my entire life as I hid in the dark countless nights as shadows moved among the darkness. The talons of fear gripped my spirit, and my hands began to shake. I sweated, even though it was a chilly night. I held a knife in my hand, but at that very moment, panic swelled up within me, and all I thought about was running, finding a hole or cave, and hiding. The way I had hid while the girl had been killed.

Someone threw more wood on the nearest fire, and the glowing light penetrated further into the darkness, increasing our visibility. Horses galloped out in the darkness somewhere, and the crackling of the fire, but nothing else. Lillian walked up quietly beside me, and I was suddenly ashamed because of the fear within me. I glanced up at her and immediately remembered what I had seen the night before but pushed the thoughts away. She stood in her nightgown beside me, a beautiful woman, not the apparition I had seen.

For the first time, I felt a bond with another human being. Even though we had only known each other for a few weeks, I was beginning to trust her more than I ever thought possible. We had spent considerable time together, and I felt like a part of her family. Whenever she was close to me, I felt nervous, but I loved her company and hated being apart from her. I had never understood love because love had never been present in my world, but now, as she stood beside me in the darkness, I think I understood what love was.

But what was I to her? I was just a fugitive, a nobody, and now I was a fugitive bound by fear and thinking of bolting like a deer, but her presence calmed me somewhat. If an attack came and Lillian was threatened, would I fight or freeze with fear and allow her to be destroyed?

"Well, Jonathan, the coward of the cave, your time is not yet, but you will have to live the rest of your pathetic existence with the memory of what you have seen tonight." The destroyer had spoken this to me in the cave. Was I about to relive that horrible night again?

Lillian stepped closer and clasped my hand, squeezing tightly and smiling at me. If she was frightened, she hid her emotions well. She appeared to be in total control with the self-assurance that she could handle anything. I looked back into her eyes and smiled nervously.

"It will be okay, Jonathan. You are safe with us. We have been attacked, but we have always chased the bandits away. No harm can come to us. The warriors are well trained; even the Sahat do not bother us."

"But what of the Bene Elohim? Your father seemed very upset. Your father said that the Bene Elohim had killed your mother. My whole life, I have heard stories about this race who are supposed to be champions of the Light. Once, only a few days before you found me on the plains, I thought I saw three of them fighting the Sahat."

"Jonathan, the legends are myths, stories told to fugitives such as yourself to give false hope, just like the stories that the Light you have can remove your chains. Yes, it is true. My father said the Bene Elohim killed my mother and forced my family from Hedone. They are a fierce and relentless race of warriors, and I am glad their kind has been banished from the realm. If they return, the nomads have sworn to drive them away."

I remained quiet, alone with my thoughts. So many things had happened. My simple world had crashed around me. The Light had once been a distant hope in a hopeless world, and when I had found a portion of it, I felt sure that I had discovered the true answer, but now I was confused. These people were free, and they did not have the Light. Were the stories only myths? The Light was upon me, and its power also pulled at my thoughts. I had to know for sure. I had to understand if the stories were true.

"They are returning!" someone shouted, and I stepped into the light.

Horses approached. At first, I only heard them, but then I saw the flaming torches and horse shadows, and they were among the camp, trotting around the scattered fires. Some rode on to the corrals, but Connelly and several others stopped at the larger fire in the center of the camp.

"You see, Jonathan, my father will take care of us. He always has."

She released my hand and approached her father as he dismounted. A bound captive lay across one of the horses, and after a sentry cut the rope, the man fell hard to the ground, unconscious.

He lay face down in the dust as if dead, but after a moment, he began to stir as the entire band gathered around to see. He was a large man, over six feet tall and powerfully built, wearing chain mail, dark leather pants, black boots, and a dark purple cloak. His hair, thick and curly, flowed down to his shoulders, a portion of it braided, and was held in check by a purple headband. A portion of it was matted from dried blood from a head wound. He pushed himself up and rolled over, and we immediately stepped back in fear and wonder as the sentries pointed their spears threateningly and encircled him. He stood up suddenly when regaining full consciousness, his arms still bound before him. One guard immediately pressed his spear against the strange warrior's chest.

"On your knees!" he commanded, and the man dropped back to his knees without resistance.

This was no ordinary man, I thought. The soldiers that I had witnessed fighting the Sahat were only fugitives like me who had somehow armed themselves, I knew now after gazing at the Bene Elohim before me. This man was a true warrior. Even though submissive and a captive, he was sure of himself with self-confidence, not of this world.

Captain Connelly spoke, breaking the spell that the sight of such a race of warriors, a warrior of legend, had placed upon us, "This scoundrel was found spying on our camp, no doubt gathering information for others of his kind. You have all heard stories about the mystical Bene Elohim. Now you see one in the flesh. He is only a man like us, but his race is a scourge upon the land. They threaten our very existence, the freedom we enjoy from the chains of death. Look closely at this man. His name is called Malak."

There was a gasp among the crowd when they heard his name.

Connelly continued, "He is the one who destroyed my wife years ago. I once vowed in front of many of you that if I ever located this man, I would kill him, but I have changed. I will spare his life, and we will take him before the Council for them to decide his fate," Connelly circled the warrior as we all looked on, "For many years, our land has been free from such as this race before you, but now we must prepare if more are in the realm. We must bind together to follow the Council and defend our freedom."

He looked down at the warrior, "Why have you returned, Malak? Can't your kind just leave us alone?"

The warrior said nothing, and Connelly waved for the guards to take him. They pulled the cloaked warrior up by the rope that bound his arms, and I stepped closer to see around the guard. The Bene Elohim bled from a wound above the ear, the blood drying in his matted hair below the headband.

As the guards pushed him toward Connelly's wagon, he looked up and stared at me with piercing dark eyes, and I jumped back. I suddenly knew he recognized me, although I had never seen him before. He looked away as the sentries chained him to the wagon wheel, and a guard was posted nearby. He gazed across the fire at me several more times but said nothing before I returned to my bed. I was tired and needed to sleep.

Lillian stood before me, holding out her hands.

"Good night, Jonathan," she said.

I blushed. Even with the excitement, she affected me, "Good night, Lillian."

I took her hands in mine and squeezed lightly. She bowed slightly and turned back to her wagon. I watched her climb up and into the wagon and then turn toward my bed. Looking back to the Bene Elohim again before crawling under the wagon to my pallet, I noticed that he continued to watch me. Two guards stood on either side of him.

An undercurrent of anxiety concerning the events of the night spread through the camp. People whispered among themselves about the presence of the mythical figure chained to the wagon. Many of the band would sleep very little. I lay under the wagon, unable to sleep despite being tired from the day's travels. Much had happened; today, much of what I understood about the realm had been questioned.

My whole life, I had been under the control of my master, who lived in another realm, another dimension. Although we were the same person, we lived independently of each other. Although everything he did in the other dimension affected me, could I not affect him? I had been taught that I could not undo the chains he created around me, slowly wearing me down, slowly destroying my strength to live. With each passing day, the chains grew heavier, even in this place among friends, although the healing ointment that I now bathed with did ease the pain and heal the wounds temporarily.

The only hope, say the legends, lay in the power of the Light, and even that belief was shaken. These people around me had helped me. They had accepted me for who I was. They did not look down on me because I was a fugitive but promised my deliverance. And now, a Bene Elohim, a race that lived only in my imagination and in stories of the forest, was chained nearby. No longer just a part of my imagination, he was now a real, living, breathing personality. He had somehow communicated through his eyes that he knew who I was and was here because of me. I needed to talk with him, to ask him what he wanted of me.

So many things had happened to me since I had found the Light. Was the Light somehow orchestrating all around me, or had it just chance led me here? In my pouch lay the most beautiful object I had ever seen, a mystery I did not understand, but what had it done for me? What had it done for me besides keeping me warm in the cave of my fears? It had offered hope in a hopeless world, and the nomads who promised to take my chains away had befriended me.

The Light had also played tricks on my sight, transforming the beautiful Lillian into the ghostly apparition I had briefly seen when she touched the Light. That transformation had frightened me, and I was not sure about the Light as I first was. How could something that was supposed to free us of the chains cast such a spell over someone as beautiful as Lillian? Was the Light just a magician's trick that I did not know how to use, or was it the source of my freedom from the chains of death? How could it free me when those around me had no chains yet did not possess the Light?

I lay in my bed under the wagon as those around me began to fall asleep under the watchful protection of the sentries until I, too, fell into a fitful sleep. Before entering the illusive world of peaceful sleep, my last thoughts were of the captured warrior who had seen deep into my soul and communicated with me through his thoughts. I needed to talk with him but knew that Connelly would disapprove. Therefore, I realized I must do it at night when everyone is asleep before I went to sleep. I needed to rouse myself and go to him! I felt that this night might be my only chance to talk with the warrior, but the more I fought the sleep, the drowsier I became until I finally stopped fighting. I was tired, I thought. Tomorrow was another day. I would have time later, but now I needed to sleep, my mind told me, and sleep finally came.

  I stood among tall stone buildings, towering into the darkened, starless expanse of space, disappearing into the mystery of a black sky. The roads were narrow and straight, proceeding in all directions from where I now stood, like the spokes of a wagon wheel, and I was the hub. All the roads looked exactly alike, each path straight, the cobblestone trails overshadowed by the buildings, the trails disappearing into the darkness around me. I stood alone at the crossroads of my existence in complete despair with no hope of ever finding my way out.

  At first, I heard no sound except my labored breathing. Although dark, the darkness was not totally void of light, and shadows danced in the night. The shadows lived, shades of gray swirling like ghostly specters of mist over the cobblestone.

  And then the faint sound of music floated in the shadows. Someone played a harp. I could not tell where the music was coming from, but I felt deep within me that if I could locate the source of the music, I could identify the way out of this maze of life that had entrapped me. I closed my eyes to regain my composure and push away the fear that steadily tried to imprison me with its' cold claws of deception and concentrated on the harp, trying to locate down which lane it was coming. The music faded away, and then a new song started, and I knew from which road it came.

  I opened my eyes and now only saw one trail leading straight and true into the darkness before me. High above on both sides of the road, the granite walls of the battlements overwhelmed me. Higher up on the walls were balconies extending out over the road and windows, all empty, the windows locked, and the balconies just out of my reach. Along the pathway were a multitude of wooden doors, all of which were locked as well, and the trail narrowed to just a few feet wide. I walked down the path with the whispering harp as my guide until, suddenly, the music stopped, and I stood in total silence for a moment.

  What was it I needed to do next? I did not know which way to go. I called for someone to help me. Fear crept over me, and I began to panic, running along the trail and knocking on the doors, but no one answered my cries for help. I hit each door as hard as I could and tried to break down the smaller ones, leaving a trail of blood from my torn fingers and hands.

Although I screamed as loud as I could for help, no one responded, and then, with a realization of hopelessness and despair, I knew that no one could hear me because I could not even listen to myself. At this point, I fell on the cobblestone and began to cry, all life flowing from me with the tears, my will to live broken and beaten. For what seemed like an eternity, I lay on the cold, hard walkway among the towering granite buildings and walls, lost and alone in a maze of my creation.

I stopped crying; no tears remaining within me, no life left to live, it seemed. Again, I heard the soft harp playing somewhere, far off, but in the darkness and confusing shadows around me, I could not locate the source of the music. It floated among the balconies and echoed off the walls. I could not find my way out, and all was lost.

Suddenly, great wings fluttered high above in the shadows among the highest balconies. Peering up into the blackness, I saw a great bird soaring among the towers. I realized that the monstrous winged creature circled the towers, slowly working its way down toward me on the road below it.

I quickly pulled myself up and, stumbling along the darkened wall, ran deeper into the maze. Death overshadowed me as I stumbled through the darkness, the shadow of the winged creature even darker than the blackness of the maze around me. I ran as fast as I could, but the road was narrow, and I kept tripping over the broken cobblestone, falling against the walls, tearing my flesh on the ragged, granite surfaces.

Complete darkness surrounded me. The monster breathed above me. I felt the foul, hot breath over me, its giant wings crashing through the wooden balconies above me, heavy beams falling around me. Death overtook me. My chains pulled me down, but deep within my soul, I wished to live.

I saw a brilliant light in the middle of complete darkness, a small white light at the end of a side road that illuminated the towers immediately around it. I turned down the road toward the light and ran toward it, but I was tired, and the great creature closed in. A balcony collapsed before me, blocking the alley with a tumble of heavy wooden beams and rock. The beast hovered above me. Fear captured my soul with its tentacles as I struggled through the rubble, fighting to get to the light. My hands were raw and bloody, and my strength failed me. With a great flutter of wings and the smell of sulfur and heat, the creature settled down on the road behind me. Still, the light beckoned me onward, and I saw a way through the rubble.

Then, a window opened on the wall beside me, revealing a room full of people with food and music. I turned to face the light from the window, but it was far too bright after being in the darkness, and it blinded me before I could shield my eyes. Unseen hands pulled me through the open window. Out on the road, the giant bird screamed in delight and flapped its enormous wings. With a great roar and a sudden crash of mighty wind, it disappeared back into the darkness from where it had come. Even though temporarily blinded, my last thought, before the window slammed shut and locked, was of the peaceful light at the end of the alley that had beckoned me. I had longed to reach that light, but at least the beast was gone. For that, I was thankful.

CHAPTER FIFTEEN

I awakened suddenly in the early morning light. My body shook because of my vivid memory of the dream that was so real to me that I looked immediately at my hands to see if they were torn and bloody.

The camp stirred outside as the nomads quickly prepared for the day's journey with renewed zeal after the happenings of the night before. Again, I had overslept. I grabbed a biscuit and washed it down with water from my canteen.

"Good morning," Lillian greeted me, "You look tired. Are you okay?"

"I'm fine. Can I help you prepare the wagon?" I asked and smiled. Her presence constantly improved my spirits.

"If that leg of yours works today, you can help me with the horses," she smiled.

"I think I can do that," I answered and hobbled behind her, crutch in hand.

Lillian gathered the horses that pulled our wagon, four huge beasts with shaggy manes and tails. I approached the corral cautiously, the nightmare still vivid in my memory, the fear intense.

Lillian did not fear the animals and quickly placed a harness on each. I, on the other hand, had great fear of them. They were powerful horses, yet Lillian handled them with confidence and authority. She led the horses from the corral, two at a time, and closed the wooden gate behind her.

Others were catching their horses, some with less success. A horse broke free, running past me as I climbed the fence. The horse trotted to the pond before being roped by one of the herdsmen and brought back to its owner. Lillian calmed her two animals as she looked at me nervously, standing nearby.

"You have nothing to be afraid of," she reassured me. "Here, take one of the reins."

She handed me the reins of one of the horses, and I took them cautiously. The horse looked down at me with black eyes and snorted, his ears back, sensing my fear and disliking it.

"It's okay. Just stroke his neck. He likes that."

I reached out and rubbed the giant beast, patting him on the neck, which calmed him.

"You see. He likes you. Now, lead him to the wagon. We must hurry. Father wants us to reach Halom as soon as possible."

I followed her to the wagon, where she hitched the horses, efficiently working the tackle.

"You are strong, Lillian. You are so different from the other women here," I commented.

Lillian laughed, "Despite Aunt Ruth's words, I prefer a man's world, Jonathan." She looked up at me with those bright green eyes, "but I am every bit a woman."

I immediately blushed and looked away, thankful she appeared not to notice, having turned her attention back to her work. Having completed her task, she climbed up to the seat, and I followed, placing my crutch next to me. Then, I realized that the prisoner was no longer tied to the wagon wheel. I knew that I still had to talk with him.

"Lillian, where is the Bene Elohim?"

"My father did not wish us to see him today. You saw what effect he had on us last night. He is tied in one of the supply wagons and under guard."

I turned, looked down the line of wagons forming, and noticed one surrounded by an armed escort. The wagon jolted forward as we began our journey. Hopefully, I will talk with him tonight, but it must be in secret. Part of me did not wish to be near the warrior, who, according to the nomads, was a fierce enemy, but deep within me, a part of my spirit called out for me to meet this man. The Light itself pulled me toward the warrior, and although I did not understand what was going on within me, I knew I had to approach him.

"Hey, Lillian!" a voice behind us broke my thoughts. It was Cristina who drove the wagon immediately behind us.

"Make sure you give Jonathan an easier ride today. He looked like he had ridden an ornery goat last night. Be easy on him," she kidded.

Lillian just laughed as we settled in for another day's journey. If we rode most of the day, we could camp by the river tonight along the edge of Halom. We would be in Halom proper in a few days, and I could be freed of my chains.

The horse stood just behind the knoll, hidden from view by a jumble of lava rocks that had spewed forth eons ago from a now-dead crater in the distance. He was rested after a night's sleep and stood silent as he watched the caravan of wagons begin to trail off into the distance in single file. Malak was in one of those wagons; if called, he would gallop in to rescue him as he had commanded the night before. The horse was an intelligent creature whose job was to support Malak, a Bene Elohim of Christendom, a job that he took seriously. He waited until all the wagons had left and the last of the herdsmen had gathered the sheep and cattle before he, too, began to follow the ancient trail of the nomads.

Patrick led his black knights across the plains at a gallop. They rode through the night across the prairie of short grass and scattered juniper, the landscape broken at times by upheavals of sandstone monuments or clumps of pine and rocky outcrops. In the early morning light, the small group galloped across a low rise and saw the ancient fortress in the shadows across the dusty savanna. They reined in their tired mounts, and Patrick dismounted to stretch. His wounded leg bled slightly again from the constant gallop.

As always, the great iron gates were shut, and Patrick noted with satisfaction that the sentries were at their post through his telescope, moving shadows on the great battlements over the gates. When Archon Krino received the news of the presence of the Bene Elohim in the realm, more sentries would be placed to protect the fortress from attack. He thought as he continued to scan the walls.

A soft morning breeze lifted the banners atop the ramparts, causing them to flutter and fall still as the breeze briefly passed.

"Shall we proceed, Patrick?" Peter asked.

Patrick placed the telescope back into its leather pouch and remounted his horse. He drank from his canteen and shifted his wounded leg a bit.

"No, Peter, we'll wait a few more minutes. You don't want to be at the gate when the sun rises and reaches the master's balcony."

The group waited, hidden from the view of the sentries by the dark shadows. Their vantage point overlooked the valley before them and the massive gates, towers, and battlements as the last of the darkness of the night receded across the plains, the morning light casting shadows from the scattered-out crops of sandstone. The shadows faded away, the way darkness always retreats when light arrives, until the sun's full glory emerged from behind the horizon.

The light gathered intensity as it reached the window at the balcony above the gates until suddenly, with a flash of brilliant, blinding light, a beam of pure white energy shot out, flooding the valley below. The light beam moved across the valley for a few seconds until it quickly disappeared into the window from where it had originated.

Patrick shielded his eyes as the light probed the valley floor. When he looked back at the balcony, a prominent, shadowed figure of a man stood there, having emerged with the light. The figure stood unmoving on the balcony for a few minutes as a detachment of Sahat approached the gate.

Patrick again looked through his telescope and watched as the guards, under one of his lieutenants' command, responded to the riders' call. The ramparts suddenly filled with archers as the gates opened. The Sahat reigned in their black horses and waited as the doors slowly opened. Patrick led his scouting party down the valley as the last riders entered, and the gates closed again.

The process repeated itself when Patrick called for the gate to be opened with great efficiency, which was a testament to the vigorous training that the men had gone through. Although well trained, Patrick thought, they had no real battle experience. They had never tasted blood, and deep within the recesses of his mind, he wondered if his men could stand up to a determined attack by the Bene Elohim. Only he and a few others had ever fought that race before.

"Good to see you back, Captain," the lieutenant greeted with a slight bow.

"I need to see Archon Krino at once, Stephen," Patrick answered. Above, the dark shadow stood motionless.

The lieutenant motioned upward, "The Master stands there many times throughout the day as if in a trance. What is going on, Captain? The whole fortress is afoot."

"Change is coming, Lieutenant, and I don't know if we can stand to it. Now tell me, where is Archon Krino?"

"He is on the mesa above by the fountains. A new detachment of Sahat arrived last night, and he is personally supervising their training."

"Thank you, Stephen, carry on. Peter, refresh the horses and get the men something to eat, but be prepared to travel again. We'll most likely be leaving soon."

Patrick dismounted, handing his horse over to Peter, and began to climb the stairway carved into the side of the cliff that ascended to the mesa above. He was tired, and his leg ached. After a few moments, he reached the top near where a fountain had been constructed beneath the shade of a dozen pine trees. Barracks lined the edge of a grove of trees, and a corral full of horses lay between the fountain and the barracks. This was the home of the Sahat.

Patrick spotted a group of warriors sparring near the tree line as Archon Krino watched close by. Unlike the other Archons of the realm, Krino did not have the customary following of bodyguards and disliked the company of women in his presence altogether. He had ruled over the plains of Sin through the cruelty of the Sahat, who claimed the chained fugitives, and the power of the Knights of Kratos, who guarded the keep and surrounding villages that spread across the plains.

Until now, he was content to allow the pompous Archon Sarkinos to control Hedone but disliked the newfound power of Archon Planos and Zanah, who were new to the realm. The Master held them in high esteem, allowing them to sway over the northern steppes and mountains to the Forest of Basar, an area he once ruled. That had to change, Krino thought as he watched the Sahat before him.

Archon Krino heard the approach of someone behind and turned to see the Captain of the Guard approaching him from the fountain.

Patrick bowed slightly before approaching his superior.

"I have come to report, my lord."

"The Bene Elohim are in the realm?" Krino asked, more of a statement than a question, for he had already sensed their presence.

"We found only one, my lord. A warrior who rode alone."

"He won't be alone for long. If a leader can be found among the fugitives, a fugitive who has the Light, then more of their kind will begin to appear. We must prepare ourselves."

Patrick wondered about that statement but only to himself. He remembered the Light as a child and a man who said he possessed it. Those were terrible memories, memories that drove him to be what he was today, one of the leaders of the Knights of Kratos, sworn to keep the Light from ever appearing in the realm again. But change was coming; his dreams were returning, and he was no longer sure within the depths of his soul.

"Come, Patrick, walk with me. It is hot and dry, and I have eaten too much dust already this morning."

Patrick followed Krino to the fountain and poured him a cup of wine. Krino removed his gloves and took the goblet.

"Do you have him?"

"No, but the nomads do. We watched as you commanded to ensure that he was captured, and we remained unseen."

"Very good. The nomads having him may be the best thing. Archon Planos has assured the Master that he can handle the situation if the Bene Elohim appears, and the Master believes him. I, on the other hand, do not." Archon Krino sighed, placing the goblet down and slapping his gloves across the rock to remove the dust.

"The Master places too much faith on him and that witch, Zanah, and has allowed them great power at my expense. There have been many signs throughout the realm that the Bene Elohim are preparing for an offensive, but the Master has done nothing. Archon Planos has promised that their power can be broken before it ever has a chance to become established, so we do nothing but wait behind our walls. "

"What do you suggest that we do?"

Archon Krino thought momentarily and then turned to face the captain, "Archon Planos thinks too highly of himself. The nomads are no match for a Bene Elohim. Even though one may be in their possession now, he won't be for long. Others of his kind are bound to rescue him, and Planos will be disgraced when that happens. They are dangerous and should not be played with."

He again turned to face the sun, thinking of some way to use what he knew to his advantage.

"Captain, take your scouts back to the realm of the nomads and follow them closely. We can do something to help break the master's trust. Before they reach their destination, take the Bene Elohim from them. The nomads are weak outside of their encampment at night. Take the Bene Elohim and bring him to me. The story will then be revealed that he escaped before Planos even got a chance to inform the Master that he had been captured. If more

Bene Elohim appears to rescue him and attack the nomads, do not assist them but get word back to me immediately. Take the tunnels to hasten your travel back. You should be able to catch up to them by nightfall."

"Yes, my lord." The captain saluted and turned to leave.

"Oh, and Captain, I remind you that this is to be kept a secret. If you are discovered so far into Planos's territory, it will not go well for you. Do you understand?"

"Yes, my lord."

Patrick turned to begin the descent back down the steps, wondering what type of trickery was happening. He had a job to do, but the more he thought about it, the more he began worrying. If caught, he and his men would be severely punished, and no doubt, Krino would not support him in any way. Krino had too much to lose. Although he was Archon Krino's subordinate, he decided he would not be attached to the losing side of a power struggle if Krino's schemes failed. He had to be extremely careful to ensure he had a way out if things went badly and the mission failed.

CHAPTER SIXTEEN

The rolling hills of Halom lay snuggled beneath the protecting arms of the ragged peaks of the mountains of Crystalline, a towering range of broken cliffs and snow-covered ridges with flanks of dark green alpine forest and scattered barren rocky slopes higher up and mixed hardwood forest on the lower slopes. A thick fog forever shrouded the highest pinnacles from view, casting a foreboding spirit on all who climbed too high up the slopes. No one had ever reached the top and returned to tell what mysteries lay hidden on the other side.

Snow-covered peaks and the abundant water available from the many mountain lakes and streams, as well as the thick groves of forest scattered across the flowered meadows, created a haven from the heat of the lower plains. Brightly colored tents belonging to small groups of nomads dotted the hillsides. Another small band of thirty nomads arrived, allowing their herds to graze freely among the meadows, mixing in with the other herds, as was the custom. Meanwhile, in Halom, each clan's herds grazed together, having been branded with the clan's mark beforehand. Halom was a happy place, a peaceful place where no enemy dared invade because of the combined power of the nomadic clans.

Nestled among a grove of large oaks against the granite walls of the lower ledges of the closest mountain stood a huge tent surrounded by a wooden palisade with a closed gate. Two large, armored warriors guarded it. This was the council tent, which only the leaders of the large and small clans were allowed to enter, except at the ceremony of the chains, where the individual fugitive could enter only when blindfolded.

Two riders approached across the plains in the early afternoon sun, a small cloud of dust marking the progression over the ancient trail of the nomads. As the riders reached the first rise along the edge of the tree-lined meadow, they were intercepted by several of the encampment's sentries who escorted the weary travelers through the maze of tents alongside a small mountain pond to the wooden gates outside the council tent.

The guards at the gate stood motionless as if no one was there.

"Two messengers from the clan of Captain Connelly with urgent news for the council," one of the escorts stated. Then he turned his mount and rode with his companion back to their position on the perimeter.

The two messengers dismounted from their exhausted horses, themselves excessively worn from the long journey. They had ridden hard through the night and all day with only a few short stops for water to reach the council as quickly as possible. The horses had been used up and would need several days of rest before being ridden again.

"Wait here," one of the guards commanded and turned to enter the gate.

One of the councils, a tall hooded man, had already opened the gate and stood in the opening.

Through the open gate, the messengers saw flower gardens and fountains among trees, with benches and tables filled with food. Several men wearing white tunics, golden hand bands, and sandals stood near the tables, and two lovely women dressed in the finest silk garments lounged on the benches by the fountains. The sight of all this surprised them both. Sensing their reaction, the councilman pulled back his hood, revealing the rugged face of an older man with blond hair and a short, graying beard. He smiled.

"My name is Theosis, a high member of the Council of Halom. You must have urgent news to have ridden so far."

"Yes, my lord," the messenger answered, "Captain Connelly sent us on ahead with great haste. We have captured a Bene Elohim."

Theosis gasped just as another man behind the gate stepped outside.

"Did you say a Bene Elohim?" Theosis asked, shocked.

Theosis looked around quickly and motioned for all to enter the gate. They entered, the wooden gate closing behind them. The two messengers had never been inside the wooden walls that separated the council tents from the rest of Halom and were both nervous and a bit frightened.

"Here, you must be hungry. Eat and drink while I gather the others. You must tell us the entire story, but not before all of the council is here to listen."

Theosis left to gather the others scattered throughout the compound as the two messengers began to feast on the food in front of them. They were hungry and had never seen so much food in one place.

A few minutes later, Theosis appeared with four other men, all wearing the same tunic and sandals. The council comprised five men, each representing one of the five great nomad clans. The messengers learned that Theosis represented their clan.

"Now then, tell us what you have seen," Theosis encouraged the councilmen as they settled on the benches.

The two messengers told their story, sometimes in unison, at other times, helping the other with missed details. They said of the Bene Elohim being captured by the sentries and that Connelly feared he was only one of many who may be hiding nearby, preparing to invade the land. When they had completed their story, the council told them to rest, but they were determined to get fresh horses and ride back to their clan in case of trouble. Their clan was still several days' travel away from Halom. The council commended their loyalty and gave them provisions for the return trip and two fresh, strong horses. A few minutes later, the two were on their way back to their clan, backtracking down the ancient trail into the lower plains.

"Bene Elohim have not been in the realm for years. Their few remaining followers are scattered, hiding in the great cities," one of the councils remarked.

"If it is true that one is among us, then others will follow," Macmara stated as he watched the two messengers disappear into the lower plains among the floating heat waves.

"They dare not show themselves. Our forces are strong. They are sure to know that. Captain Connelly could be mistaken?" another member questioned.

"No, Phagan, Captain Connelly is not mistaken. Rest assured, if he sent messengers on ahead with such news, he wanted to prepare us for what is to come," Theosis answered and looked toward Macmara, "And you are right, Macmara, if one Bene Elohim is in the land, then others will follow, but only after a leader is found. The rebels must be unified to be effective. Our lord has taken great steps to disband them. As you know, we have already converted many. The messengers said that the warrior had been captured. That is unusual. The Bene Elohim are very resourceful and make few mistakes."

"Then possibly they are weak. If this one was easily captured, what have we to fear?"

"Our very existence, Phagan, if the warrior finds who he is looking for. To be a powerful force, they must have the strength of a devoted follower. They can only be effective if they have disciples. The power of the Light can be very strong. It can destroy us all, but only if they know how to use it. If the Bene Elohim is in the camp, the fugitive is the one. He is of the realm of the plains of sin but is scheduled for the ceremony of the chains as soon as they arrive. After that, he will become one of us, and we will have nothing to worry about."

"What if there were more of them, and the clan is attacked before they reach Halom? Should we not send a troop out to intercept them?" Phagan asked.

Theosis thought for a while before shaking his head, "It took the messengers all night and most of the day to reach us, but the clan has been traveling this way all day and will continue to do so until dark. If a detachment leaves at once, it may be able to intercept them during the night or early tomorrow morning. The nomads do not travel by night even though we protect them from the Sahat of Krino by treaty. They still fear the darkness. He will stop for the night; hopefully, the detachment will reach him before he resumes his journey tomorrow.

"Our nomadic warriors are no match for the Bene Elohim if they attack in strength," Macmara stated.

"But surely our lord's knights can stand up to them."

"Yes, but they are few. His power is strong over the inhabitants of this land, but I am unsure if his knights are strong enough to defeat a full detachment of Bene Elohim."

"But you said they only appear in numbers when they have a following. There has been no sign of such," countered Phagan.

"You speak out of fear," a voice spoke from behind the fountain, startling all the men.

A form began to materialize from within the cascading water, at first just the changing shape of the water itself and then a soft green hue until the figure of an overwhelmingly beautiful woman stepped out from the water. She had long black hair and green eyes and wore a dark green silk dress tied at her thin waist with a black sash, the dress accentuating her perfect figure. She pulled back her wet hair from her face, and immediately, she was completely dry. The very sight of her beauty was intoxicating, as she well knew.

The woman walked up to Theosis, gently pressing her body up against his, and lightly, seductively kissed the older man on the neck just below his ear. All the men stepped backward and fell silent as the courtyard immediately filled with the fragrance of her perfume.

"The Bene Elohim do not threaten us as long as the people are kept blinded to the truth," she spoke in whispered, mesmerizing tones as she walked among the councilmen, playfully caressing each of their necks and shoulders with her small, delicate hands. "But you are right in saying that your brave nomads are no match for them."

She closed her eyes dreamily, "They are beautiful creatures, strong and masculine, but even the Bene Elohim can be seduced and charmed."

Finally, Theosis regained his composure, "My Lady Zanah, of course, you are right, but the fugitive Jonathan is among them who may have a portion of the Light. If the Bene Elohim can free himself and the fugitive before the ceremony of the chains, we may have a problem."

Upon hearing this, Zanah stopped her dreaming and opened her eyes, staring directly into those of Theosis, almost burning them with her glare, "My dear man, when were you going to inform me of this?" she asked.

Theosis suddenly became frightened. This woman could tantalize and threaten you with her voice and those brilliant green eyes.

"We were not sure, my lady; we are still not sure. We only suspect that he is the one."

"You were at the camp just a few days ago. Did you not find out if he indeed possessed the Light," Zanah asked, and then, seeing the fear on the man's face, she continued, "Oh, I see. You still fear the Light, even after all this time. Theosis, it has no power!" Zanah shouted and then regained her composure.

"Lady Zanah, we must see Archon Planos. We ask for...."

"I know, I know. You ask for a detachment of knights. Go to him, Theosis. I am tired of this. It brings me no pleasure, and pleasure is what I desire."

The woman again seductively moved among the men, weaving her charms. Just as quickly as she appeared from behind the fountain, she disappeared into the mist, leaving the intoxicating scent of spices and flowers.

For a few seconds, the men stood, totally seduced by her fleeting presence as she wanted them to be before, finally brought out of their trance by the approaching guard.

"Our lord has requested your presence. You are to come at once, " the guard said and turned to exit out the back door of the courtyard.

The councilmen knew they were expected to come right away if summoned in this manner. For years, Archon Planos had protected them and had given them special favors and power to rule over the nomads of the plains. They all knew he also had the power to destroy them if he chose. So, they followed the guard warily.

The back exit from the courtyard led into a winding, narrow tunnel that extended back through the very base of the mountain. Torches set in ornate golden brackets lit the walls of the underground hallway with flickering light, the pungent smell of pitch strong in the otherwise dead, still air.

At first, the guard filled the entire opening with his armored form, but after the first turn, the hallway widened. The torches cast shadows across the bare granite walls. They turned another corner, the hallway suddenly in total darkness, and then turned again and entered a large room lit by the same torches as before.

The room was round; the floor smoothed white marble, the walls pink stone polished and smooth. Four larger torches lit the room well, situated at each cardinal point, north, south, east, and west, although no one in the room but the guard knew which was which. A total of sixteen iron, locked doors surrounded the men, four between each of the flickering torches. Here, the air was fresh and clean, the pitch lending its fragrance to the smell of rose blossoms and the faint, almost undetectable, salty smell of the ocean.

A polished white marble fountain trimmed in gold dominated the center of the room, the massive stone disappearing into the darkness above where the light from the torches could not reach. Sparkling water cascaded over a series of ledges carved into the stone, originating from an unknown source above, before splashing into a basin surrounding the rock on the floor.

"Drink from the fountain of life to cleanse yourself before entering." The guard commanded.

Each council member drank from the fountain. At first, the water was bitter, but after a moment, it turned sweet. The water was poisonous to any council member who was not genuinely loyal to Archon Planos.

After assuring himself that everyone had drank from the fountain, the guard unlocked one of the great doors and opened it, stepping aside to allow the men to enter.

They proceeded through the open door, which immediately closed behind them. They had entered a broad, hidden valley of nearly a hundred acres. All around them rose shear, granite walls of the mountain. A stream with trees flowed from a spring and emptied into a cavern that led deep into the wasteland of broken rock, ledges, and towering granite peaks. The towering Crystalline Mountains surrounded the valley, the highest ridges hidden in the foreboding fog. The meadow before them was covered with blue and yellow flowers in complete contrast to the desolation high above. Elk grazed far across the meadow. Several horses stood near a small corral next to a log stable. Built against the valley wall near the entrance was a two-storied stone house of perhaps ten rooms with a separate kitchen and dining hall. Above the front door over the porch hung a bronze shield with a green star painted across the front. This stone structure was the headquarters of Archon Planos.

The five men stood by the door, overtaken by the beauty of the valley before them. No one else knew of this place, even their women and servants. The winding tunnel was constantly guarded, and death came instantly to anyone who entered the tunnel's outer door unless Archon Planos himself requested. The guard who had summoned them had not entered the valley but had closed the door behind them and locked it. This was discomforting to the council, who stood silently waiting for their master. Each time they had been summoned to this place, it had always been this way. They would sometimes wait up to an hour before the master appeared.

To one side of the stone house stood a veranda shaded by several large oaks, and on the table lay an assortment of fruit and several bottles of wine. The table was set for six with beautiful, sparkling crystal plates and glasses. Somewhere far off, the faint sound of harp music and laughter floated in the air. Horses stood lazily in their corral, enjoying the cool afternoon breeze. In this place of tranquility and beauty, time seemed to stand still, and all five men began to feel a sense of well-being, having forgotten their former apprehension.

"Come, Council of Halom. You wish to speak to me?" Archon Planos beckoned suddenly from the veranda.

They turned to see that he sat at the table, pouring himself a glass of wine. Behind him stood two bronze warriors, and Zanah lounged on a chaise lounge. She appeared to be sleeping, unconcerned with those around her, undoubtedly caught up in her fantasy of dreams. The five bowed and seated themselves at the table.

Archon Planos motioned to the food, "Here, eat. You were interrupted from your meal. Zanah has said you received word that a Bene Elohim has been found on the Plains of Apistia."

"Yes, my lord. Captain Connelly has captured him."

"Captured!" Archon Planos drank from his goblet. "Well, well, that is highly unusual. She also told me that fugitives have a piece of the Light among them."

Theosis hesitated, "Yes, my lord, but he has consented to the ceremony of the chains and will no longer be seduced by that Light once free of his chains."

"That may be true, Theosis, but seduction is a very powerful force," Archon Planos pointed to Zanah, "as you know. She is beautiful, is she not? But beware of her. She can be very dangerous as well."

He drank again, "But seduction works both ways. The Light can also seduce with its beauty. Archon Krino has failed yet again to destroy all the fugitives who have somehow received the Light, and he has also failed to find the source. Even Archon Sarkinos has failed to find the source, even though it is rumored that there are followers of the Light still in the great city of Hedone. But no matter, charms, seduction, and deception will work in our favor. We can unite the nomads together against the Bene Elohim if need be. Hopefully, this will not be necessary."

Archon Planos sighed, "I am tired of this game, but it is necessary to ensure victory for the great master. I will give you six knights. Take a detachment of nomads and intercept Connelly in case there are more Bene Elohim out there. When the fugitive appears before the ceremony of the chains for their removal, we will ensure the Light is destroyed."

What a victory over Krino that will be, he thought to himself.

"Then the Bene Elohim will be powerless and can be banished from the realm as was done those many years ago. Now leave me."

With a flick of his hand, the five men were again in their outer courtyard, among the fountains.

"Phagan, gather a dozen of the best nomadic warriors we have with the fastest horses. We will leave immediately," ordered Theosis as they regained their bearing.

If Bene Elohim were present, Theosis wanted to see for himself. He hurriedly changed into more appropriate riding clothes and packed an overnight bag.

Outside the gate, the warriors waited, led by a young clansman named McConnell and six bronze knights who stood off to one side, mysterious and aloof. Phagan had also retrieved Theosis, a horse.

"Thank you, Phagan. I will see you the day after tomorrow," and with that farewell, Theosis mounted his mount and led the band of warriors and knights off across the plains, following the same trail the two messengers had taken an hour before.

Standing among the rocky ledges overlooking Halom, Archon Planos, and Zanah watched as the band rode off into the heat waves of the lower plains, their dust clouds the only evidence of their existence from this distance. Below them scattered the beautifully decorated tents of the nomads. From their vantage point high above, they saw the sentries, the women cooking, the children playing. To one side, a group of young men wrestled. They all appeared happy and content, precisely what the two wished for them to be. Happy subjects create very few problems.

"They have such weak minds, don't you think?" Archon Planos remarked dryly.

Zanah said nothing but continued to stare down into the encampment below.

"There are many whose time has come. We must be cautious about how we cleanse the land. If the Bene Elohim resume an offensive, we can pre-empt their struggle for the nomads by further deception."

Archon Planos turned to face Zanah, who looked up to him.

"Take a detachment out right away. It should be done before Captain Connelly arrives. His hatred of the Bene Elohim will do the rest for us."

"Yes, my lord," she responded, and they both turned and proceeded back down the ledge to their hidden valley below.

CHAPTER SEVENTEEN

Connelly pushed us hard, allowing very few stops.

The river marked the border of the hills of Halom, and if we reached the river by nightfall, we could reach Halom by the following night. We traveled through a vast expanse of desert country covered with scattered short grass, yellowed by the summer heat, and occasional areas of barren sand and broken rocks. I had never traveled through this country before. Just a few weeks before, my entire existence had been within the forest, prairie, and the city called Hedone.

Before meeting the nomads, I had never heard of Halom, but the more Lillian described the place as we rode over the endless desert trail, the more I longed to be there. To be free of my chains and live among the nomads, befriended by these people, especially Lillian, was more than I had ever hoped. And now I was but a day away.

A great, red-tailed hawk followed us the entire day. Otherwise, I saw no living creatures out across the barren desert.

Cristina had seen the bird first and had yelled for us to look up as it passed overhead. When I first noticed the bird, my first thought was of the dream of the night before, but then I remembered the eagle that had followed me in the forest before I had injured my ankle.

On that day, which seemed like an eternity ago, I had wished that I, too, could fly and be free from this world of death. The hawk circled above, occasionally swooping behind the low ridges to the west and returning shortly afterward.

So much had happened, and I had so many questions, but one thing was sure. I would not do anything to jeopardize my chances of getting the chains removed. The people around me were free, but as we continued to ride and Lillian became very still, lost in her thoughts, something deep inside me cautioned me to be wary. Everything was not what it appeared to be.

"Jonathan, you must see through the power of the Light to see the truth of what is around you," a ghostly voice whispered.

I looked around, expecting someone to be immediately behind me, but no one was there.

I reached into my pouch and pulled out the Light by the leather band that held it. The Light was very small and dull, but as soon as I touched it, it reacted to me and increased in intensity. I was very hot, yet the Light was cool, which surprised me. The Light kept me warm When I was wet and cold. Now, it cooled my hand. I had to understand the truth behind the mystery. Was the Light just a magician's trickery, or was it the wondrous power the legends spoke of? I slipped the Light back into the pouch again.

Malak sat, bound, and gagged in the back of the wagon, armed escorts surrounding the wagon. It was sweltering, and thirst dried his lips, but no water had been offered. The tightly bound canvas cover over the opening kept even the soft desert breeze out of his prison cell. Outside, the constant creak of the wagon as it jolted across the rocky desert became his only companion. Now and then, one of the riders mumbled something unintelligible. Otherwise, everyone was quiet, all enduring the constant travel over the ancient trail.

Malak remembered hundreds of years before, when a different race of people had traveled the trail. Now, it was the trail of the nomads, a scattered people lost in a world of deception. Malak could see their true form but could do nothing to save them until the Light was freed and an Apostolos Or found.

"Jonathan, you must see through the power of the light to see the truth of what is around you," he spoke softly, pushing the thought through time and space toward the fugitive.

Suddenly, a surge of energy pulsed through his veins, filling him with strength and refreshment as if the winds off the snow-covered mountains of Crystalline had blown through the closed canvas. He knew that Jonathan was touching the Light. He could feel the strength that it gave him. There was still hope. As long as the fugitive continued to be interested, the Light's power could still be unleashed, and he would gain strength. Malak also sensed that his horse was nearby, and from the occasional call of the hawk above the caravan, the black knights of the night before were close as well.

The wagon viciously bumped over a large rock, and the driver swore. The road was rocky, not the well-smoothed surface when it was first used many years ago. He thought it was time for a change, time for the veil to be lifted, exposing the deception. First, though, he had to talk with the fugitive directly, but for that conversation to be meaningful, it had to be initiated by the fugitive himself. All he could do now was make suggestions, which was what he had just done and with some success, he thought.

"Did you say something, Jonathan?" Lillian asked.

"No, I was just thinking of how hot it was. How long do we have yet to travel?"

"I'm not sure," she answered. "I'm worried about father. He never pushes us this hard. He seems afraid, and that is something that I've not seen before."

Connelly rode in front of us, his shoulders slumped. Like all the others, his horse walked lethargically, taking one tired step at a time across the desert, pressing through country that became more desolate as we continued.

Distant rocky crags and ledges of a mountain range loomed on the horizon, their highest peaks hidden in a thick fog, only occasionally revealing the glisten of snow and ice. This sight gave all of us hope because we knew that at the foot of those mountains lay the hills of Halom.

The hawk again swooped low over the wagon trail, and even Malak caught a glimpse of the bird through the small opening in the rear canvas as it glided behind the ridge and disappeared. The bird landed with a flutter of wings on the outstretched, gloved hand of the scout Peter.

Peter placed the bird on a perch fastened to the back of his saddle. Four other knights, including Patrick, trotted up to his position. They had just exited the tunnels from which great distances could be traveled quickly, but only if Archon Krino opened the gate. That shortcut had allowed the group to catch up to the nomads in just a few hours.

"The nomads are pushing themselves very hard, Captain. They usually do not travel at this rate," commented Peter.

"They fear the Bene Elohim. Even Archon Planos' power over them cannot free them of that fear. They must be trying to reach the river Dolios before dark. If I were their leader, I would try to cross the river before dark and that will take some time as well. There is a ford, but the river is deep. It will be difficult to get the wagons across safely."

Suddenly bored of the conversation, the bird launched into the sky again on his constant trail of the nomads.

Peter laughed, "He never liked the back end of a horse."

Patrick stared off into the distance, remembering the subtle threat from Archon Krino.

"Peter, you know that we are in a precarious situation so far into the realm of Planos. Since the great council, new control boundaries were set, and we have crossed them."

"Surely, Archon Krino has cleared this with the Master?"

"I don't think so. Our mission is to expose the deception for Krino's gain. A power struggle is going on, and we have been cast in the middle. If Krino fails, we may be left hanging out to dry," Patrick answered. We must be extremely cautious. We are being pulled into their struggle, and I do not wish to be the scapegoat if things go wrong."

"What should we to do?" Peter asked.

"We are to shadow the nomads and keep our eyes open for any attack from the Bene Elohim. If the nomads are attacked, we are to offer no assistance," Patrick shook his head in disgust, "It appears we are nothing but lowly spies, but we must be cautious spies. If the Bene Elohim escapes, we are to capture him. If not, we will sneak into the camp and take him by force. Krino wishes to discredit Planos."

"Do you think that there are others?"

"No, I do not. They are a strange race with strange beliefs but usually work alone. Many years ago, in Hedone, I knew those who followed the Light before I was recruited and freed of my chains. I saw the Light once, but I had no respect for the man holding it." Patrick did not say that the person was his father, who used the Light for his gain and abused him as a child.

"I paid it no mind, but the Light has haunted me. If we can rid the realm of its evil, we will all be the better."

Patrick spurred his horse forward, and Peter thought that maybe his friend was not as sure about that statement as he let everyone believe him. He, too, had been dreaming a lot as of late, dreams that confused his thoughts, casting doubts on the mission to which they had all sworn allegiance.

"Come," Patrick called over his shoulder to the others, "Let's ride ahead to the next oasis and wait for them there. They have to stop for water soon."

As they rode, Peter glanced up at the afternoon sun, "They might just make it across the river by night, but it will be a close-run thing."

The five knights rode on a parallel course hidden from the caravan's view by the low sandstone ridge. Although they were several miles away, they still had to be careful not to be seen, especially since a constant cloud of dust marked their progression across the desert as they rode.

CHAPTER EIGHTEEN

The horse stood under the shade of a gnarled pine, waiting for the caravan to proceed onward, hiding from the afternoon sun within the limited shade of the tree and dozing. Above, she occasionally took notice of the hawk that followed the path of the wagons. However, He did not see the small group of bedraggled fugitives quietly approaching her.

Two men and a girl cautiously crept toward the horse. The process was made extremely difficult by the heavy burden of the crossed chains. Filthy, torn, and bloodied clothing barely covered their emaciated bodies. Having picked up the caravan's trail earlier in the day, they followed, hoping to sneak into the camp at night for food. They, too, were searching for freedom from their chains but had no clue which way to go.

And then they saw the horse, a beautiful, saddled stallion with a golden shield attached to the front flank, a sword, bow, and quiver of arrows, and canteens and saddlebags attached to the leather saddle. This horse carried treasure that they had never seen before except in Hedone. If they could capture the horse, they could ride to the camp and possibly trade the weapons for food and safe passage.

It was now late afternoon. With darkness would come the Sahat. The night before, one of their numbers had been taken as they lay terrified behind a cluster of large boulders. They did not wish to succumb to the same fate and desperately needed shelter before another night began.

One of them had fashioned a crude rope from torn clothing, and they hoped to catch the horse while he slept in the shade of the pine tree. The three spread out and slowly crept forward within a few feet of the horse.

Finally sensing their presence, the horse suddenly bolted toward the trail, but not before the girl threw the rope looping over the shield. The woman desperately held on to the rope as she fell violently to the ground as the two men chased her and the horse. The horse dragged her across the desert until she could no longer hold on, her hands torn and bloody.

The men caught up to her as she lay on the ground. The horse continued to run, panting for air and covered in dust. In a rage of anger, the two men kicked and beat her as she tried to stand, knocking her back to the ground among the ragged rocks until she finally collapsed, unconscious. They thought she was useless to them now, having befriended her only because she had a bit of food and the rope. Stripping her of her tattered clothing, they left her lying in the middle of the trail to die and proceeded on their way after the horse.

The two nomadic herdsmen worked hard to keep the herd together. They had been stationed at the back of the herd, a very unpleasant position, but the herdsmen rotated the position throughout the day. At the back, one had to constantly watch for stragglers, protect the slower and weaker from the wolves that followed the herd, and eat the dust of the herd. That was especially difficult in a desert country. The two were teenagers accustomed to the arduous duties of the herdsmen, but after several hot, dry hours on the trail, they were wearing down.

"Captain Connelly has been pushing us hard today," commented the oldest.

"I heard that he fears the Bene Elohim," questioned the youngest.

"I don't know why he would be here in this miserable place. Nobody in his right mind would travel across this place on such a day."

"I guess that makes us out of our mind," the younger said, and they laughed.

The two rode a broad sweep around their herd's rear to ensure no stragglers. One good thing about the herd being tired was that they tended to stay with the group. Some of the weaker ones lagged, but they did not stray. They followed the path, heads down, determined to reach the next watering hole. As the two herdsmen rode up on a low rise behind the cloud of dust created by the herd, the youngest noticed movement far off along the trail.

"David, is that a horse back there on the trail?" the younger herdsman asked.

The older one turned his mount and looked in the direction his younger assistant had pointed out, "I believe it is. It's saddled and appears to have weapons attached to the saddle. Do you see that?"

"We should take a closer look," Nate said hopefully.

"Yes, but we best be careful. Suppose there are more Bene Elohim close. I'll take the rope and see if I can catch the horse. You stand watch."

They trotted their horses back down the trail into the small valley, keeping a wary eye out for whatever it was that had startled the horse and caused it to run. As they rode closer, the horse pranced nervously, looking back down the trail toward the two herdsmen. The horse didn't mind the approaching herdsmen so much but was wary of the two fugitives hiding in the rocks nearby. He thought of bolting and running away for a moment, but he calmed and stood watching the two riders approach. Noticing the rope still looped around the shield; he backed up a few steps until he could place his hind foot on the rope. He then turned himself until the rope slid off its perch across the shield and fell to the ground.

The two herdsmen stopped a few hundred feet away.

"Did you see that?" David whispered, "That is one smart horse. Look at the weapons. That is truly a warrior's horse."

"Yes, but where is the warrior?" Nate whispered back.

"He must belong to the captive. He surely had a horse. Only the fugitives travel across the land on foot."

The horse lifted his head toward them, smelling for them, and then neighed a greeting to the herdsmen's horses that answered in kind. The two fugitives remained hidden in the jumble of rocks nearby, powerless to approach the horse now and frightened by the presence of the herdsmen, thinking at first that they were soldiers. When the two strangers walked their horses in closer and stopped, the fugitives realized they were not armed.

The first fugitive whispered to the other, "If they dismount, we may have a chance to surprise them. The older one has a rope, and both have food and water. If we take them, we can capture their horses as well."

The second she acknowledged him, greed overcame their previous fear.

"Okay, Nate, dismount and hold back our horses. I will try to get close enough to him to take the reins. Hopefully, I will not need the rope. He appears to be settling down and likes the company of our horses," David ordered and dismounted slowly, careful not to make any sudden movement that may scare the horse away. Nathaniel also dismounted and collected his partner's horse.

The two fugitives plotted their attack.

"You charge the younger one holding the horses. He already looks frightened. When the older one turns, I will kill him. We can both take care of the other and capture the horses."

David slowly walked up to the horse, who stood his ground.

"Okay, boy, easy now. I don't want to hurt you," David spoke softly, trying to reassure the horse. The boy slowly made his way up to the horse and patted him gently on the neck. The horse pushed his nose against the boy's chest in greeting as David collected the reins and fed the horse a small piece of sugar that he carried as treats for his horse. He turned to Nathaniel, who stood holding the other two horses, "Well, it looks like we have gained a new friend."

Suddenly, the horse jerked violently free from his hold, knocking the young man down. The two fugitives jumped up from their hiding place, screaming. The suddenness of their attack caught both herdsmen off guard. Nathaniel had been so intent on watching David with the strange warrior horse that he had not seen the two rise from behind the rocks.

"Watch out!" Nate screamed as one fugitive knocked him to the ground among the hooves of the two horses. Kicking wildly, they managed to break free, but not before hitting Nate with a sharp blow across the ribs. Nate felt the sharp pain of what had to be broken ribs before he fell hard on the desert floor as the foul-smelling, chain-covered fugitive attacked him.

The fugitive grabbed a rock to hit him across the face, but Nate dodged the hit. Nate struggled to escape, but the fugitive hit him again in the ribs and then once against the side of his head with the rock as they rolled beneath the horses.

David quickly regained his composure and stood up as the second fugitive swung at him with a branch. He ducked under the swing and drew his knife from the sheath at his waist. As the fugitive pressed forward, the herdsman struck hard with the knife toward the man's heart, but the chains deflected the blade, and the knife tore a wound across the exposed stomach instead.

The fugitive gasped in pain and fell away from the herdsman. Forgetting his companion, he regained his footing, and clutching his wound, he turned to run back down the desert trail from where he had come, leaving a blood trail to mark his way.

David turned quickly, knife in hand. Nate struggled with the other attacker. He ran toward his young assistant, who freed himself from his assailant and managed to hit him across the head. The fugitive fell away from the herdsman just as David approached.

The man stood up, panting. The boy tried to stand, but he had been beaten badly and tumbled back down headfirst into the sand.

The fugitive stood half naked and starved, massive chains covering his chest and shoulders, molding themselves, it seemed, into his raw, bloody skin. David suddenly felt sorry for the creature before him.

"Your friend has left you."

Nate struggled again to stand up.

Without turning, David asked, "Are you alright?"

"I'll be fine. But I think I have a few broken ribs."

"I should kill you for attacking us, but that is not our way. We are free of our chains."

"You are not free," the fugitive interrupted, "No one is free in this land. You have been deceived. I was once like you, but it is all a lie."

"You will die here in the desert," David answered.

"Death would be a welcome thing," the man said and suddenly charged David.

He grabbed the knife and thrust it deep into his chest. David let go of the knife and backed away in disbelief, astonished as the man fell to his knees. He pulled the knife from the wound and threw it to the ground in front of him as David rushed up to the fugitive and knelt beside him.

"Why did you do such a thing? I offered you freedom?"

"You offered nothing. All is hopeless. I am a prisoner of my master," the man gasped and coughed blood, "My time is near, and soon the Sahat will overtake me. I tried your way once, and it did not help me. You have been lied to."

"What do you mean? Look at me. I don't have the chains of death. My people are free from them," David answered him. "Your time is not over. There may still be a chance. I can take you back to camp, where we have medicine that can help."

"No, yours is a false hope. I once rode with the nomads until I saw the Light, which showed me that it was all a lie. I ran away from the Light and the nomads with more chains around me than ever before. I was frightened by your false hope, but I was more frightened by what I had seen."

"The Light is evil, but I can show you a way to freedom. Come with us," David pleaded.

"No!" the man yelled, standing back up. There is no hope! Leave me be, for I wish to be alone. I will reason with my master. The Sahat will soon take me, and then it will finally be over."

The man walked away into the shimmering heat waves.

David retrieved his knife and cleaned it with the sand. He then helped Nate over to the shade of a gnarled pine tree.

"Hold on, my friend. I'll get the horses and then clean your wounds."

"What did the fugitive mean when he said we were not free?"

"I don't know. He has been blinded to the truth," David answered as he watched the chained fugitive disappear behind the rocks. He looked up at the sun. He had to get the boy back to camp.

"I'll be back with our horses and some water."

Luckily, the horses were not too far away and were easily retrieved. David ignored the warrior horse and returned to the tree. He gave Nate a drink from one of the canteens and then took one himself. The water was hot but wet, which eased the cracking of his lips caused by the heat, low humidity, and sand of the desert. Taking a cloth, he wetted it and washed the boy's head wounds. He then tore strips of fabric and wrapped the young herdsman around the chest. It appeared he had several broken ribs. Each rasping breath caused sharp pains, and the boy gasped.

"Can you ride?"

"I believe so. I surely don't want to stay out here," the youth replied.

"Okay, let me help you mount up. We'll take it easy."

David helped the young herdsman mount his horse. "Now, hold tight; we'll travel slow."

Nate pointed," Look, the mare is still here. Can you lead her back to camp as well? Then these broken ribs won't be for nothing."

David walked his horse over to the horse that stood in the trail.

"Easy boy," he said as he reached across and gathered the harness. It was then that he saw the woman in the trail. She was a fugitive like the others but with fewer chains around her thin frame. She lay face down on the trail, her arms outstretched in front of her. She had been stripped of her clothes and lay naked under the glare of the afternoon sun. At first, he thought that she was dead, and then he saw her stir.

"What do you see?"

"Another fugitive, but this one is a woman.'

David dismounted, wary that this was a trap. He watched the girl as he searched through his saddlebags and found a long cotton shirt. The woman stirred, trying to push herself up. She realized with terror that she was not alone and pulled herself over against a nearby rock, pulling her knees up against her chest to cover her nakedness. Her eyes were wide with fear as she looked from one of the strangers to another and then all around her.

"Easy now. We won't hurt you," David reassured.

He handed the shirt to her, keeping his head turned away. She hesitated at first, then quickly snatched the shirt from David's hands and put it on.

"Who did this to you?"

She did not say a word. David returned to his horse and retrieved his canteen and some fruit. He brought them back to her, laid both on the ground in front of her, and then backed away. She grabbed the fruit, quickly ate it, and then drank from the canteen, the whole time watching the two herdsmen warily like a caged animal.

Seeing that she was drinking too quickly, David reached for the canteen, "Slow down, not so much at first."

"Thank you," she finally spoke, her voice raspy from lack of water.

"We have an encampment nearby with plenty of food and women who can treat your wounds. Let us help you."

"You are a strange race and have no chains. Do you have the power to remove these from me?" she asked hesitantly.

"We do not, but we know of those who do," David answered, reaching out his hand.

This time, she also reached out with a glimmer of hope.

David picked her up and placed her on the saddle of his horse. He now had two wounded people to get back to camp. He then mounted the warrior horse.

"What happened to the others?" the girl asked as they rode toward the distant dust column marking the caravan's location.

"We ran them off," the younger herdsman answered, a bit proud in spite of his many wounds. He had never been in a fight before.

"They used me, like all men before."

"You are among friends now. I am David, and this is Nate. What is your name?"

"Heather."

"Well, Heather, you will be safe with our clan."

Heather had heard that line many times before by bands of fugitives, merchants in Hedone, and even the Knights of Kratos, but it had always been the same. Men used her and promised her freedom, shelter, and food for her body, but in the end, it was always the same. When they tired of her, they forgot her. She was used to it and would do whatever it took to be taken care of. Sooner or later, the men would tire of her, but until then, she would not starve in the barren desert.

CHAPTER NINETEEN

The faint outline of trees created a black ribbon against the horizon below the even more distant mountains, and with renewed hope and strength, we knew that water was near. Connelly, leading from a distance ahead of us, suddenly turned and trotted back to our wagon.

"Water is near daughter. We will rest for a bit. The river is but a few more hours beyond the trees," he said reassuringly and then rode past us along the caravan with the news.

With renewed strength, the caravan lurched forward faster than before. Several sentries rode ahead to scout the oasis and establish a protective perimeter.

"Look, Jonathan, the horses can smell the water," Lillian struggled with the reigns, "We must be careful to hold them back. Can you help hold the reins?"

I slid closer to her on the seat and clasped both reins tightly in my hands. The horses, alert to the nearby presence of water, wished to run and we both pulled back hard against their great strength to keep them in check. Clear, refreshing water sparkled in the afternoon sun among the shade of scattered trees.

The sentries motioned for us to continue, and we turned the wagon to one side, allowing the horses to walk up the water's edge but keeping the wagon on dry ground. The others behind us pulled their wagons alongside ours as people began to jump off their horses and climb out from the wagons.

Lillian set the hand brake, and we climbed down from the seat and splashed into the pond. My ankle gave way, and I fell face-first into the cold water with great embarrassment. Regaining my footing, I stood up, totally wet but rejuvenated by the cool, clear water. Lillian rolled her pants leg past her knees and walked deeper into the pool. I watched as she dunked her head to wash the dust from her hair and face.

Her father rode up then, allowing his mount to drink. He dismounted and refilled his canteen. He splashed a little water across his face, took a quick drink from the canteen, and remounted.

"Spread the word. We rest only long enough to drink and must be on our way. The river is close, but we must cross before dark. Then we will be safe and can rest for the night. Tomorrow, we'll be in Halom," he stated and rode off to the other wagons.

The herds were coming in from the trail, and soon, the watering hole would be filled with goats and cattle. Lillian watched as her father rode off.

"You, okay?" I asked.

"Yes, but I am worried about father. I have never seen him this way."

"I'm sure he'll be okay. When we cross the river, we can all rest. He'll feel better then," I assured her, but I had also noticed a melancholy change in the captain since the Bene Elohim had been captured.

I could not stop thinking about the warrior, who seemed to have communicated with me as the sentries dragged him away. I had decided that as soon as possible after we crossed the river, I would try to talk with him. I didn't know why, but I felt deep inside that he would hold the answers to the questions that stirred within me. I understood that I would have to be extremely careful not to be noticed and I could tell no one of my plans, not even Lillian, but I had to settle the confusion, or was it longing, in my heart and mind once and for all. Tonight would be my last chance to talk with him, and I knew what to do. I began refilling the canteens. The voice I had heard had told me to see through the power of the Light, but I did not know how. Hopefully, the Bene Elohim could answer that. I refilled the last of the canteens and turned toward the wagon.

A small dust cloud marked the presence of several horses, and I strained against the afternoon sun to see who they were. They trotted their horses toward the camp, two herdsmen, by the look of their clothes, and a small woman. And a warrior's horse! The three reined in their mounts near the wagons, and the first dismounted.

"I need help. I have two wounded," he shouted as he gently lifted the woman from the horse and placed her on the ground next to the water across from where I stood.

She sat down shakily and reached her bloody hands into the water, and with cupped palms, she splashed the life-giving element across her face and drank deeply. She had been beaten; I noticed and then realized that she was a fugitive, wearing several chains under the cotton shirt that was several sizes too big for her and covering her knees.

At first, the nomads rushed in to assist her, but they held back upon seeing that she was a fugitive. Only the clan leader could give the nomads permission to assist a fugitive. Captain Connelly rode up as the second herdsman dismounted with the help of his friend.

"What happened?" Connelly dismounted and reached for the reins of the warrior horse. "Well, look what we have here, the horse of a Bene Elohim."

Others gathered around the horse to see the splendid animal and hear the tale of the two herdsmen, seeming to forget the woman near the pond who continued to drink. But I pushed my way through the gathering crowd to the young woman, a fugitive the same as I. The two herdsmen began to tell me what had happened to them as I knelt beside the girl. She was younger than me.

"My name is Jonathan," I spoke quietly, not knowing anything else to do.

By the look of her, she had been mistreated. She looked up at me through a tangle of blond hair, covered in dirt and matted with filth and dried blood, revealing a beaten face with one eye swollen shut, a bloody lip, and a half-healed scar across one cheek of her face that appeared to be from a previous wound.

"My name is Heather," she said softly and nervously, then realized I was chained. "You are a fugitive?"

"Yes, but these people have taken me in, healed, and protected me. You are safe here."

She drank from the canteen that I gave her.

"There is no safety anywhere in this realm, only hopelessness."

"I thought that once, but you will see. Here, let me help you up. I will take you to the wagon, and the women will assist you."

I reached over and picked her up into my arms as she placed her arm around my shoulders. She was light, and although I still limped, I could easily carry her.

"Hold!" a voice boomed from among the gathered crowd.

I turned abruptly to face Captain Connelly, watching me with the girl. The crowd quieted as he walked up to me. At first, I thought he was angry. Heather nervously held tightly around my neck, fear rising within her spirit.

"What is your name, fugitive?"

"Heather, sir," she answered softly, frightened.

For a moment, I thought the captain would deny her assistance, as was his right as clan leader. I determined then that I would not allow him to do that and stared boldly into his eyes.

He looked back at me and smiled, "Heather, you are welcome here. Jonathan, take the girl to Ruth's wagon. She will be cared for."

He turned to face the crowd, "Prepare to pull out. David, take the warrior's horse and tie him to my wagon. He is too good a horse to leave, and the gear will fetch a fair price at the market. The Bene Elohim will have no further use for him."

He mounted and rode off as we made haste to prepare for the rest of the day's journey.

"Ruth will take good care of the fugitive girl, Jonathan," Lillian said as we climbed back up the wooden bench on the wagon.

"Here, let me try a go at the reins," I said with new confidence.

I had taken a stand and had helped others, such as myself. She was among friends now, and I had helped to save her. The caravan formed along the trail with the sentries out in front and along the flanks, and we left the small oasis and once more traveled across the ancient, dusty trail across a barren, rocky landscape. The black ribbon of trees loomed in the distance but appeared closer.

Malak had been given no water at the stop. His throat remained tight and raspy, his lips cracked and bloody, but he continued to endure, knowing that he was in the plan of his Master. An opportunity would arise, he knew. A door would open, and the master's plan would begin forming. Over the years, he had learned to allow events to happen, trusting his instincts and knowledge to lead him when it was time to act. When he had first entered the Plains of Apistia several days before, he had been aware of many obstacles before his mission could become a reality.

A commotion outside interrupted his thoughts, and straining against his chains, he saw the crowd gathering outside through the canvas flap. A fugitive had been brought in. She was ragged and filthy and appeared to have been beaten. Another lost soul wandering in desperation, Malak thought. But he knew that hope was nearby. His time would come, and then the Light would be able to penetrate the deception and show all who would see what manner of men they were. He could see their true form because he was of a race not of this realm, although similar in appearance. But until the Light pushed back the darkness and revealed the truth, all of them were deceived and believed a lie.

Looking at the girl as she sat by the pond, Malak saw a soul that had given up on ever finding peace. He saw a girl who had been abused by all manner of men, a girl who gave her body to any who would take it to stay alive. He thought she would be hard to reach but knew that the Light could break down the barriers she had constructed around her. He could see the barriers around her heart, barriers of hurt and pain, distrust and unforgiveness. He watched as Jonathan handed her over to others who carried her to one of the wagons to tend to her wound, the blind leading the blind, for he could see that the one that had the girl was wounded even more than she was, but did not know because of the illusion that held their minds captive.

Malak saw the heart of compassion that Jonathan had for the girl. The Light was beginning to affect him, even though the boy did not understand it. The more the young man paid attention to the Light, the more influence it would have on him. But he would never be able to utilize its true power until that power was revealed to him, which was why Malak had been sent. The time was near, which gave the Bene Elohim renewed strength. He could continue to hunger and thirst with the assurance that his time was near.

And then he saw the horse! There he stood, his companion for his entire existence in the realms of men's souls since, from the beginning, his most faithful friend. The horse was being led to another wagon, where they tied him to the back, all his gear still attached. The horse could sense his presence, her ears alert and eyes searching.

"Easy, boy. I'm here and alive. Our time is near," Malak spoke softly.

The horse turned quickly and stared through the opening in the canvas, stomping his feet to acknowledge his friend.

"I got tired of waiting alone, and I'll get fed here. It's good to see that you're alright."

Malak laughed and leaned back against the seat, closing his eyes to rest. Tonight, he would make his escape. Tonight, he would find the Apostolos Or, he thought as he drifted off to a peaceful sleep.

CHAPTER TWENTY

Finally, after traveling the entire day over an endless desert, we reached the river Dolios. The river flowed swiftly, lined with brush and occasional trees. Lillian remarked that we would have to cross the river at a ford, which at this time of year was not very deep but could still be treacherous to cross with the wagons. Also, the band could be easily attacked at the crossing while struggling across the ford, so we must cross quickly.

To ensure our safe crossing, the sentries splashed into the river and quickly crossed the swift current to the opposite shore, where they fanned out and scouted for any sign of a potential enemy. Others formed a rear guard behind the caravan.

Lillian snapped the leather whip over the horses' heads to push them forward, and with a great jolt that almost knocked me off the bench, the wagon dropped off the bank and into the muddy waters. Immediately, I felt the river's power as the current pressed against the wagon's side. Water lapped at the wagon's edge, and some splashed over the side, but the horses were strong and strained against the flow.

Fear motivated the horses more than anything to fight the current and press across the deepest and strongest portion at the center of the great river. The current slowed as the water receded, and we safely climbed the opposite shore. Immediately, I noticed the landscape had changed dramatically.

The vegetation here differed from the barren desert across the river behind us. Lush, green grass with red, blue, and yellow flowers blanketed the rolling hills. Sections of the meadows before us were covered with flowers, their brilliant, multicolored petals fluttering in a faint, cool breeze. Scattered trees dotted the landscape with dark clumps of pine spread across the upper flanks of several of the low ridges.

A herd of deer grazed among the flowers in the distance beneath the pine forest. Most trotted off into the protective shadows of the tree line as we crossed over the river, but a few lingered behind, watching as Lillian reined in the wagon near a small clump of oak trees.

The mountain range we had caught glimpses of while crossing the desert loomed more clearly against the horizon, a great expanse of ragged, rocky cliffs and pinnacles, the ledges covered in snow, and the upper peaks shrouded in a thick fog. They reminded me of the mountain range that had haunted my dreams, with the twisting trail from which so many had fallen, the deceptive trail to supposed safety on the peaks that led to death on the other side.

"Welcome to the low hills of Halom," Lillian announced as she climbed down from the wagon, breaking the spell cast over me by the mountain range.

I climbed down to stand beside her.

"How far to the summer encampment?" I asked.

"Another day's journey," she pointed toward the mountain range. "The clans gather at the base of the mountains."

We watched as the other wagons each crossed the river without incident. We were all safely across the river in Halom.

Just the thought of being on the north side of the river among the lush grass and trees brought us a sense of security, but Captain Connelly was taking no chances. We were still a long day's journey from the encampment and the combined protection of all the clans. The Bene Elohim could still be out there, hiding in the desert, waiting to attack us with the coming darkness, even though it would be more difficult because there were few places to cross the river.

Overhead, the same hawk trailing us across the desert circled once above and then disappeared across the river. I watched the great bird fly high among the clouds, wondering why he had been our constant companion over the past few days. The bird dropped low over the trees lining the riverbank and disappeared. I turned to assist Lillian with the horses.

Peter sat tall and strong on his horse, his arm outstretched as the bird landed on his gloved hand. He petted the bird and placed him on the perch behind the saddle.

"They made excellent time," Patrick commented. "I wouldn't have thought they could have made the river by this time, but they have."

Peter dismounted, as did the other knights in the party. Patrick led his mount up to the riverbank, followed by the others who allowed their horses to drink. The hawk sat motionless on the saddle, only his head turning from side to side.

"There's another crossing upriver where we may be able to cross, but we will be in Halom, which the bronze ones patrol."

Patrick thought momentarily before answering, "Let's camp here tonight and watch the river crossing. If the Bene Elohim escapes, he will cross over, and we'll be ready. If not, then we can try to enter the camp tonight and take him ourselves if the chance arises."

Patrick turned and began to unsaddle his horse.

"We will take turns watching. Leave the horses here, and we will walk the rest of the way on foot. We can hide among the brush and watch the camp closely. The sentries will not venture far from the camp's fires," Patrick chuckled, "It amazes me how much the nomads fear the night, but that is to our advantage."

The warriors rode hard across the rolling hills, forty men led by Zanah, the warrior woman dressed in black. They rode parallel to Theosis and his band that followed the two messengers, all three groups converging on the river crossing. They were engaged in a race, although only one of the groups knew its true importance. The two messengers wished to return to their clan as soon as possible. The second group was riding to assist another clan against a potential attack, and the third was in a race of deception and destruction.

Zanah led her troop on a wild ride across the meadows and scattered trees with the power and strength of a higher realm of her own making so that the group quickly overtook the other bands and passed the nomads as they rested at a small stream to refresh their overly tired horses. They also passed the two messengers and approached the river several miles south of the ford.

The great river flowed among the thick brush that lined the banks, and they reined in their tired mounts among a grove of trees, allowing the horses to drink from the river before the warriors dismounted as a unit.

Zanah removed her helmet, shaking loose her thick black hair. The ride across the hills of Halom had been hot and dusty. She dismounted, splashed water from her canteen across her face, and then poured the contents over her head, allowing the water to flow through her curly hair and down across her face and neck. She wore black armor that fit her form perfectly, leather pants, knee-high, and black riding boots. A wide, brilliant crimson belt buckled in the front along her thin waste held a dagger and short sword.

She was as dangerous a warrior as she was seductive a lady. Sometimes, it was tough to tell the difference, for she could kill a man with her sword while seducing him with her dark green eyes. She smelled lavender and flowers even in the armor and after a long ride. As spirited as she was seductive, her horse pranced about her as she bent and refilled her canteen from the river.

"Easy girl," she calmed the horse with her soothing words, laughing softly. "Has the ride across the hills energized you even more than usual, or is it that you smell the blood of the lost?"

She patted her horse and turned to address the soldiers under her command who tended to their mounts. The warriors around her wore knee-length chain mail and a bronze helmet that covered their faces except for their eyes, mouth, and chin. They each carried a shield as well as a variety of weapons, depending on their preference. They owed their allegiance to Archon Planos and no one else.

"We camp here tonight, my fair warriors," Zanah addressed her men. When the other nomads arrive, we will attack the camp. There are many there whose time has come, but be wary of the sentries. They will fight back, and remember, if it is not their time, you will not be able to kill them."

A mounted warrior rode up and interrupted, "My lady Zanah," he said as he dismounted and bowed before her.

"The nomad camp is just a short distance to the north alongside the ford. They circled their wagons to prepare for the night, and I counted a dozen sentries on the perimeter. There is a place near the river where we can come to within just a few feet of the guards without being noticed, from which to stage the attack."

"Excellent, my dear Troy. You have done well."

Zanah thanked the young scout, who saluted her with a bow. Then, she turned back to the warriors gathered among the trees. "Rest until the arrival of Theosis and his band. Place a watch and prepare yourselves for battle."

The woman warrior handed the reins of her horse to her second in command and personal bodyguard, an aged, bearded giant of a man called Mackenzie.

"I wish to take a bath, Mackenzie. You watch for me. I do not want to go into battle with the filth of a day's journey over me."

Zanah left the men to find a secluded place within the cottonwoods where she could bathe, knowing that her trusted aide would watch over the camp and her. The men began to prepare for battle, many wondering how it would be to partake in their leader's beauty but knowing that it would be instant death to do so. Mackenzie would make sure of that, they all knew.

Patrick walked up to the river's bank to peer across the water to the opposite shore for any sign of horsemen. He thought he had heard horses a few minutes before and retrieved his telescope from his saddlebags. He searched the bank carefully but saw nothing out of the ordinary. Then he heard a splash upriver. He quickly looked toward the sound and saw nothing until he peered through the telescope's magnification.

Someone swam near the opposite shore several hundred yards upstream. The person ducked entirely under the water and remained under the surface for a full minute. The person vanished beneath the dark waters. He scanned the shoreline but saw nothing, and then he heard another splash closer than the first one and focused closer toward his hiding place.

A woman emerged back from beneath the water. Her long hair covered her face, the thick locks floating over the water around her shoulders. She stood near the opposite shore, revealing her body down to her waist, the long, black hair covering her breast. The woman pulled back the wet hair from her face and chest, and with a start, Patrick recognized the woman as the enchantress, Zanah.

He quickly lowered the eyepiece and looked away as Zanah swam the short distance to the shore and climbed out from the water to where a large, bearded warrior stood holding a robe and towel, respectfully looking away as the beauty emerged from the water and wrapped the robe around her. She dried her hair with the towel as the man vanished into the undergrowth from where he had emerged moments before.

Patrick again watched through the eyepiece as Zanah carefully navigated the rocks to where her clothing and full armor lay in the warmth of the late afternoon sun. How could something so beautiful be so full of evil? Patrick thought as she let the robe slip to the ground and picked up her clothing from the rock. Patrick quickly lowered the glass and again looked away. She was indeed a beautiful creature, radiating a feminine glow of pure sexuality, but he was wary of her seduction and did not wish to be enslaved by her magic. He had seen enough.

Zanah, with full battle gear, commanded Archon Planos's warriors, who had to be nearby. He swore to himself as he quietly backed along the trail away from the river.

The question was why they were here. He had hoped not to encounter any of Archon Planos's warriors and especially did not wish for Zanah to know of his presence so far into the bronze one's territory.

Peter stood near the riverbank as Patrick emerged from the brush. Constantly vigilant, the scout had also heard the approaching horses and was preparing to let loose his hawk to see who was across the river.

"Hold the hawk, Peter," ordered the captain as he approached his friend.

Seeing Peter's questioning stare, Patrick answered, "Zanah is among them. She knows of your bird. Tie him to the perch. If she sees him, she will know that we are close."

"What is Zanah doing here? She leads the bronze ones only in battle."

"I don't know, but this game is getting risky. Hopefully, the Bene Elohim will try to escape across the river, and we can take him by using our nets and leave this forsaken country. If she has arrived to escort the nomads or commandeer the Bene Elohim, it will be tough to sneak into camp and take him ourselves. But I don't think the nomads know of her presence, which puzzles me."

Refreshed from her bath and fully dressed in battle armor, Zanah emerged from the brush and walked into the circle of bronze knights. They ceased whatever they were doing and turned to face her. The giant, Mackenzie, stood nearby as he always did, a constant protector of Lady Zanah, although she needed little protection as a warrior. Unlike the other warriors in the band, the bearded warrior wore no helmet, revealing curly red hair streaked with gray and a weather-beaten face. He stood motionless as Zanah addressed the soldiers.

"Troy, gather the scouts and secure the riverbank. Please eliminate the nomad sentries and open a way to their camp along the shoreline. I will lead the rest of you in an assault on these nomads. We will ride through the camp, searching for those whose time has come," she smiled wickedly. "Dispatch them with great cruelty so that all nomads will forever curse the Light."

She raised her gloved hands and closed her eyes, circling her head gracefully with her tiny hands as the bronze knights stood silently and still. She lifted her head to the evening sky and blew softly across her outstretched hands, invoking a swirling cloud to take shape around her hands. The mist circled her body, transforming her into a female Bene Elohim.

The cloud of mist then spread across the warriors, changing each of them into Bene Elohim, wearing silver body armor and purple capes. Zanah lowered her arms and opened her eyes to look upon her handiwork approvingly.

"Now, my brave warriors, you will masquerade as warriors of the Light and strike great fear among them. But beware of the true Bene Elohim held captive. Do not seek him out to fight. Only defend yourself if he is near."

Patrick and Peter walked back to their camp, where the others waited. The horses were hidden among a great tumble of large boulders.

"We must be careful," the captain warned his troops, "I have seen the bronze warriors across the river. They may just be a patrol or escort for the nomads, but we will all be in grave danger if we are seen. It will be dark very soon, so we had better get going. Peter will brief you on your assignments."

After Peter passed the orders, the group slowly edged toward the ford downriver from their camp, moving with great stealth. From then on, there would be no verbal communication; the knights use sign language to speak with one another. Peter disappeared over the small hill, marking the trail for the rest to follow. One of the men was to remain with the horses with orders to rendezvous at the ford if given the proper sign.

CHAPTER TWENTY-ONE

We all pitched in with great energy and enthusiasm to prepare the evening encampment—the long and arduous journey across the barren desert but a memory. Among the tall, lush grass growing on the low hills of Halom, our spirits immediately rose. We were safely across the river, separated from the barren desert. To the north, I gazed in awe at the snowcapped mountains that berthed the cool breeze swirling around us as we worked to set up the camp.

Across the river, the air was stale and very hot. No breeze caressed the land. Very little life, only rock and sand, and an occasional gnarled pine lived a torturous life in a land of death. But on this side of the river, scattered trees flourished among a bed of thick green grass with islands of purple, yellow, and crimson flowers. The scent of flowers and rich soil floated on the cool breeze among many living creatures. Many songbirds inhabited the brush along the river, their multicolored bodies darting in and out of the greenery as they flew in happiness and contentment.

I could not believe the wondrous beauty surrounding me on this riverside. As we led the horses to one of the corrals, I saw the sweltering heat and harshness of the barren desert across the river. How could such a drastic change occur just because of a river?

"Isn't it beautiful?" Lillian asked as I assisted her with the horses. I watched her and thought she was beautiful, but she was talking about Halom. I no longer feared the great beasts but still didn't trust them.

"Yes, I have never in my life seen such beauty," I talked of her as well as Halom, "The Forests of Basar are nothing compared to your hills of Halom."

"It is life, Jonathan. Halom is filled with life. This is where we are renewed each year! It is where we were all freed of our chains, and soon, you will also be free!"

Lillian suddenly grabbed my hands, "Come, Jonathan. Before dark, let's go down to the river. The water is cool, and I would love to go swimming."

"Are you sure it's safe?" I questioned.

"Yes. We have but a few minutes, though. There are sentries across the river, but the river will be off-limits after darkness. But we can go now!"

She was like a child, full of enthusiasm. I had never seen her so excited. Looking toward the river, I saw others playing in the water. We were exhausted and thirsty several hours earlier, fearful of being attacked. Now, because of the beauty around us, we felt relaxed and safe. Even Captain Connelly appeared to have overcome his dark mood and laughed with several other men nearby.

The sentries, as always, were posted around the camp, watchful. Across the river, several of them on horseback guarded the swimmers from the dangers that lurked in the desert.

"I'll race you!" Lillian exclaimed and began running toward the river, bunching her dress around her waist.

Although my ankle prevented me from running very fast, I tried my best to keep up with her, and with a great splash, we both dived into the cool water.

"The current is not strong here, but don't go past the large trees, or you will be pulled into the deep water." Lillian pointed to the narrow channel.

The water was cool and refreshing; we swam and played for several minutes, forgetting the past problems. Suddenly, Lillian ducked under the water. I circled, looking for her. With a great splash, she emerged behind me and pushed me face-first into the water and to my knees. I fought to regain my footing and reached for her, grabbing her arm and pulling her into the water, laughing. I had never been so happy.

Life was worth living again, I thought, as she regained her footing and pulled me up. We stood there, face to face in the middle of the river, other nomads playing around us, and for the first time in my life, I felt genuine love for another person. I gazed into her green eyes, and something deep inside me surged forward through my heart; warmth flowed through my veins that I had never felt before.

My heartbeat, my breathing deep. Locks of wet hair stuck to her face, partially covering her eyes, strands across her cheek and neck. I held her tiny hands at our side, her face only inches from mine. The top of her head lay even with my nose, and she tilted her head upward toward me, staring back into my eyes. I released one of her hands as she stood there before me, breathing heavily as well. I carefully pulled the errant strands of hair from her face and then placed my hand across her cheek, lightly rubbing her chin with my thumb below her lips. She nervously licked her lips and placed her free hand on my shoulder above the chains.

At that moment, my most inward spirit reached outward to hers, connecting through the portal of our eyes that are the gateways to our souls. I peered deep into her eyes and saw her spirit, and we connected in a way that I would never be able to explain. And suddenly she kissed me quickly, and, like a shy doe, with a soft laughter, turned and ran out of the river.

Turning to face me at the riverbank, she spoke, "Come, Jonathan, if you can still walk. Supper will be ready soon."

She turned and hurried across the meadow to her wagon. I stood in the river for an eternity, staring after her, my heart pounding.

"Fugitive Jonathan of Basar," a passing sentry said from above on his horse as he crossed through the water. "You have been enchanted."

He laughed, "You can stand here all night if you wish, but if I were you, I would pursue the one that has enchanted you."

Embarrassed, I regained my composure and quickly exited the cold water. The sweet aroma of food roasting over the open flames reminded me how hungry I was. But deep inside my spirit, a new hunger was birthed, one that I had never experienced.

The sun melted over the horizon, washing the desert in gray shadows as the Knights of Kratos crept up to the edge of the river at the ford the nomads had used earlier to cross the river. At this point, the river flowed several hundred yards wide. There was very little vegetation on either shore, the banks sloped back by years of use, covered in gravel and larger boulders.

Peter hid behind a large tree trunk that some past flood had lodged against the riverbank among large rocks. The scout raised his arm, and the approaching knights froze. Peter watched as a single, mounted sentry crossed the river to the other side, passing a fugitive who followed him. When the two emerged from the water and entered the circle of wagons, Peter lowered his arm, and the knights continued forward.

Patrick motioned for the others to spread out along the shore to begin their vigil and wait until the sun had disappeared entirely, casting the river under the umbrella of another night. They then positioned a large net across the ford along the edge of the water among the shadows of the approaching darkness that could be used to catch a rider. The net would snare him if the Bene Elohim escaped across the ford. The captain crawled up to the log where Peter lay hidden only a few feet from the dark water.

Dark shadows engulfed the far riverbank. Across the river, several large cooking fires within the circle of wagons illuminated the darkness, revealing shadowy figures that moved back and forth across the light as the nomads prepared to meet for their evening meal.

They had circled their wagons about a hundred yards from the river, a ring of sentries posted just outside the wagons. Patrick heard but could not see the herds of goats, sheep, and cattle in the corrals nearby.

The captain thought the nomads were very predictable. They always camped at the exact locations when they traveled, circled their wagons, posted their sentries about one hundred yards outside the wagons, and never ventured outside their camp at night.

Like the fugitives, the nomads feared the night, even though the Sahat never bothered them. The captain had once feared the night as well, but over the years, he had learned to embrace the darkness. The night was a comfort to him and his kind. Because of his allegiance to Archon Krino, he did not worry about the Sahat, and there were no known warriors as well-armed and trained as he and his men. He had learned to use the darkness to his advantage, but with a shiver, he realized that deep within him, there was a growing hunger for something else.

"Their spirits have improved since crossing the river," Peter whispered.

They could hear music and laughter floating across the night air.

"What did you say?" Patrick had been in deep thought.

"Their spirits have improved."

"Oh yes, they know that Halom is but a day's journey."

Peter pointed to one of the wagons near one of the fires. "That one has an armed guard. That must be where the Bene Elohim is being held."

Patrick looked through his telescope for a closer look. Even though it was growing darker, the fires illuminated scattered locations throughout the encampment. He could better see the sentry stationed outside the rear of the wagon and the legs of another sentry standing behind the wagon across from the river. The canvas was closed, and he could not see inside.

"I believe you are right, my friend. Keep a close watch on that wagon. If the Bene Elohim wished to escape, the two sentries would be no match for him. The way the wagons are situated, his quickest escape route would be straight into our trap." The captain's spirits rose, "Maybe we can nab him and get out of here after all."

"Maybe you're right," Peter answered. He, too, was beginning to worry about this mission, but he trusted his Captain.

Lillian stood at her wagon wearing a simple dress. She looked lovely in the soft blue fabric, small yellow flowers in her braided hair. I, on the other hand, only had the one outfit that I now wore; therefore, I had to sit close to the fire to dry out. While eating, we learned that the two messengers had returned with news that a group of nomads were close behind them to escort the clan safely to Halom.

We ate well, Lillian and I casting frequent glances at each other across the fire. I had never felt this way before, but deep within me, I knew I had several questions I needed answered. I was scheduled for the ceremony of the chains, but the experiences with the Light and the Bene Elohim over the past few days challenged my desire to go through with the ceremony. I had to talk with the Bene Elohim and answer the question of the Light once and for all.

Ruth took a plate of food to the wagon, giving it to one of the guards who placed it inside the closed canvas. There were two guards stationed by the wagon, and Connelly had forbidden anyone else from nearing the wagon. I did not wish to break his command, and I knew I risked much by trying to see the Bene Elohim. But the memory of the vision the Light had cast of Lillian still haunted me, and I needed to know.

Part of me wanted to forget the Bene Elohim. I didn't need the Light to be free of my chains. After all, these people around me appeared free and did not possess the Light. Yet I knew something was not right. Even this place where we camped was strange. Could it be an illusion?

The voice had told me to see through the power of the Light. What did that mean? A few days before, I had seen Lillian through the Light as a disfigured woman covered in chains, not the radiant beauty I had this night come to love. That memory still haunted me and caused a pull deep in my soul. I yearned to know the Light.

I knew I had to answer that question, no matter the cost. I finished my dinner and excused myself from Lillian. I left the circle of light around the fire to sit by a tree near the guarded wagon where I could watch discreetly. There had to be a way to get close enough to talk with the stranger.

"There is a way," the ghostly voice spoke. It was the same voice I had heard the day before in the wagon.

"Trust in the Light. It will lead and guide you."

I reached into my pouch and retrieved the bit of Light, careful that no one could see me. Its soft, white light illuminated the small sphere of space around it. It grew as I held it in my cupped hands. The Light pushed back the darkness around my hands and then my arms.

"There you go, Jonathan," the voice spoke again. "See how the Light grows the more that you study it."

I continued to look at the Light's wonders and suddenly realized that the Light was not white but a combination of all the colors: brilliant reds, soft blues of the sky, the dark green of the hemlock, and the purple of the mountain flowers, all swirling within the sphere in my hands. The many colors seemed to dance within it as the Light spread slowly over my arms and reached toward my chest and heart, exposing the chains across my shoulders. Suddenly, a shot of hot pain, like a flaming arrow, pierced my heart, and I quickly pulled the Light away so that only my hands were illuminated.

"Hold on, Jonathan," the voice reassured me. Sometimes, the Light will hurt as it breaks the bondage, but it will eventually free you. Just hold on."

I covered the Light with both hands, reducing the illumination to only the sphere in my hands, and looked around. I sat alone in the darkness behind the wagon, hearing the river that flowed in the blackness beyond me. No one could see me now, but someone may if I allowed the Light to grow like before. I had to talk to the Bene Elohim first.

"I am the one talking with you now," the voice whispered again.

I quickly glanced over to the wagon. The sentries stood there, oblivious to any sound. How could he talk with me, and the sentries not hear him?

"Who are you?" I spoke softly, questioning the darkness, or maybe I was questioning the Light.

"I am Malak, the one that you wish to speak with. I have been sent to help you activate the power of the Light, but the real One you need to talk with is within it."

I remembered one other time that I had witnessed the Light. It was while hiding in the tree before I injured my ankle.

"The fourth man in the fire?" I asked.

"Yes, the Light is the answer. It alone will free you of the chains of death," Malak answered.

"What about these people around me? They are free of their chains yet do not know the Light."

"Some do but choose not to look through the Light's power. All around you is an illusion. These people are deceived. They think they are free, but they are worse off than you. They do not see the chains around them because of the deception. You know that what I am saying is true, Jonathan. You have seen this before in the young woman you love."

I thought horses approached. It was a faint sound, but horses ran in the meadow. My fear of the Sahat returned, and I quickly put away the Light and stood up.

"Jonathan!" the voice spoke urgently.

I turned and investigated the small opening of the canvas door. I stared directly into the Bene Elohim's piercing eyes. He opened the canvas further and stood at the door. His guards did not notice that he was free of his prison cell. I began walking toward him even as I heard the approaching horses.

Someone shouted a challenge, and the nomads from Halom were allowed to enter the perimeter with a great commotion from the nomads of Clan Connelly. Captain Connelly greeted the leader of the band with an embrace, and the people cheered.

I was aware of all that was happening but continued walking toward the wagon, my inner soul reaching outward for answers that only this servant of the Light could have.

I stood directly before the warrior, who stood head and shoulders over me. I looked deeply into his eyes of kindness, and my spirit jumped inside me, coming alive with a new life for the first time. I reached and pulled the Light from the pouch and held it out in front of me.

The Bene Elohim smiled, took my hands that held the Light into his, and placed them over my heart. The Light suddenly shot upward, startling me at first, almost blinding me with brilliance. It covered my entire body as thousands of indescribable colors, like a flood of rainbows, cascaded across me, radiating from my heart, warmth flowing through my veins. The colors wrapped around each chain link individually, melting the links from me one at a time as the colors moved across them until all of the chain links had disappeared from my body.

I could not move, did not want to move, as the lights continued dancing around and through me. Malak stood before me, holding the Light to my heart with his gloved hands.

I remembered the dream from the night before about the huge, flying beast and the maze. I had searched for a way out and had seen the light, but before reaching its peace, I had been pulled into one of the rooms that had saved me from the beast. There was one part that I had forgotten. The beast had screamed in delight when I had been pulled into the room, even though he could no longer reach me. He was delighted I had been dragged into the room without reaching the light. I knew then that if I allowed the ceremony of the chains, I would fall prey to the deception. The room had been a false hope; it demonstrated not the true salvation but a cleverly constructed counterfeit.

"Those dreams were the thoughts of your master in the physical realm," Malak answered my unspoken question. "He was desperate and hopeless, but now you will control your destiny and his."

My spirit, long dormant for my entire life, began to awaken as the chains fell from my body and the Light fully engulfed me. My soul, which the sins of the physical realm had always chained, was now free and able to allow the spirit man to take control over my existence both in this realm and the other.

"Behold the Fourth Man!" Malak proclaimed as he released my hands and knelt before me in a vanishing mist. Suddenly, I no longer stood by the wagons. I stood among the clouds, overlooking a never-ending panoramic view of the valleys below, for as far as I could see stood snow-capped mountains and timbered slopes, lush mountain meadows, and pristine, crystal-clear lakes. A faint breeze stirred around me, carrying the faint scent of the sweetest incense. I stood all alone on the rocky slopes of a mountain.

Behind me lay a tormented, disfigured, rocky landscape, void of any living thing, barren and burned, covered with the stench of death. But before me was the mountain range of beauty and glory, full of life and purpose.

A winding, narrow path emerged from the desolation behind me and, like a thin ribbon of hope and peace, extended upward along the spine of the ridge to the summit higher in front of me. The path was the only way to reach the summit because the ridgeline was narrow, only the width of the trail itself, a great void of space on both the right and the left down to the dark timber far below. I continued the gradual climb to the highest point on the mountain, where the trail ended at a rocky ledge.

Far below me, a silver ribbon of water marked the winding course of a great river. Across the river, I thought I saw thin trails of smoke rising from a small meadow, marking the presence of a village in the darkened forest. What country was this, I wondered.

I stood for a moment at the great precipice of life. I was first perplexed because there seemed no place to go but back down the trail from where I had come, and I did not want to go there. I closed my eyes and opened them.

Before me stood a lamb, pure and white. I reached down to pet the lamb, but the animal disappeared, and before me stood a cross covered in blood, more blood splashed across the rock in front of me. I knew in my heart that the blood had come from the innocent lamb standing there before. I knelt before the cross and began to cry first for the innocent lamb that was slain and then for myself, who had been the cause of the lamb's murder. I was why the sacrifice had been made, myself and all of those like me, fugitives searching for truth and freedom in the Shadow Realm.

I stood up again, wiping the tears from my eyes with the palms of my hands. The cross disappeared in a swirl of silver, sparkling mist like ice crystals. Below me lay the great expanse of the beauty of the forest and plains, but now I saw thousands of people, small like ants, traveling across the country below me. They were fugitives who had not been freed of their chains. My heart broke because so many needed to know the truth of the Light. I looked away and turned to the side of the trail. Standing next to me was myself.

"My only regret is that I took so long. I almost destroyed you, but now the spirit is alive, and the soul can also be free. I must continually die so that you may live," I said, and the self-figure before me disappeared.

I stood alone once more, but was I alone?

A presence stood behind me then, with a radiance of pure love, and my spirit pulsed within me, pulled toward the all-consuming glory, and I turned to see the fourth man in the flame standing there. He placed his hand on my shoulder, and I looked at his eyes. Eyes filled with love and peace, eyes filled with compassion and strength. When I looked into the eyes of my Savior, who had been slain from the foundation of the world for all such as I had been, I knew that I was healed and whole when I looked into those eyes filled with love more than I would ever see. I understood that no matter what happened, I would never again be alone.

"I am the Alpha and Omega, the beginning and the end. You have been made complete in me. I have chosen you, Jonathan of Basar, to be the Apostolos Or in this realm. Your chains of death have been forever removed, and your spirit is one with me. Now you must be totally united, body, soul, and spirit." He said and touched my heart. Suddenly, I stood again by the wagon, holding the hand of the Bene Elohim called Malak.

CHAPTER TWENTY-TWO

I could not speak for a moment and then asked, "What happened?"

"Just as He said, you have been freed of the chains of death. You have been chosen Apostolos Or. My work here is done for a season, but yours is just beginning." Malak bowed before me, a great smile on his face.

"But what am I to do now? If the Light has set me free, all these people have been deceived."

"Yes, they have. You will lead them to freedom in time, but that time is not now. It would be best if you left this place. There are others out there," he waved a hand across the dark river, "that need the truth first."

"What do you mean, leave? These people are my friends. They have helped me," I thought of Lillian most of all. "I must show her.... them that they are deceived."

"Jonathan, the deception is strong, the power over this land great, and tonight, things are about to happen that will challenge your freedom and further deceive those around you, but remember, look at everything through the power of the Light and you will always see the truth and will know what to do."

Horsemen rode somewhere out in the night again, but I was not afraid this time. I could hardly comprehend it; I was not scared anymore!

"They are coming now," Malak warned, "You must take the fugitive girl and flee across the river and into the desert. Her time for freedom is at hand, and you can give it to her, but you must leave now!"

He spoke urgently, but I protested, "Who is coming? And why flee? What about Lillian? Malak, I love her. I can't just leave her here knowing what I know!"

Horses were approaching!

"After what is about to happen occurs, she will not understand your freedom; she will despise you for it. You must leave and take the girl Heather with you. Lillian's time will come, but not now. In due time, you will have a chance to show her the truth but remember; it will be her choice to believe or reject it. Only she can accept the Light and be free of her chains of death."

He clasped my hand firmly, and I felt a great surge of power flow from him into me. My chains were gone! Still, I could not believe it!

There was a great commotion throughout the camp. Blaring horns echoed through the darkness, similar to those used by the Sahat but different somehow, and I saw the emerging forms of charging knights outside the circle of wagons. They appeared to be Bene Elohim. I looked back at Malak.

"They are not of my kind, Jonathan. Look through the power of the Light, and you will see the truth. Now go! Quickly! There are horses by the wagon next to this one. Take them and cross the river. Your time to expose this deception is not yet, but soon. Now go!"

He suddenly jumped away from the wagon, startling the sentries, who appeared to have been in some trance. Malak gave a shrill whistle, and a horse galloped out of the darkness toward us. The sentry struck with his spear, but Malak blocked the blow and struck the guard in the jaw with his fist, knocking the luckless sentry to the ground. All around me, people were running. The camp was under attack!

"Did you see that?" a startled Patrick asked Peter, who lay behind the other end of the tree trunk across the river from the encampment. The two had been watching the camp as the nomads ate their evening meal. They could smell the food from their location, reminding both that it had been a while since they had eaten a hot meal. They had seen nothing out of the ordinary until just then.

"What is it?" Peter asked, turning his head toward where the captain pointed.

"A strange light by the wagon. There, you see it illuminating the person holding it. Over by the wagon with the Bene Elohim."

"Yes, I see it now." Peter turned his whole body toward the strange light to see it better, "That is not fire. I have never seen such as that."

The captain had, a long time ago as a child, a different time and place.

"I have seen that Light. It was many years ago when I was a child. It is the Light of the World, or so the heretics of Hedone once claimed."

Peter looked at Patrick questionably, thinking of the Sahat, who had been searching for those said to possess the Light.

Captain Patrick continued, "It is the Bene Elohim's Light, great magic in the hands of those who understand its power. They say that it has the power to remove men's chains."

Memories of his father flooded Patrick's consciousness. He thought of the abuse he had suffered as a child at the man's hands. His father had had the Light and claimed to understand it but only used it to hold his family in bondage. As a boy, Patrick swore that he would resist its evil and intolerance because of what his father had done to him and his mother in its name. But seeing the Light now also awakened a deep desire to understand it. He pushed that thought away and watched closely as the Light grew in intensity, revealing the shadowy figure of the fugitive who held it.

He had heard rumors of a fugitive in the realm who possessed the Light. Could this be the one? The captain knew now why the Bene Elohim had allowed himself to be captured by the nomads and had not tried to escape. He was in the camp to show the fugitive the power of the Light. The captain chuckled at the irony of what was happening. Krino and Planos were involved in a game to win the Overlord's favor, and both failed to eradicate the Light from the realm. He who had been sent as a pawn to try to discredit Planos now had evidence of both their failures. Krino had been tasked with destroying those who had the Light before they could understand its power. Planos ensured the masses followed him and would not need the Light to remove the chains. But now the Light was in the land, and a Bene Elohim was nearby to activate its power.

"The Light grows, Captain," Peter whispered, usually unemotional and stoic but now fully engrossed by what he saw. It is the most beautiful thing!"

Patrick started to rebuke and warn his friend not to investigate the Light because of its seductive power, but he became pulled into its charms. It was a beautiful thing to look upon. His spirit struggled to come alive at the sight of the Light, causing an inner desire to grow. Suddenly, the Light disappeared, and only darkness remained.

The two watched intently to see if the Light would reappear.

A rustle of branches immediately across the river near the sentries standing watch close to the shore alerted both knights of another band of shadowy figures across the river. Peter spotted a dark figure running across the sandy shoreline and quickly pointed him out to Patrick. They watched as the figure struck the sentry, which fell hard.

"Archon Planos's men, Peter. That is why Zanah is here," Patrick whispered, then thought for a moment, confused. But why attack his subjects to take the Bene Elohim when they are bringing the prisoner to the council?"

Something foul was happening here: "Whatever is happening, remember our orders. Peter, go pass the word to the others."

"Yes sir," Peter replied, quickly melting back into the shadows, leaving the captain to watch.

The high moon cast an eerie glow across the water, but the light was not strong enough to penetrate the dark brush on the opposite shore. Only the open riverbank and the areas immediately around each fire could be seen. Patrick noticed several more figures moving through the open space at the river crossing before disappearing into the darkness beneath the trees. The nomads continued to eat around their fires, oblivious to the approaching soldiers. What was going on? Why was Zanah attacking the nomads whom she was supposed to protect? What trickery was this? Patrick had never trusted the woman or her master. He watched closely, wondering about the moving shadows that continued to cross the opening.

Suddenly, a brilliant, lightning-quick flash erupted near the prisoner's wagon, shooting toward the starry sky. The light almost blinded him, and, at first, Patrick shielded his eyes from its glare. Then, the light dimmed somewhat, and he removed his hand to stare in disbelief at the mystery before him. Thousands of colors swirled around the figure of a man from where the light had originated, first covering his arms and then his neck and shoulders until his entire body became one with the lights, the figure's outline wavering until he seemed to melt away, becoming a part of the light itself.

Then another figure of a man appeared in the light, and for a moment, two figures were standing in the light before the light suddenly vanished into the darkness. Startled by the suddenness and beauty of the Light, Patrick was surprised that no one else seemed to have noticed it, including the sentry standing nearby.

Without realizing it, Patrick stood when the Light first appeared and left his hiding place to walk out into the water as if a force pulled him toward the Light. In his reverie, he was unaware of the sudden rush of horsemen upon the nomad's camp. Peter ran behind him and stopped at the river's edge as horns blew across the river, piercing the quiet night air with their booming echoes.

"They are attacking!"

I turned quickly as a large horse galloped past me in a cloud of dust. Malak grabbed the horse's long mane and promptly mounted it.

Malak unsheathed a two-edged long sword from the scabbard attached to the back of the saddle as he mounted. He parried the attacking blow from a sentry and, with the flat side of the blade, hit the man across the chest, knocking him against the side of the wagon to fall unconscious by the wheel.

I turned to face a mighty silver knight riding a dark horse and carrying a sword like Malak's. The horseman leaped his horse over the front of the wagon and turned toward me, the sword lowered. I stood transfixed at the sight of such a mighty warrior. Why were the Bene Elohim attacking us?

But then suddenly, I knew the truth. Before my eyes, the knight transformed into a hideous creature riding a black horse with fiery red eyes that glowed. I could see through the deception.

"Go quickly, Jonathan! You must not be taken!" Malak shouted as he bravely blocked the charging beast with his horse, his golden sword raised over his hand, shining brightly in the fire's light.

The beast appeared to be a hairy, manlike creature with the same glowing red eyes as the horse. He wore knee-length bronze chain mail and metal leggings to protect his thighs and knees. A spiked helmet covered his head, and he carried an axe in one hand and a bronze shield in the other, a red dragon emblazoned across the front of the shield. The warrior's horses collided with a stunning blow, neither horse giving ground. Brilliant sparks of red and gold showered across both warriors as the Bene Elohim broadsword clashed against the axe's metal.

All around me was confusion. People ran past, screaming as more horns blew out in the shadows of the night all around us. The sentries formed ranks, but other panicked nomads ran through the ranks of the soldiers, hindering their attempt to protect the camp from attack. The great rumbling of galloping horses mixed with the crashes of wagons overturned and the clash of metal as combat was joined across the camp.

I ran, searching for Lillian, even though Malak's orders still rang in my ears. I could not leave her. I had to take her from this place. I had to show her the truth of the Light and free her from the deception to escape with her from this nightmare. Then I would find Heather, and we would all escape across the river.

The animals stampeded through the camp, adding to the confusion and panic. More wagons overturned as the cattle crashed against them. One wagon overturned as a panicked steer pushed through the blockade, knocking over a torch that immediately spread its burning fuels across the canvas. Another wagon burst into flames from a thrown torch. Those hiding inside jumped out from the wagon. The cooking fires began to spread across the grassland.

Most of the attackers were still outside the perimeter of the wagons, having dispatched many of the sentries outside the camp. I ran past Captain Connelly, who shouted orders to his men. They reformed their ranks to protect themselves from the attack as the horsemen broke through the wagon barricade.

I stood in the open beside one of the fires, breathing hard, searching for Lillian. The last I had seen her, she had been eating by the fire, but now she was nowhere in sight. The horsemen broke through the wagons in force to attack the ranks of sentries standing in squares in the middle of the camp.

My breathing slowed, and I blinked my eyes, looking from side to side. It took a few minutes to understand what was happening to me. Through the power of the Light that was now a part of my spirit, I saw the forms of all the nomads and attacking soldiers around me. The view was disorienting as I looked from person to person, turning in a slow circle and adjusting to the new vision.

I saw Captain Connelly as he battled one of the horsemen. He was not the strong, brave leader I had come to respect. He appeared to me instead as a crippled old man in ragged clothing, his body covered with chains that dragged the ground around him. His face and arms were covered with open sores and disease. I feared that he would be struck down severely in this fight.

The sentries and other nomads around him all wore chains around their bodies. They were not, in reality, the armored and fiercely muscled warriors I had first seen on the plains weeks before. Now, I noticed they were fugitives, just as I had been. They held battered, rusty weapons with beaten shields. The women were filthy with matted hair and festering sores across their faces and arms. The children were half-naked and starving.

I stood, heart pounding, horrified at the spectacle around me. Even the tall grass and beautiful trees I had seen when we first crossed the river were an illusion. We were camped in a barren desert with no vegetation. All these people were living a complete lie. They were fugitives just as I had been, but because they were deceived that they lived in the truth, they could not see that they needed the chains of death removed. They had no chance to escape the chains because of the deception. I had to show them the truth!

In desperation, I began to shout, "No! These are not Bene Elohim! The Light is your salvation!"

But, of course, no one listened. They were too busy defending against an enemy that to them was of the Light itself. The attacking enemies had transformed into warriors of the Light to confuse the deceived nomads further. How could I reach them with the truth? I ran among the wagons, searching again for Lillian.

A woman screamed behind me, and I quickly turned to see one of the bronze beasts ride past me. Another horse leaped over the wagon, knocking me to the ground as the maddened beast charged over me.

A sentry tried to defend himself against the charging horsemen but was trampled over by the horse as the warrior continued to charge past the wounded sentry, chasing another sentry. The man attempted to slash at the horse's flanks with his rusty blade, but his chains prevented him from swinging the sword correctly. In desperation, the sentry turned to flee, but the chains that dragged along in the dirt tripped him, and with a scream of terror, the sentry fell to the ground.

The horseman reined in his horse and turned the mount back to the sentry who lay on the ground before him. He spurred his horse on, and leaning down as he rode past the sentry, the warrior slashed down across the neck of the man. The sight sickened me, and I turned my head, doubling over with great heaves that emptied my stomach and left me breathless. I whispered, "May the Light help me, as I pulled myself up.

The horsemen quickly overran the defensive ranks, and individual horsemen targeted certain nomads, who I now understood to be fugitives whose time had come in this realm. Just like the Sahat had done on the Plains of Sin, these warriors were doing here. They searched out and destroyed those whose time was at an end. They only had the power to take the lives of those fugitives, although they could, and did, wound many others.

Finally, I spotted Lillian across the opening in front of me. She stood over her cousin, Cristina, who lay dead at her feet. Lillian held her small knife, screaming at each of the horsemen as they rode past her. She was not the radiant beauty I had come to love but a weakened, hollowed shell of a person in ragged clothes, yet I still loved her. Our spirits had connected in the river this very day. I could still barely see a glimmer of the radiant spirit in her darkened eyes. Somehow, it cried out to me from some distant place for help. But her spirit had no power because her soul was enslaved by the chains of death formed around her by the flesh that lived in the other realm.

"Lillian!" I screamed over the sounds of battle, but she did not heed my call. "Lillian, you must come with me quickly. We have to leave this place!"

I ran to the place where she stood, shaking with grief, and grabbed to pull her away. She resisted at first before realizing who I was.

"Jonathan!" she cried, "They killed Cristina. The horrid Bene Elohim killed her. They will kill us all!"

"No, Lillian, you are wrong. This is all an illusion. Nothing is at it appears!" I held her shoulders, trying to look her in the eyes and connect with her again.

She looked down and noticed that my chains were gone. The Light around my neck glowed, and she suddenly pushed me away.

"What has happened to you? Oh my! Of course, the Light. You brought it to us! You have brought them all to us. We allowed you to come among us. We trusted you. Jonathan, I loved you, but you brought the Light among us."

She began to sob, holding her face in her hands, and then she looked back up to me, rage in her eyes, "Look what you have done!" she screamed and slapped me.

"No, Lillian. You must believe me. The Light has removed my chains. It is our salvation."

I pulled her toward me, holding her hands, my heart aching for a way to show her the truth, but she resisted me, and then the Light glowed stronger, and she looked down into its warmth. I thought I felt her dormant spirit come to life for a moment, but just as quickly, it ebbed, and the Light faded. The nomads ran past us toward the river, and her brothers pulled Lillian from my grasp, and a mob began to push her away. I ran after her, but the crowd closed in, and I could not reach her.

I gazed into her eyes for a moment, and she looked back. I saw her broken spirit, bound and gagged and pleading for help. But she turned away, running with the crowd toward the river.

CHAPTER TWENTY-THREE

I ran after her but was suddenly blocked by a horse. A warrior woman turned her mount toward me and pushed me back toward the darkness near an overturned wagon. The nomads continued to run past me to the river as horsemen rode among them. I was powerless to assist them. I knew the truth, but no one would listen to me.

The woman spoke to me, toying with her short sword, "You are different than the others." Her voice was soft, seductive. She looked over at me with a confused interest.

"I am not a nomad but a fugitive recently freed of the chains of death," I answered her boldly. I felt no fear; instead, something about her eyes intrigued me. She smiled and lowered her sword.

The battle moved away toward the river as the nomads retreated. I heard the screams, the clash of arms, and the thunder of the horses, but the sounds were more distant, obscure. The battle around me did not seem to matter anymore as I gazed into her eyes, deep green pools of mystery, more beautiful than even Lillian's had been.

"So, you are the one who has the Light. A rather handsome young man you are," she commented as she sheathed her sword and leaned down to caress my cheek with her gloved hand, her hair cascading over my forehead.

I could say or do nothing but stand there and breathe in the intoxicating fragrance of her beautiful hair. I tried to see if she was what she appeared to be but could not see clearly. She was a woman, of that, I was sure.

"Can I see the Light? I hear that it is truly a marvel to behold." She held out her other hand, and I looked back into her face.

She removed her helmet, and I beheld the most beautiful woman I had ever seen. Something within me urged me to run away from her, not to be seduced by her charms, but her eyes held a power over me, and I reached for the Light on the chain around my neck.

"No! Zanah, you are too late. Your seductions will not work with this one now!" A strong challenge broke the spell that her seduction was weaving over my soul.

The woman hissed in anger like a cat, quickly drew her sword, and pulled her horse to one side, knocking me to my knees beside a wagon.

"So, we meet again, fair Malak," the woman taunted.

"Jonathan, you know what you must do. Now go!" Malak ordered as he swung his mighty sword.

The woman parried his blow and backed her horse away just as one of the bronze knights galloped beside her. This warrior was a giant bearded man carrying a sword as large as Malak's. He reined in his warhorse between the woman and Malak as I scrambled under the wagon to escape.

"Please help me," a small, shaking voice spoke, "I do not wish to die."

It was Heather, curled up under the wagon by the rear wheels.

"Here, take my hand. I know a way out."

I pulled her up, and we crawled out from the wagon. Malak had told me where to find horses for my escape, and I led her through the darkness near the river. Behind us, Malak and the giant warrior battled. I looked back but could only see fleeting shadows in the fire's light and the cascading shower of red and gold sparks as the weapons hit. He had saved me from the seductions of some form of magic. I prayed that he would escape as well. To save Lillian and these people, I had to escape and trust the Light to lead me.

Captain Patrick of Kratos and his men stood in the shadows across the river, watching the spectacle in disbelief. Why were Archon Planos's soldiers killing his subjects? Masquerading as Bene Elohim, they were pillaging and burning the camp, chasing down selected nomads and killing them with cruel efficiency. The captain was sickened by what he witnessed. He had never trusted the light, but before him, he saw his allies killing those who trusted them for their safety.

Alarmed at the nomads' flight, he turned to Peter, "All is lost here. We need to get away. Signal the horses. I am tired of this game and wish to have no more part in it."

Peter made a shrill whistle from a small horn, and the group retreated quickly back to where their horses were waiting. The captain had seen enough. Who could he now trust? If Planos could turn on his people, Krino could do the same. The black knights rendezvoused with their horses as planned and rode a short distance to wait for their leader to decide what to do next.

As Malak told, two saddled horses stood tied to a tree near the corral. How had he done that?

"Can you ride?" I asked Heather.

"Yes, I think I can. But you will have to help me."

I picked her up, lifted her onto the saddle, and handed her the reins. Taking a small rope from the nearby wagon, I tied her securely to the saddle because she was weak, and I feared the horse might throw her as we crossed the river. I then mounted the second horse and turned him toward the river. I had never ridden a horse before.

"Hold on, Heather," I managed to say, unsteady in my saddle. With a sudden leap that almost flipped me back off of the horse, both horses galloped through the camp toward the dark river.

A few of the bronze knights spotted us, as did the warrior woman, who shouted for them to intercept us. They spurred their horses toward us, but we had a slight head start, and our horses were sleek and fast, anxious as we were to leave the destruction behind. Instinctively, I leaned into my horse, holding securely to the reins of Heather's mount, and we splashed into the river at full stride, the horses straining against the current past the nomads struggling through the water on foot. Behind us, the battle subsided, but the nomads continued to press across the river to the desert, some being dragged into the turbulent, deeper water to disappear downriver into obscurity.

"Horses crossing the river, Captain," a knight pointed out to Patrick.

"It's not the Bene Elohim?" asked the scout.

"No. I see the Bene Elohim back in the camp," Patrick replied, his gaze still focused on the activity across the river. "He is among the burning wagons. Two horsemen in battle."

They could vaguely make out the shadowy figures of two horsemen dancing among the firelight, red, and gold sparks bursting into the night as their weapons clashed.

"He is fighting for his life?"

"No. He is fighting for time, time for those two horses to carry their burdens to safety," Patrick looked over at Peter standing next to him, "We have witnessed the conversion of a fugitive this night, Peter."

Memories were surfacing, memories long locked in a bound spirit but was now desperately trying to break free.

"I have an idea," the captain continued. "We will follow the two horses. If I am correct, one of them is the fugitive with the Light we saw earlier."

The captain turned his mount toward the open desert. He was on a personal mission now, a mission that was decided when he had seen the Light explode around the fugitive, a mission confirmed when he had witnessed the carnage across the river. If the Light was genuine, he wanted to confront it once and for all.

We finally pushed our way through, the horses struggling to fight the deep current across the middle of the river, and eventually gained the rocky shore opposite the camp. Soldiers entered the river behind us as our horses climbed out of the water. I did not look back but kicked my horse onward, holding Heather's reins in one hand and mine in the other. I clung desperately to the saddle, leaning low against the horse's neck, the thick mane blowing back across my face.

Behind me, the cries of the nomads retreated into the shadowy night as we fled. I heard the pounding of our horses' hooves, plus the more distant rumbling of horses behind us, and turned to look back briefly. The fires illuminated the far side of the river. Nomads ran among the wagons, struggling through the water. Horses, cattle, and goats added to the confusion and panic. I could no longer see the brilliant flashes of gold and red that marked the position of the two battling warriors. Had Malak escaped?

A small cluster of horsemen rode hard after us across the open desert country. I knew that I could not outrun them for long. I needed help. Heather clutched desperately to her horse, still weak from her past ordeal, the ropes securing her on the saddle. But how long could she last?

Our horses ran in unison as if pushed by an inward fear of what lay behind, their hooves beating against the rocky ground, their muscles straining to outrun the horsemen. I felt labored breathing as they continued to press onward. Searching red beams of light flashed overhead and past us, the red eyes of the Sahat and I could better hear our pursuers' heavy breathing and clattering hooves. They were gaining on us!

My Lillian. I had left her, the only person that I had ever truly cared for, back amid slaughter. What would she think of me now? I had to return and save her from the deception but knew I had to flee now. Malak had said that others needed to understand the truth first, and then I could one day return. I had to get Heather and myself to safety. Time was short.

Up ahead, I saw a low rise, and as we reached the summit, our vantage point revealed a great pile of rocks and massive boulders that looked as if the ancient giants of legend had scattered them across the flat desert floor. I quickly turned and rode into the maze of giant rocks. There was a winding corridor between the rocks, and we followed it for a few seconds until we were safely hidden from the open country.

The two horses stopped, lowering their heads, chests heaving, and sweat running down their flanks. Heather lay slumped across the horse's neck, exhausted, possibly unconscious, but I could not tell. We had walked into a maze of rocks absent of any light. I sat in complete darkness, listening above my difficult breathing for the sound of approaching hoof beats. I heard each horse clearly as it passed the rocks until they all passed. Heather moaned in pain beside me, the horses heaving beneath us.

It was quiet here in this place void of light, and for the first time in my life, I did not fear the darkness. A peace beyond all comprehension enveloped my heart and mind, and I knew that I was truly safe. My chains had been removed! The light was the same as the fourth man in the fire. It had removed my chains and awoken my dormant spirit. I was finally free from the chains of death and was in control of my destiny. But what was I to do now? I had left the only friends I had ever known because of the power of the Light that now lived within me. There were still so many things that I did not understand, but that was not as important as the fact that I was free from the chains of death, and my spirit was alive now, controlling my soul.

I waited in the darkness for several minutes, hearing nothing. I slowly worked our horses back to the entrance. We had only traveled a few hundred feet into the maze and I knew that the entrance was close, but after traveling several hundred feet, a hard granite wall blocked our way. I felt forward along the wall, yet there was no opening. The rock was smooth and cool to the touch. Confused, I turned the horses and proceeded back. The corridor was narrow, and there was minimal space to turn the horses. The way had not been so tight when we had ridden in just moments before. It was as if the walls were closing in around us. The horses disliked the cramped quarters and darkness and pranced nervously.

"Easy now," I patted my horse on the neck to reassure him, even though I too was becoming nervous.

"Jonathan?" Heather was awakened, her voice trembling in the darkness.

"I'm here, Heather. We have taken refuge in the caves from the soldiers. We'll soon get back to the entrance. It's but a short distance."

My horse suddenly stopped, refusing to step further in the complete darkness. I was sure that the entrance was very near. We had only ridden in the maze of rocks a short distance. Why couldn't I find it? I kicked the horse, upset with his disobedience, but he refused to move. Disgusted, I dismounted in the narrow corridor and stepped forward to lead him to the entrance. It had to be just a few more feet ahead of us.

I tied Heather's reins to my saddle, and holding one hand out in front of me and drawing the other along the warm side of my horse, I slowly inched forward to the front of the animal. I felt his moist breath against my face but could not see him. I reached out, feeling for his nose, and then gathered the reins in my hands, wrapping them around my right wrist so as not to lose them in the darkness. High above, a crack in the blackness revealed several stars that peered down but offered no help with light to see how to get out of the maze.

"Jonathan, I'm scared of the darkness," Heather whispered, her voice faltering.

I, too, feared this place. I pulled on the horse, but he resisted, refusing to take a step forward. With a snort, he pulled his head upward and away from me, stamping his front hooves.

"What's wrong?" Heather asked out of the darkness.

"This crazy horse refuses to go any further. The entrance has to be very close, but he will not budge."

I pulled again on the reins, frustrated. This time, he jerked his strong head up violently, pulling me up against his shoulder, causing the second horse to turn nervously.

"Whoa, now!" I worried that the horses would panic and hurt themselves and us in the cramped space, which seemed to get smaller the longer we remained in the rocks.

"Hold on, boy."

I patted him, and he calmed down a bit. Why didn't he want to continue? Did he know or sense something that I could not?

"PROBABLY SO JONATHAN."

I stepped back quickly against the horse. Who had spoken?

"Did you hear that, Heather?"

"No," she answered.

But a voice had spoken from somewhere, a voice from someone.

No matter, I thought, dismissing the warning. The entrance had to be just a short distance ahead.

"Okay, let's try this again," I spoke to the hot breath blowing across my head and reached up to pet the horse again. Holding the reins tightly with one hand and reaching out in front of me with the second, I walked forward, hoping the horse would follow me.

The darkness pressed in on me, and before I had been freed, I would not have had the strength to proceed onward but would have been paralyzed by fear. But now, although nervous and feeling the weight of oppression of the darkness and the towering granite walls above me, I knew I could make it. After all, I had been freed. I was strong enough to overcome anything that came my way, or so I thought.

I bravely stepped out into the darkness and realized too late, with terror, that there was nothing below my extended foot. The soft ground gave way under me, and although I desperately fought to regain my balance, I fell into the dark Abyss of Pride below me.

I twisted around, clawing the rocky soil with both hands as I slid down the broken wall of the pit, desperately trying to grab anything that would save me. Heather screamed, and then, with a sharp jolt, the reins wrapped around my wrist pulled me back against the wall of the pit. I grabbed them with both hands as more dirt and gravel fell across my head and shoulders.

"Jonathan?"

"I'm okay," I answered, holding the reins, hoping they were securely fastened to the harness. Below me, rocks and debris fell a great distance before splashing into a pool of water. Looking up, I could barely see the silhouette of the horse's head and neck against the vague light from the aperture in the towering outcrops. Stars stared back down at me but offered no help.

"Heather!" I called upward, straining to hold the reins. "Can you find the reins to your horse and pull him back? I can't climb up. The ledge has broken away, and I can't get a foothold."

She responded with silence. I discerned that she must be terrified of the darkness and could be paralyzed by fear. I remembered a time in the cave of my fears when I could have helped the girl who held a small portion of the Light but did not because the tentacles of fear had obsessed my mind.

Of course! The Light! How could I have been so ignorant? The Light could pierce the darkness and show us the way out. But first, I needed to get back out of this pit of pride I had fallen into.

"Heather, you need to try to find the reins to your horse and pull him back. I can't get up any other way."

The leather reins bit into my hands and wrist, cutting me. Warm blood flowed down my arm. All was silent above me except for the breathing of the horses. I tried to swing my legs to the side, but the ledge kept breaking away, and I could not gain a foothold. I had no strength to pull myself up with just the reins.

"Heather, you are our only hope. I know you are afraid, but you must try to get your horse back up and pull me out."

I saw the silhouette of my horse's head, most likely staring down at me, wondering why I had done such an ignorant thing as step off a cliff.

"Okay, you have made your point! Now back up and get me out of here," I said to the shadow. The beast did not move, except to lower his head, lowering me deeper into the pit. There was still silence above, and then I heard Heather crying softly.

"Heather, it's okay to be afraid, but please try to pull the horses back. Can you do that? If I can get up, I know how to get us out of here. I tried to do that in my strength before, but now I know what I must do." I tried to speak calmly.

"I'm too frightened. The walls are closing in. The darkness is suffocating me."

"Heather, you must overcome the fear, or we will not be able to leave. The ledge may break away soon, and we could all fall."

My strength drained away. I could not hold on any longer, and the horse refused to back away.

"Heather?"

Silence

"Heather!"

"Yes, I'm here. I have dismounted, but I can't get past the horse. The corridor is too narrow."

"It's okay. Try pushing your horse to the side and feeling forward along his neck until you find the reins." My voice came out in gasps as I stretched to hold on.

I heard her now, straining against the horses that were paralyzed by the oppressive darkness around us.

"Okay, I have the reins," she spoke, her voice trembling and soft.

"Good girl. Now take the reins and pull back on them."

"I'll try."

She overcame her fear of the dark, the first step to freedom. Slowly, I felt myself being pulled upward.

"Come on, you stupid beast, back up!" I shouted in frustration.

My horse backed a few feet more, and I grabbed the ledge and pulled myself to safety. I carefully walked around my horse to where I was safe, feeling out for the second horse and the girl who had saved my life.

I clasped her tiny hands in mine, both shaking from fear and relief, "I'm fine, Heather. Thank you. You have saved us both."

"What is this place, Jonathan?" Heather asked, still clinging to my hands.

"I don't know, but I know how we can get out." I pulled gently away and reached into my pocket, carefully retrieving the Light by the leather band.

"What is it, Jonathan?" she asked me.

I opened my cupped hands, revealing the warm, white glow that illuminated the area around me. I immediately pushed back the darkness of depression until Heather and I, plus the horses, were encased in a circle of light. Heather gasped in awe.

"It is beautiful," she said in wonderment.

"Yes, it is," I remembered with great pain the first time that I had shown the Light to Lillian. Now she hated me because of the lies of deception.

"I have heard of the Light, but have never seen it," said Heather, and she looked up to me, a glint of hope in her brown eyes, "Is it true then? Can this Light remove the chains of death?"

I thought about that question. I still understood so little, but I knew what the Light was. The Light was the Light of the World, the Redeemer of man's soul.

"Yes, that is true. My chains have been removed this very night. My master no longer has control over me. I am free, and my spirit is alive."

Heather reached out her frail, trembling hand to touch the Light and then quickly pulled her hand back. I knew the battle in her mind. I, too, battled the mystery of the Light. I saw the years of pain and abuse in her eyes and knew that a wall had been built around her soul because of it.

"You have been hurt?" I asked, not fully understanding what was going on.

"Yes," she began to cry.

"The Light can take your pain away."

"But my mistress has done so many things. And I have even lost all hope. When the herdsmen found me, I wished to die."

"The Light can give you new hope. Even now, the sight of its wonder and warmth is healing your spirit. Can you feel it?"

"Yes, but how does the Light work? How can it remove these chains," She pulled at the chains around her. I sensed walls of distrust and guilt, pain and abuse around her heart, each one a barrier to the Light.

"That I do not understand, but you must trust me on this one. I know that it can remove your chains. Even before its power removed my chains, it gave me warmth, light, and peace."

"But how do you know it's real! The nomads have no chains, and you saw what the Bene Elohim were doing. How could they be associated with something you say is so pure?"

The Light dimmed around her, and I saw the walls of distrust grow stronger around her spirit.

"I asked that question but took a step of faith to believe in the power of the Light. When I did, I saw through the illusion. Heather, this Shadow Realm is a world filled with deception. Everything is not what it appears; the Light has shown me this. Just now, I could see a wall of distrust around your heart, and it was weakening. Don't let it grow strong again."

She gasped, and the wall of distrust immediately lowered because she knew what I said was true.

"Those warriors were not of the Light. I do not know who they were, but they were not Bene Elohim. Did you not see the true Bene Elohim by the wagon fighting their leader?"

She nodded.

CHAPTER TWENTY-FOUR

Patrick reined in his horse on a small knoll, the moonlit swept valley of monuments below him. Behind him, the commotion in the camp continued, although the attack had ceased. The mounted knights melted back into the forest, leaving the scattered, mutilated bodies among the burning wagons, the survivors stunned and frightened, but that was not his concern. Peter pulled in his mount, as did the others. Would they understand his decision, he thought as he studied the ground before him. He had seen several horsemen riding across the valley but not of their prey. Where did the fugitive go?

Sensing the Captain's unspoken question, Peter commented, "If I were trying to escape, I would hide among the monuments. Don't you agree, Patrick?"

Only Peter called the captain by his real name. "What are your plans?" the scout continued.

His great bird fluttered behind him in the darkness, anxious to be flying once more. Patrick was not ready to state his sudden change of heart because he knew that it was dangerous, that, if wrong, he could get himself as well as his men killed. He did not fully understand what he was doing himself. All he knew was that when he saw the rainbow-colored light engulf the fugitive at the camp, something deep inside came alive. A long, suppressed spark of life suddenly emerged in recognition of the Light, and he had to settle the chaos in his mind once and for all.

But could he trust his men? Would they understand? Only one will, a voice within him spoke.

"Peter," Patrick broke the silence as they watched the horsemen suddenly stop and turn back to search the area that they had crossed before. "Did you see the second light before the attack?"

"Yes, but I don't understand what it was," Peter whispered a reply.

"The last time I saw such a light was when I was a child. I have tried to forget about the Light, but I never really could. And then, when I saw it earlier, I knew I had to capture it to see if it was true. Lately, my mind has been in chaos. All that has happened these past few months since the Light was first reported to be in the land again has troubled me."

Peter did not comment.

"If the fugitive has entered the monuments, then that is where I must go. I don't fully understand, but I must find the Light. Then, I will know if it is true or not. If it is the Light my father had, I will destroy it and take the fugitive back to Krino."

"And if it is not?" Peter asked.

"I don't know. But you have been relieved of this mission. Take the others back and advise Krino of all that has happened. I will return as soon as I conclude this battle within me."

"Patrick, you know that I have always followed your orders. I have always trusted your instincts, but I cannot do so now. There is much danger in the monuments. I cannot let you go alone. I am also confused at what I have seen tonight," Peter answered and turned to the others, "Darius," he motioned to the oldest of the band lined behind him, a dark-headed youth with blue eyes, "Lead the others and return to Archon Krino. Advise him of what has taken place. The captain and I will search the monuments for the light we saw. We have failed if we have not returned within the next two weeks."

Darius saluted and rode quickly back into the barren desert, the other knights behind. Peter looked back toward the monuments below, "I, too, have tired of the game, Patrick. When will Archon Krino do to us what Planos has done this night to his own? If we perish, so be it. At least the misery will end."

A distant trumpet blast echoed across the desert floor, and towering rock and the horsemen below gave up their search and turned their horses back toward the river. Patrick and Peter waited quietly until Planos's warriors disappeared into the shadows of the night. Peter untied the hawk, allowing it to fly above again as their sentinel.

"The Light is too bright, Jonathan. Please lower it from my face," Heather said as she turned. "I wish to leave this awful place, but where will we go? How will we survive?"

I lowered the Light, and as if it understood her fear of its brilliance, it dimmed to a soft glow that illuminated the darkness around us. Because of the Light, we could now see any hidden traps that might lie before us, but I had no idea how to leave this place. We had only ridden in a short distance, but the entrance was now nowhere to be found. One way along the trail led to the pit, and the other way was a dead end of granite walls. But I could not let Heather know of my confusion.

"We'll make it. Don't worry," I told myself and Heather.

I searched among the saddlebags and found bread, dried meat, and fruit. Malak had provided well for us.

"We have food and water enough for several days of travel," I reassured her and myself, but the obvious question now was, where to go?

As fugitives, we had always lived day to day, having no home and few, if any, friends. And now, I had left my only friends and a girl I had fallen in love with. I had left them only because of the voice that reassured me that I was now a part of a new race, a new creation with a destiny of greatness before me.

But now, after escaping into the desert, I stood among the great towering maze of life with no direction of where to go. I had narrowly missed destruction in the pit of pride because I had felt sure that once free of the chains of death, I could do anything I wanted to do within my own power. But now I knew that it was the Light that had freed me, and it was the Light that would have to help me through the monuments of life that now surrounded me.

"FOLLOW THE LIGHT. SEE THE WORLD THROUGH THE LIGHT, AND YOU WILL SEE WHERE YOU ARE TO GO. THE JOURNEY WILL BE ACCOMPLISHED A STEP AT A TIME. THERE WILL BE TIMES WHEN YOU SEE FAR AHEAD, BUT FOR THE MOST PART, YOU WILL ONLY SEE THE GROUND AT YOUR FEET. IN ALL TIMES, YOU WILL BE ABLE TO SEE EXACTLY WHAT YOU NEED TO SEE TO LIVE THE DESTINY SET FOR YOU BY THE LIGHT ITSELF. BUT YOU MUST HAVE FAITH IN THE LIGHT OF THE WORLD TO BEGIN THE JOURNEY. YOU MUST TAKE THE FIRST STEP."

The voice was strong within me, and I was now accustomed to it.

"Heather. I don't know where we are going, but I know now the One who will guide us there. Don't worry. If we trust in the Light, it will show us the way."

We ate a small amount of the food, which improved our spirits. The Light pushed the darkness from us as if a protective wall had been constructed. The horses were also calmed. I placed the Light around my neck so that it would continue to guide us.

"Which way do we go?" Heather asked.

The pit, broken ledge, and black abyss lay before us. There was no way to cross, and the corridor was blocked behind us.

"I'm not sure."

I still did not understand how we had gotten lost among the towering monuments of life, but somehow, I had taken a wrong turn. I had entered the monuments to escape my trouble and now was trapped by the illusion of safety that they had offered. There had to be a way out. I looked down at the ground below and, for the first time, glimpsed a narrow trail leading toward the pit, where others had traveled before. The worn path disappeared in the wall of blackness before us. I walked cautiously forward, and the wall receded. I now saw two trails, one disappearing into the abyss and the second running along the cave wall, bypassing the pit below along a narrow ledge just wide enough for the horses to walk.

"Heather, there is a trail that travels a ledge by the pit, but we have to lead the horses across."

Heather left her horse and walked up to me, grabbing my hand.

I clasped her hand in mine, and with the reins to my horse in the other hand, I cautiously stepped out onto the ledge. At first, the trail was several feet wide, but it appeared to narrow as we proceeded alongside the pit. We reached a point where there was barely enough room to walk, and I stopped.

We could not back up, and it appeared we could not go forward, but the Light had led us this far. I glanced back at Heather, who stood with her back against the cave wall, staring in horror at the abyss below that even the Light could not penetrate at this point. What was I to do now? I looked back along the wall and noticed writings carved into the granite.

YOUR WORD IS A LAMP TO MY FEET AND A LIGHT FOR MY PATH. I HAVE TAKEN AN OATH AND CONFIRMED THAT I WILL FOLLOW YOUR RIGHTEOUS LAWS.

"Don't worry, Heather, the Light is a lamp that will lead us."

I knew that I needed to continue along the path laid out before me, so I took another step forward, and the trail began to widen once more. This new walk required total faith and trust in the Light.

The horses no longer resisted my leading, unwilling to be left in the darkness behind us. There were a few places where the trail had broken off, but after several hundred feet, the trail widened, and we were past the pit and safely on the other side.

Looking up, I saw a vast star-filled sky and realized we were now in a large opening. The moon hung just above the cliff above, casting a dull glow in stark contrast to the darkness in the caves. Ghostly outlines of trees lined the opposite wall and scattered shrubs grew nearby. Lush mountain grass cushioned our feet, and our horses began to crop as we stood.

Somewhere, I heard the cheerful bubbling of water. Towering cliffs surrounded us, creating a hollow bowl of several acres. A few black, foreboding openings in the broken rock marked the locations of other caves, one of which had to be our way out. I did not know which to take but knew I had to search until I found the correct one. With the Light as my guide, I felt confident I could lead us to safety. We had to continue.

"Can we rest?" Heather stopped behind me.

I was also tired but wanted desperately to be free of this maze that I had entered and commented that we should continue. She said nothing, and I led her to the nearest cave opening. The cave entrance loomed black before me, and the Light did not penetrate the opening. I stepped into the doorway, expecting the Light to push the darkness away and reveal what was hidden inside, but the Light did not. I quickly stepped backward into the meadow. Why did the Light not illuminate the opening? I stood there for a moment, perplexed.

"FOLLOW THE LIGHT. IT WILL LEAD YOU."

The Light did not illuminate the cave, so I tried another and the third one and finally backed into the cave from where we had just exited. In all cases, the Light did not penetrate the darkness. At first, I was angry, and then, sheepishly, I realized that the reason the Light did not work in the caves was that I was not to go.

Heather had given up on me and sat in the center of the meadow with the horses as I tried the different caves. When I returned, she had fallen asleep.

"Did you find a way?" she asked through a drowsy fog.

"No, but we are safe here in this place. I'll build a small fire, and we'll camp for the night. Tomorrow's light should expose the way from this place."

She stirred and settled down against one of the trees, exhausted. She was still frail from her past ordeal in the desert, and the chains tore at her flesh, causing her pain. I knelt beside her and noticed that she looked very pale. She couldn't last much longer, I thought. I had to find her medical help, a warm bed and good food, none of which I had.

"That sounds fine. I need to rest." She spoke softly, leaned back against the tree, and was soon asleep.

I unsaddled the horses and looked from where I had noticed the noise of moving water. The moon's reflection glowed through an opening in some brush, sparkling on the water's moving surface. I walked the horses to the place and allowed them to drink from the cool water. Then, I let them loose to graze on the heavy grass. I then gathered sticks from beneath the trees and built a small fire near Heather. A soft breeze blew in from one of the cave openings. It chilled me some. I placed a blanket over Heather and sat beside her, leaning back against the tree's trunk. Exhausted myself, I, too, dozed off quickly.

CHAPTER TWENTY-FIVE

Patrick was a Captain of Kratos, a trusted leader of Archon Krino's castle guards who, for years, had ruthlessly obeyed his master's orders. He had run away from a drunken father who claimed to be free of the chains of death and had been recruited at a young age in Hedone to be a knight of Kratos, keepers of the gate of the prince of this realm. He had proven a powerful asset to Archon Krino and fought in the Light Wars years ago. For years since the Light had been driven from the realm, stories of the Light were treated only as myths. None had seen the Light until recently when several fugitives had been found with tiny slivers of the Light at their capture.

But conditions were changing in the realm. The captain had watched as the Sahat would ride through the gate each night in search of the fugitives on the Plains of Sin. He had seen the nomads lose their chains through the magic of Planos. He and his men did not have to worry about the chains as well because of their allegiance to Archon Krino, but the stories of the Light continued to haunt him, casting doubts in his dreams about whether he was truly free of the chains of death or not.

And then he witnessed the colored lights cover the fugitive, melting the chains around his body and leaving him free of the chains that had enslaved his soul. He had to find peace. He had to locate the Light once and for all.

"Peter, the cave opening is this way. Keep a close watch," the captain whispered to his friend as they walked slowly searching along the massive walls of the desert monuments.

They carefully inspected the cliff wall for signs of an opening that the fugitive had entered. They worked their way through the jumble of boulders and broken rock that littered the ground at the cliff's base. The hawk circled overhead to warn them if someone approached as they searched. The fugitive had found the opening as he rode past. Surely, they could find the same opening. Then Patrick saw a black hole in the cliff wall, contrasting the granite walls illuminated by the moon's light.

"Do you see it, Peter?"

"Yes, but be wary. The monuments are said to be filled with traps. Many have gone in, but I know of no one who has ever returned," Peter warned as he led the two horses behind the captain.

"Just stories to scare the children," Patrick replied confidently, but upon entering the cave opening, he quickly backed back out into the moon's light.

"There is no light inside the cave, not even at the entrance. Light one of the torches, Peter, so I can take a closer look inside. There are horse tracks here. This has to be the place."

Peter reached for one of the torches he carried tied to his saddlebags after confirming that two sets of tracks were in the sand at the cave entrance.

"That will not show you the way through the monuments," a voice spoke from behind the boulders near the cave entrance, startling both men. Peter quickly grabbed his crossbow and side stepped behind his horse as he loaded the weapon. The captain stepped back into the cave, drawing his sword.

"The rocks must know the secrets of the monuments," Peter remarked as he finished loading and cocking the crossbow, laying the weapon over his saddle, and peering into the shadows among the boulders.

Patrick said nothing, hiding in the darkness of the cave entrance. He knew that he could not be seen and did not wish to give himself away.

Peter continued, "Or you must be a man who has been inside and lived to help others through."

The person laughed, "I am neither, but I do know that only one light will lead you through the dark monuments of life. Your torch will illuminate the maze but not show you the way through it to the other side."

Patrick began to feel the heavy burden and oppression of standing in complete blackness. It was like he had stepped through a portal where only blackness existed. He stood in total darkness just inside the doorway, totally absent of any light. Just inches in front of his face, he saw the outside, but it was like he was standing in a mirror where he could see out of it, but no one could see in. There was no transition between the moon's light that cast a pale glow across the desert immediately outside the entrance and the blackness inside.

"Patrick, be careful where you step inside the cave. It might be your last," the voice spoke again.

Patrick stepped from the portal and instantly felt the oppression lift, "Do you have a suggestion then, my friend?" he called to the voice in the shadows.

"Yes, I might have the answer to your question, but tell me first, Patrick, why do you now search for the Light? You have denied its truth for many years, vowing as a child to destroy it."

Peter glanced over at the Captain, seeing that the man's words visibly shook him. Who was this stranger among the rocks that knew so much about them?

"How do you know that we are searching for this Light? Maybe we are just wanderers seeking a safe night's sleep. After all, the Sahat rule the night in this realm."

"You do not fear the dark ones," the voice answered, "but you are searching, of this I am sure. Now, tell the other one to lower his weapon so we can talk face-to-face. I have information that you may find useful in your quest."

Patrick motioned to Peter, and he lowered the crossbow. A dark figure emerged from behind the rocks.

"Now, who are you?" Patrick asked.

"My name is Malak," replied the dark figure.

"Have we met before that you know of my past?"

The figure chuckled, "Yes, I believe that we have. How is your leg, Patrick? I hope my arrow didn't cause much damage."

The Bene Elohim!

Peter quickly raised his weapon again as the hooded figure stood quietly.

Patrick shook his head at the scout. "Put it away, Peter, " he ordered. Patrick stepped closer, sheathing his weapon. "We have been trailing you for several days."

"Yes, I know. You were quite formidable. You almost snared me that night." Malak looked at Peter, pulling the hood from his head but remaining in the shadow of the rocks. "Your hawk is a beautiful creature, but he failed you on this night."

"You have killed him then," Peter spoke quietly, saddened at the thought.

"No, no, of course not. He will continue to serve you well," Malak answered, backing into the darkness behind the rock.

He immediately appeared again in the shadows, holding the great bird. Stroking the bird's head and neck, Malak released the bird that, with a great flutter in the night, returned to its master's upraised hand.

Peter placed the bird on the perch behind the saddle. "How is it, Malak? Do you know so much about Patrick and me, and how did you catch the bird? He goes to only me."

"Let's just say I have a gift of knowledge and wildlife, but that is unimportant. What is important is that you are searching for the fugitive and his Light, and I have a dual mission. The first is to protect that boy," he pointed into the cave, "and the second is to assist anyone searching for the Light to find it."

"The last we saw you was at the camp under the axe of the bearded giant. How did you manage to escape with your head?" Patrick queried.

"We wore each other out, and I have the bruises to prove it. Then the horn blew, and he disappeared into the forest with the others."

Patrick stepped further from the cave entrance toward Malak, taking a chance, "Listen to me, Bene Elohim! I am indeed searching for the Light, as you say. If it is the Light of my father, then I will destroy it, and you as well." Patrick's voice softened, and he stepped closer. "But, if it is the truth, I wish to understand it. If you know the way through that oppressive place, I ask for your assistance."

Malak did not flinch at the initial threat. He could see Patrick's mask of distrust and hate over his soul, enslaving his spirit. Even then, Patrick struggled to free himself and reach the Bene Elohim nearby. Patrick was a brave man who would make a strong disciple of the Light.

"Patrick, the Light is both the Light of your father and the truth, as you will eventually realize. I will help you. I am grieved that your father caused such pain to your spirit. Yes, he held the Light in his hands but never truly placed it in his heart," Malak explained softly. He momentarily looked at the cave opening, then turned back to Patrick. "You cannot go into the caves at night. Camp here, and you will know the path to take in the morning."

"But the fugitive could escape at night," the Captain urged.

"Trust me, Patrick. I have told you the truth, and you know it deep within. Camp here tonight and in the morning. Seek your answer." Malak commanded, and then suddenly, he was gone.

"Malak?" the captain called. "Peter, where did he go?"

Peter lit the torch and carefully walked toward where Bene Elohim had stood. They saw footprints in the sand and a few drops of blood. He had been wounded then. And then they heard a shrill whistle out in the open desert and the beating of hooves receding into the night, fading away until there was no sound but their breathing and the crackling of the torch.

Both men stood silently, listening for any sign that Malak was close, but heard nothing.

"That was strange," Peter broke the silence.

"Yes. I guess we camp here tonight." Patrick wearily agreed and walked back to his horse.

"But what if it is a trick? The Bene Elohim said that his mission was to protect the fugitive. Maybe he told us to stay so the fugitive could escape through the maze as we waited here."

Patrick pulled his bedroll and saddlebags from the horse, allowing them to slide to the ground. "That is a chance that we will take, but I think that he told the truth, and besides, I do not wish to enter the monuments in the dark."

Peter looked at his friend closely. He had never seen Patrick fear the darkness but knew he had been shaken when he had emerged from the cave the second time.

"As you wish."

Peter turned to unsaddle his horse and prepare the camp.

"I'll take the first watch, Peter. Get some sleep. We will trust this Malak."

Patrick touched the wound that was healing on his thigh. So, the Bene Elohim were in the realm once more. Maybe he would finally learn the truth. He settled down among the rocks as Peter found a hidden place to sleep. Both men shied away from the cave entrance. Patrick watched the blackness of the cave warily. What mysteries were inside? What dangers lay waiting within the maze of towering granite? A chilly breeze blew from the open desert, and he pulled his cape close and thought he smelled smoke. He felt it must be drifting smoke from the smoldering fires across the river.

CHAPTER TWENTY-SIX

I woke up startled in the dark. Next to me lay the girl, Heather, asleep, her breathing labored. A bed of twinkling embers glowed from the fire pit. A soft breeze stirred the light smoke. The night grew chilly. The horses also stood nearby, asleep, although my stirring had awakened the closer animal that stomped his foot and snorted disapprovingly at my interruption.

I did not fully trust the beasts; I feared them to a point, but it was easier to ride across the desert than to walk so I would learn to trust them. I gathered more firewood, placing several small sticks on the hot embers, which immediately rose with renewed life and pulled the fuel into its embrace of golden and red flames. I set back toward the fire's warmth, my back to the horses. I did not know how long I had been asleep, but by the darkness of the night and the quiet, it had to be sometime during the morning hours before sunrise.

Soon, the sun would cast a soft glow across the eastern sky, ushering in another day. Another night of fear of the Sahat would be replaced by a day of survival, but I thought my life was different now. In one moment, when I placed my trust and faith in the Light, my chains melted away, and my spirit was free. But free to do what? I had run from the only family I had ever known and was now trapped in a maze of monuments where any wrong turn could lead to disaster.

"NARROW IS THE PATH AND FEW THAT FIND IT, BUT THE LIGHT IS A LAMP UNTO YOUR FEET," a deep voice within spoke.

I clasped the Light tightly in my hands, and its soft glow immediately covered my hand and filled me with peace and joy. Heather stirred and suddenly awoke, at first frightened. She sat up, took the blanket, crawled to the fire, and huddled by its warmth. I noticed that the chains had torn her garments from her shoulder during the night, and she was bleeding from the new wounds created. If I did not get her help soon, she would die.

"You say that the Light took your chains away?" she asked softly, tremblingly. She was cold.

"Yes, it did. I don't know how, but it removed my chains." I answered as she moved closer beside me.

"Show me, Jonathan. Please show me the Light. I fear the darkness. The chains are so heavy now."

She began to cry then, a hopeless cry of despair. I saw the walls wrapped around her soul, but the wall of distrust was now gone. I moved closer to her and held her close in my arms. She laid her head against my chest, and we gazed into the fire. I did not know what to do. I did not understand how to help her. Malak had said that I was chosen to be an Apostolos Or, but what was I to do? How could I give the light to anyone?

With a start, I pushed her away, and she looked up into my eyes, and I saw the fear that I had caused. The Sahat would come! They would kill her, and like before, I could do nothing. Suddenly, I was afraid. No, I would not let them take her. She had placed her trust in me, which I knew was hard for her to do. I could not let her down. I thought of the small knife that I had found months ago. I could do something. I would fight them off. They may kill me, but I was not going to hide like a coward while the Sahat destroyed her.

Just then, both horses jumped, instantly alert; their ears laid back, and their eyes glared past me into the shadows! The Sahat must be nearby, I thought.

"Heather! We must..."

I looked down at her and realized what had startled the horses. The Light glowed brilliantly like a crystal, shimmering with all the colors of the rainbow. Heather reached a frail, trembling hand to hold the Light.

"I have never trusted men, Jonathan. They have always used me, but I trust you. If you say that the Light will remove my chains, then I believe," she said and touched the Light.

The Light grew more extensive, and I slipped the necklace from my neck and placed it securely in both her hands. The horses bolted to the opposite side of the small meadow. Horses galloped somewhere out in the darkness. Tiny red beams of light appeared on the horizon. Where had the cliffs gone? The Sahat had found us! No! Not now! She is almost free. I turned to face them to give Heather time to be free of her chains of death.

"NO!" a voice shouted from within, "THEY WILL NOT HARM HER OR YOURSELF. I HAVE PROVIDED FOR YOUR PROTECTION. STAY WITH THE GIRL."

I turned back to Heather and helped her stand to her feet. I saw two warriors emerge from behind the boulders in the early morning light. A great bird swooped down from the trees out of the gray sky, and then the Light suddenly blanketed Heather with all its majesty, knocking me to my knees.

Captain Patrick, one of the leaders of the knights of Kratos and probably unemployed, sat in the darkness, keeping watch as his companion slept nearby. There was no sound, nothing to indicate that anything was alive nearby, and then he faintly smelled smoke again as the breeze increased. At first, he considered that the lingering smoke was from the dying fires at the nomad camp, but then realized that the wind was blowing toward the camp, not from it.

Someone must be nearby. He slowly stood up with heightened alert and backed toward where Peter slept. The two horses slept, and the great hawk appeared to be as well, but then the bird stretched out his wings, waking the horse on which he perched. Neither animal seemed to sense the presence of strangers, Patrick gathered from their apparent lack of interest.

"There is a very small fire, perhaps one hundred yards along the monument wall, hidden behind the boulders," a whispered voice said in the early morning quiet.

How did he do it? The captain thought. "Don't you ever sleep?" he asked.

"Someone has to look after you," Peter joked as he stood beside Patrick.

"Who do you think it is?"

"He is most likely the fugitive, but how did he get out of the cave without us noticing him?"

"You were the one on watch, Captain, or maybe you fell asleep. It's a good thing I smelled the smoke," Peter continued to joke. He loved it when he got the better of his friend.

"It could be others," Patrick commented, disregarding Peter's suggestion.

Then they both saw the bright light grow from behind the rocks, the colors of the rainbow dancing among the shadows, and knew it was indeed the fugitive. Their two horses were also awakened, and they heard distant hoofbeats.

"Release the bird, and let's have a look," ordered the captain.

Red beams of light penetrated the morning darkness out on the open desert. Peter quickly released the bird, giving him the order to hunt, and both ran across the scattered rocks toward the light growing in intensity, just as they had seen it do in the nomad camp last evening.

The two searchers emerged into a small meadow just in time to see the light encircle a girl. At that moment, a man standing next to her collapsed to his knees. Across the meadow, a dozen black horsemen reined in their battle steeds, their red probing eyes glaring through the darkness for their prey.

"We can't allow them to be killed," the captain shouted as he drew his sword from the sheath.

The hawk flew low over the two individuals, and the light completely encircled them just as the Sahat charged into the meadow. Peter whistled, and the bird immediately gained altitude and disappeared into the darkness above.

I knelt transfixed at the sight before me, frozen on my knees by the power and beauty of the Light, oblivious to what was happening around us. The myriad of colors covered Heather's arms and then her shoulders as she stood in a trance, her eyes closed, and her head tilted upward toward the heavens, her small hands raised. The lights circled her head and shoulders, surrounding her chest, waist, legs, and feet until she seemed to merge with the lights.

Her form shimmered like a ghost, and then a second figure, the figure of a man, appeared in the mist within the lights. He stood facing her, and she turned to face him. I saw the walls that had been woven around her heart from past abuse, walls of hate, unforgiveness, hopelessness, and depression, melt away as the lights broke her chains one by one. They fell to the ground and shattered before completely disappearing at her feet.

Peter quickly shot one of the horsemen through the chest with his crossbow as Patrick raced forward to stand between the remaining Sahat and the two forms, or was it three surrounded by the Light? He dodged the blow from one axe man but was knocked back by a second, just as the hawk soared out of the morning sky and attacked the axe man, tearing at the rider's face with his sharpened talons.

Peter stood beside his beleaguered comrade, brandishing his two-edged sword. The Sahat stopped their attack suddenly and backed away as the light intensified. They could not look directly toward the light and had to turn their horses to one side.

"So, you have turned traitor, Captain," the leader spoke, "You have signed your death warrant then."

"Maybe, but you will not serve the warrant today. You are no match for my blade."

The Sahat turned toward Peter, his twin red eyes focusing on the scout's face, the red casting an eerie glow across Peter's forehead. "You stand with this traitor as well, Peter?"

"He has never led me wrong. I go with the captain," declared the scout.

"So be it!" the leader shouted, "We will feed your corpses to the dogs of Hades and then take the girl."

The horsemen urged their horses forward, and the captain and scout stood side-by-side with great swords. Still, suddenly, the light exploded outward, engulfing everyone in the meadow, knocking Patrick and Peter on their faces, unconscious.

The evil horses screamed unearthly cries of pain as their riders turned desperately to escape the rush of white-hot light but to no avail. They immediately disappeared, wholly incinerated by the light's power, leaving only the smell of sulfur and red smoke behind, and then, just as quickly, the light disappeared.

I watched as the second form waved his arm in a slow arch toward me, and a brilliant white light shot forward, knocking me back to the ground. The multicolored light was also gone, leaving Heather standing in the meadow, holding the soft, glowing white ember I had given her, plus a second light in her other hand. I stood back up, trembling at what I had seen.

The light grew steadily among the boulders as Malak looked on from his vantage point among the tall pines along the ridge overlooking the valley of monuments below. In the east, the first signs of dawn lit the heavens with a pale gray light. He watched as the light exploded in a swirl of thousands of colors, and then a brilliant stream of light emerged from the heavens above, intersecting with the light from the ground, and Malak fell to his knees on the ground. The horse lowered her head in honor as well. A bolt of lightning struck out from the source, covering the entire hidden meadow that Jonathan had found, and then just as quickly disappeared. Malak stood and mounted his horse.

"You are a quick learner, my dear Jonathan," he murmured, climbing through the thick pine forest. His work was finished here for a season, he thought. Now for the woman.

"You are a quick learner, my dear Jonathan," I heard audibly as I stood up. I looked around me, thinking Malak was nearby, but I did not see him. How did he do that?

Before me stood a new creation, not the sick, bleeding, chain-covered creature of before, but a strong, healthy, radiant, beautiful girl with long, flowing, blonde hair. Her chains had disappeared, and she no longer wore the tattered garments of a fugitive, but a white dress with a purple sash, and in her hair was a sprinkling of yellow flowers. This was her proper form, the way her Creator had meant her to be. It was how she had always been, but in the Shadow Realm, the deception changed her form by the chains. Now, she was fully restored.

"He gave me flowers, Jonathan. He kissed my cheek, wiped away my tears, and gave me these beautiful red roses, one for every year of my life, he said."

She held the roses nestled into the crook of her right arm and twirled in glee, laughing and crying simultaneously. Then she ran to where I stood and embraced me, showing me the bright bouquet.

"Thank you, Jonathan. You have given me the Light of the World. Because of you, my spirit is alive. I am no longer a slave. I am free!"

She kissed my cheek, and I embraced her in return. My spirit rejoiced with her. I knew that I had to give this Light to all of those like me who once had been a slave to the chains of death. I had never felt more alive, knowing I was responsible for sharing the Light of this World with another fugitive.

"YOU ARE A NEW CREATION; THE OLD HAS PASSED AWAY; ALL THINGS HAVE BECOME NEW!" the voice within me spoke.

Yes! Yes! We have become new. It was then that I noticed that we were not alone. Two warriors lay face down in the tall grass among the scattered pines. I remembered seeing two shadowy figures emerge from the rocks just as the light had overtaken me. And what of the Sahat? I gently pushed Heather away, who was still blissfully ignorant of her surroundings.

"I'm free, I'm free!" she said as she twirled around, laughing and skipping around the meadow. She held her roses before her, smelling their wonderful fragrance.

I hated interrupting her bliss, but I needed to so we could assess the situation. The Sahat was nowhere in sight, and with the early morning light appearing to the east, they would not return. But two strange warriors were lying next to the weakening fire that had to be dealt with, and overhead, I heard the shrill whistle of a hawk. Could it be the same one that I had seen earlier?

The sun peaked a golden eye just over the red canyon walls. With the new day, I realized that we had somehow emerged from the maze, and the meadow was at the edge of the great wall of the monuments among a jumble of giant boulders scattered across the ground.

"Heather," I reached for and grabbed the girl's hand.

"He gave me roses, Jonathan," she said breathlessly.

"Heather, we have a problem," I stated, and she suddenly stopped dancing and stared over my shoulders toward the two soldiers. I saw the dance of fear in her blue eyes.

"Kratos!" she gasped at once, trembling in my arms.

"It's okay, Heather. They are unconscious. They cannot hurt you now. I think they may have saved us from the Sahat," I reassured her.

She looked back at me, the fear gone from her eyes, "The Sahat were here?"

"Yes, but they are gone now. They may have been destroyed, but I'm not sure. They can no longer harm you. Your chains are gone, remember. You are free from the chains of death."

"Yes, but I feel my time in this realm is near. My past life has greatly damaged my body."

"No, you have been freed. They cannot take you now!" I objected, and she took my face in her tiny hands.

"Jonathan, it is okay. All is well with my soul. Each of us must travel through this realm and into the next one. Before, when the chains of death bound me, I had no hope. The Sahat would destroy me when my time came, as they would have you. But now my soul will leave this realm for a far better one, where we will be at one with our creator," she kissed me on the cheek again," and I have you to thank for my freedom."

She better understood the Light than I, even though I had held it for these past few months, and she had just received it. I understood then that her time might be close, but as Malak had told me, I could save her. Could I somehow save her body as well and prolong her life? If I had not listened to Malak's command and left the camp, she would have been taken by the Sahat and destroyed, her soul lost forever. But now, she was a new creation, beautiful and healthy, fully alive for the first time in her existence.

She looked past me again to the two men, "We must help them, Jonathan. They, too, have saved my life."

"Do you know them?" As I gathered their weapons, two large swords, and a crossbow, I asked, "You spoke of Kratos. What is that?"

They were strong warriors, but under their chain mail, I saw the chains of death around them. Their weapons were forged with solid steel, unlike the weapons of the nomads. They lived a life of illusions in this land of shadows, thinking they wore no chains as did the nomads, but for some reason, their weapons were razor-sharp and strong.

"I lived with their kind before. They used me at their parties but grew tired of me and left me to starve in the desert. I have never seen these two, but the larger one may have been at one of the feasts."

She looked away, saddened, "I would sell my body to those such as these warriors. My flesh would do terrible things, which is why it is so weak now."

"But you are now in control, Heather. You are no longer that person," I reassured her.

"I know, and that is why I have to use what time I have left to ensure that others are free of their chains of death."

She pointed to the chains as we pulled the second warrior against the tree next to the smaller one and tied them with rope I had found on Heather's horse. Malak had provided everything we needed as if he knew what would happen.

"For some reason, these two attacked the Sahat who had been sent to kill me. There must be good in them somewhere. I must forgive them because we were once just as they are now, lost without hope."

She stood then, smiling, "You and I are free. We must help others to be free as well."

She gave me back the Light I had given her and tied hers around her neck.

I placed their weapons across the small fire from where the two warriors were bound and gathered our two horses nearby. One of the packs contained dried meat and bread, and I brought Heather some while I ate a portion. We waited for the two to awaken.

The sun had cleared the top of the cliffs, spreading its life across the desert floor, driving the last shadows away from the broken landscape. I placed more sticks on the fire to push away the morning chill and watched the men carefully.

CHAPTER TWENTY-SEVEN

The smaller of the two began to stir, and with a sudden jerk and shake of his head, he opened his eyes. At first, he struggled against the ropes until he looked at me and stopped. His companion was also awake. We stared at each other for a few seconds, and then Heather spoke, breaking the silence.

"Are you hungry?" she asked.

"Yes," the smaller man replied, "and thirsty, but we cannot eat or drink with our hands tied. We mean you no harm." He held out his bound hands.

I took the knife and cut the rope that tied their hands, but not the one that secured them to the tree. Heather gave them meat and bread as well as water. The water she brought in a small, earthen jug was cold from the stream, and the two men each drank greedily.

"Thank you," the smaller one said with a nod.

They ate as Heather and I watched. We were both unsure of how to proceed.

Then the smaller warrior looked up from his food and said, "My name is Patrick; this is Peter. You must be the fugitive who holds the Light."

"Yes," I answered, "My name is Jonathan, this is Heather."

The larger of the two, the one called Peter, looked around anxiously, "The Sahat?"

"They disappeared in the bolt of light that knocked you out, or at least that's what I think happened," I explained.

"How did you control such a powerful weapon?" Patrick asked.

"I did nothing. I do not fully understand the power of the Light," I held it to show them as its intensity increased. "I was once like you, covered in the chains of death with no hope in this realm. Then I found the Light, and when I truly believed in its power to redeem my soul, my chains, as were Heather's, were removed. We both have been freed from our chains and are no longer fugitives."

Patrick grunted in disbelief, "My father said the same years ago, and I felt the leather strap of the Light's hypocrisy. He was an evil man who used the magic of the Light to gain power and riches and destroyed my mother and family in the process. I vowed as a child that I would never yield to the Light."

He pulled at his chains, thinking they were part of his armor, "See, I have no chains and did not have the Light to remove them. The Light may have the power to remove your chains, but there are other ways. Mine were removed through the disciplined life of a soldier."

For some reason, I had difficulty seeing through the two warriors and could not discern the condition of their souls. However, I could tell their spirits were searching and fighting for freedom.

"You both live an illusion," I continued. "The other ways that you refer to only lead to your deception. I can see the chains around you, but I can also see the inner turmoil in your spirit. You saw something last night that has changed your mind. If you despise the Light, why did you fight to protect us? Why have you come in search of the Light?" I asked.

I could tell that my thoughts confused him as he looked back to the ground. They were both searching for truth, just as I had been. The four of us sat awkwardly around the fire for a moment. So much had happened to each of us over the past few days. So much had changed. Our lives would never be the same, and the enormity of the changes weighed heavily on my heart. What was I to do now?

Peter broke the silence, "I have never seen such beauty before. I have trained in the camp of the Knights of Kratos my entire life. I know only war and violence, but deep inside, I am an empty shell. One look at the power of the Light, and I knew that I must seek its truth."

Patrick looked up at his friend in surprise. Peter turned to him and began speaking in a language I could not understand.

"Patrick, you search to see if the Light is true. I believe now that it is true. I do not understand what we have seen, but I feel a great heaviness in the Light's presence as if the chains have not been removed. Malak said that the Light was both the Light of your father and the truth. Your father abused the power, but that does not make the Light wrong. It made your father wrong. I chose to follow you last night because I saw the Light. Surely, by now, you know that Krino knows of our treason against him. Even though he is far away, he has always known when his subjects disobey his commands. How many have we captured over the years? We have no place to go. Either the Light is truth, and we give ourselves to its power, or it is not truth, and we still suffer because of the quest itself. We have nothing to lose, brother. At least if we have seen the truth and these two have been freed from their chains of death, we have a chance."

They were silent for a while as Patrick studied whatever Peter had told him, drawing circles in the sand at his feet with a small stick.

"Peter, I know. I, too, have felt the heaviness around me. The Light has plagued me since I was a child. I thought I had pushed the memory back into the recesses of my mind, but several months ago, when we first heard that the Light was present in the realm again, I was also plagued with dreams. And when I saw the Light, I knew I would have no peace until I confronted it face to face."

Both men looked at me, and Patrick spoke, "You say that we live in an illusion. Then show us the truth," he pulled at the ropes that bound them to the tree, "and cut the ropes. We are tired of being tied up like cattle."

I quickly cut loose the ropes that bound the two, and the Light shone brighter.

Archon Krino, dark overlord of the Realm of the Plains of Apistia to the River Dolios, stood upon the battlements of the ancient fortress. For years, his army of Sahat and Kratos knights had ruled all the country around the great city of Hedone and into the forest. The Sahat were evil hunters given to him by the Overlord to use as he saw fit to search out and destroy the fugitives whose time had come, but they had no real connection with him. They were soulless creatures created in the dark underworld of caverns beneath the great fortress that lived in the shadows of the night. They obeyed his commands only because they were programmed to do so.

On the other hand, the Kratos Knights were men who owed their allegiance only to him. They were handpicked and well-trained at a young age. He hid their chains from them and gave them strength to overcome the destruction of the chains to their souls. They would eventually die like all of mankind, and their souls would be eternally lost, but at least in this realm, they lived a life of luxury. He gave them anything they desired: riches, food, shelter, women, and power. They were well-armed and lived better lives than those around them only because of his power. He made them what they were. Krino was connected to each of them so that his magic would continue to cover them with the illusion; therefore, he knew the moment when the Captain and the scout had decided to turn traitor.

So be it, Krino thought. Without his protection, the chains would reveal themselves soon enough, and when their time came, the Sahat would take them.

Then Krino remembered that Patrick was one subject he had trusted with information, and information was power. If the Captain succeeded in his attempt to reach the Light and the Light worked the treachery to its completion, the Captain could use that information against him. He had to be destroyed. Once and for all, the Light that had entered the realm would have to be eradicated like the plague that it was.

Archon Krino tossed the remaining blood wine from his golden goblet over the tower walls to rain down on the courtyard below and turned to make the preparations. He would lead the men himself, vowing that when the two traitors were captured, they would be used as examples to all who dared have thoughts of rebelling against his rule. The two would endure such pain and torture as no man had ever dreamed of, and all would again fear him, as was his birthright.

CHAPTER TWENTY-EIGHT

It is truly unique how the fortunes of a man's life can change in just a flicker of time. Once a vagabond wearing the chains of death, I was now a new creation. My spirit was alive for the first time. It now seemed so long ago when I hid in the cave of fear and first met the Light. Even though I did not fully understand its power, I saw the world in a way I had never noticed before.

For years, I had been searching for the truth with little contact with others except in Hedone when I traveled there for the census. In that great city, many fugitives were begging in the streets. Others worked for the merchants or city officials. They made a life for themselves, living in homes and raising children, working jobs, and attending schools. Many in the city were never as needy as I had been, but all wore the chains of death. Some tried to hide the chains under their delicate garments and expensive jewelry, but others did not care. These even fashioned their clothing to accommodate the chains, and I wondered how they could live such a life. Didn't they know that they were in a doomed condition? I had constantly feared the night when the shining crimson eyes of the Sahat searched for those such as myself. They did not enter the city, which was why so many fugitives would travel there each year and try to secure a job to live within the protective walls.

Then I met the nomads who appeared to have found the truth and wore no chains, but now I knew they lived a lie. They lived in a world of illusion, lost as I had been, and with a sudden pain of guilt, I remembered that I had left them, the only friends that I had, amid carnage and death. I thought of Lillian. Had she survived? I prayed that she had. Was I a coward to leave? I could have pushed through the crowd and rescued her, bringing her to a safe place where I could have given her the Light. I had given the Light to the young Heather and, more recently, to the two warriors who now led us across the desert country to the shadowy mountains far to the south, where this had started.

I had watched in awe as the Light had engulfed both men simultaneously. Each met their Savior face to face and had a separate tale of their encounter with their Creator and Redeemer. We rested at the camp the rest of the day and night and began our journey the morning after. During that time, I learned a lot about the realm we lived in. I knew of the evil leader of the Sahat and the great cliff dwelling of the Overlord.

They told me of Archon Planos and the Crystalline Mountains, foes of Krino in a power struggle for the realm. My first wish was to travel to Hedone for food, supplies, and safety within the walls. I knew of no other place to go. After all, I had never seen the enemy within the city walls and had been traveling there my entire life. It was where I used to feel safe from the Sahat, and I wished to be safe now.

But the Captain told me of the great council and the ruler of Hedone, Archon Sarkinos. They knew of the power of the Light. They understood they had to keep the realm's people disunified and weak. The council had agreed not only to destroy the weak and murder the children but also to deceive those who were trying to break free of the chains, to cause the people of the realm to despise the Light through deception. That was to be their ultimate weapon. Then, the captain told me of a leader among the people who would usher in the Light and open the door for the Bene Elohim to invade the land.

"You, Jonathan, must be the leader spoken of in the council. You have ushered the Light back into the realm. You freed me of the illusion that held me captive," Patrick had told me in the darkness of the morning by the warming fire, "I fought the Light and what it stood for all of my life because of the abuse of my father. But in one night, you have shown me its truth. You have the gift to lead souls to their freedom. Look around you. The girl Heather, who had no hope, was left beaten and naked in the desert. The elusive Peter who banished many of the followers of the Light many years ago because of his loyalty to me. And I, who vowed to stamp out the Light from the realm once and for all. I was sent to capture the Bene Elohim and destroy the Light. I would have killed you as well," he continued. "You have given each of us freedom and peace, and this, only one day after you yourself were freed. You are the one, Jonathan. You are the Apostolos Or spoken of."

As I rode under the afternoon sky, I doubted those words. I was no leader of men. My whole life, I had been searching for my freedom without thinking of anyone else. I had watched in terror as the fugitive Gloria had been killed on that rainy night months ago, as I had done countless times before. I had fled the nomad camp, possibly leaving Lillian to die. How could I be the leader to usher the Light back into the realm?

"BECAUSE YOU HAVE BEEN CHOSEN," the voice spoke to my spirit, "YOU ARE NO LONGER WEAK. YOU CAN DO ALL THINGS BECAUSE OF THE LIGHT'S POWER WITHIN YOU."

"But how?" I spoke back.

"ONE STEP AT A TIME," the voice responded, "TRUST IN ME. I WILL GIVE YOU EVERYTHING THAT YOU NEED."

The shrill scream of the hawk above startled me.

"Hold!" Patrick ordered, and we obeyed. Now that was a leader, I thought to myself. How could I do such a thing, command men, and they obey?

Peter rode ahead and dismounted just under the low rise of ground before us, barren of all vegetation. We stood still as the scout crawled the rest of the way up to the crest of the ridge and peered over to see what was on the other side. The hawk soared overhead, vigilant as always.

I turned to see if Heather was well and noticed that she was dozing atop her horse. She looked peaceful, and even though radiant with the yellow flowers in her hair something appeared to be wrong. I nudged her gently. She opened her eyes, looking at me.

"You, okay?" I whispered.

"Yea, just tired." She answered.

I worried about her health. She seemed to be so weak.

Noticing that we had stopped and Peter was out ahead of us, she asked what was going on.

"I'm not sure. The bird spotted something ahead and Peter is checking it out."

It is strange. Before yesterday, I had never seen the two men before us, but now I trusted them completely. I trusted them with my life. The Light within each of us had bonded us together.

Upon hearing last evening that I wished to go to Hedone, Patrick had cautioned against it, telling me of another place, far off in the forest above the Forest of Basar, a place where a remnant of the people of the Light were said to live.

"It is many days journey, possible weeks. I do not know for sure, but the forces of this realm do not reach that far. There is a river, a great river that I have only seen once years ago. The river cannot be crossed except at one location. As a child, I remember seeing the people of the Light standing on the other side, waving back to my father, mother and myself as we left. I don't know why, but my father was traveling to Hedone. He spoke of spreading the Light in the realm. That was years before the Light was driven out and the Archons of the Realm took full control. I saw the crossing again during the Light Wars, but that was many years ago in my youth. I had forgotten that until just now, but I know that this place is where we must go."

"Do you know the way?" I had asked.

"I think so, but the voice inside me says to follow the Light and it will lead the way."

So we were traveling toward the south, into a new realm that I had only heard about in legend.

"YOU HAVE SEEN IT."

Of course, I saw a village in the forest while standing on the precipice of life. It had appeared to be so peaceful. Malak had told me that there would be a time when I would return to help Lillian and the others, but I now knew that I first needed to find the village across the river where I would learn the ways of the Light. I would return, but first I needed a place in which to prepare. I did not know my destiny and did not truly believe that I was the leader foretold, but I did know that I had to do something to destroy the illusion and show the people that they could be free if they would trust in the power of the Light and embrace its beauty.

Peter turned and made a hand sign that only Patrick understood. Patrick turned to Heather and me to interpret: "Soldiers riding from the east, twelve of them. We should wait here a bit before continuing. They are passing to the west."

Peter slowly backed down the hill through the rocks to his horse and rode back to where we waited beneath the shade and cover of a grove of juniper and pinion.

"Who were they Peter?" Patrick asked when the scout rode up beside us.

"A patrol from Hedone. It appears Sarkinos must have gotten word of the fight by the river. I have never known his soldiers to ride so far from the city. It must be at least three days ride from here."

I was thankful now that I had listened to Patrick and not traveled to Hedone. During my whole life, that city was the only bit of protection that I had ever felt, and I had been tempted to yield to its familiarity.

Peter continued, "They usually stay within a day's ride from the city. They don't care much to be outside their protective walls at night."

"They are searching for us, my friend." Patrick glanced over at me and then Heather, "It appears that we have brought more problems for you and the girl. When the Light broke our bond with Krino, he must have felt it. He knows that we have turned against him. I do not know how, but the Archons of the Realm can communicate briefly with each other from anywhere in the realm."

"There are hundreds of soldiers in the city Patrick. I have seen them. How can we hope to evade them in this barren wilderness?" I asked in fear and unbelief.

Patrick smiled, a confident smile full of power, "You must have more faith in yourself, Jonathan. You are the Apostolos Or. We'll make it to the river before they catch us."

He spurred his horse onward as I called after him, "But do you know the way across the river?"

"We will when the time comes. Have faith in the One who saved you," he shouted back over his shoulder, a wide smile across his face.

He may enjoy grand adventures and chases across the desert, I thought, but I was still afraid of the horses. With a jump, my mount galloped to catch up to the others, and I held tightly to the reins. Heather rode beside me. Somewhere, there was a great river, with safety on the other side and no way to cross it.

"THERE IS ALWAYS A WAY."

CHAPTER TWENTY-NINE

A vast, thickly forested wilderness of rolling hills spread out beneath a snow-covered mountain range covered in dark spruce and fir with veins of white-barked aspen, their bright yellow leaves shimmering among the deep gorges that fell sharply down to the valley floor below. At first, from his vantage point high among the rocky crags of a cliff overlooking the great river of turbulent, rushing water, Malak saw no sign of life except for the lush vegetation and occasional birds. Even though he stood several hundred feet directly above the river among the broken red cliffs, the roar of the rushing river assaulted his ears.

Malak searched carefully among the trees lining the opposite riverbank below him for the sign that the river crossing was near. Though he rode a powerful horse, they could only cross the river at the designated place. As he searched, the horse nudged him gently and he looked further up the sandy shoreline.

On his side of the river, the great cliffs extended far off into the distance in both directions, but across the river lay a shoreline of smooth white sand and scattered deciduous trees with occasional rocky outcrops and narrow flower-covered meadows. Near one of those meadows, a polished white stone, standing twenty feet high, marked the crossing. A narrow trail extended from the water's edge by the stone and disappeared into the dark shadows of the great forest. The crossing would be directly next to the stone.

Malak turned and mounted his horse to begin the descent down the narrow cliff trail, "You have good eyesight, my friend."

The horse nodded his head approvingly and led his master down the treacherous, winding trail down to the river below.

The great river had many names, depending on those who beheld its beauty and feared its power. All fugitives, once free of their chains had to cross the river sometime in their life. Few had ever witnessed its power in this part of the realm, although in other areas, great civilizations flourished in places where the Light was strong, and the power flowed freely. Here, on the other hand, there was only one crossing, known only to a few. It took great faith to cross the turbulent waters, even at the crossing because of the violence of the river.

Through the great river flowed all of the temptations of men, all of the fears, all of the concerns, all of the powers of the world that strived to pull man's soul back into bondage once he had been freed. The strong current roared by at incredible speeds, seething and churning, crushing all with its power, yet at the point of the crossing, the river could be traversed with ease, even by the smallest and weakest child.

Once free from the thin ribbon of trail that descended the cliff wall, Malak trotted his horse up to the crossing marked on this side of the river by the same white polished stone. Directly across the river stood twin sentinels that marked the true course to the safety on the other side. He rode calmly through the water, emerging on the opposite shore completely dry as if he had never entered the river at all.

Like many of the wonders of the realm, Malak trusted in them and marveled at their beauty and power but never truly understood them. He often wondered how humanity could better understand the power of the Light than he could, but often did not have the faith or courage to take advantage of the gifts given to them by the Creator.

The Bene Elohim halted by the polished stone next to the dim trail, knowing that his passing would alert the guardsman of his presence. The trail was dimly marked and covered with leaves, testimony of its lack of use. He remembered long ago when it had been a wide trail. Hopefully, that time would come again if the plan worked.

The trail extended into the forest until it turned and was lost from view by the massive tree trunks of the ancient oak trees. The trail, he knew, wound through the great forest for a distance until it emerged in a series of small woodland meadows where a village lay nestled in the security of the forest, protected by the evils of the Shadow Realm by the great river that he had just crossed.

In the village lived a small community of people of the Light who, although free of their chains of death, feared to cross back over the river again, content to live out their lives of freedom and peace among the beauty and safety that the forest offered.

Malak knew that in the great scheme of life, the village had been used as a haven in the past and would be used as such in the future. With the right leader and at the right time, the villagers would, again, cross the river to expand their territory. It was one thing to use the village as a haven and place of rest; it was another thing entirely to never leave and cross the river, as was the perfect will of the Light of the World.

Over the years, there had been a few who had ventured across the river to try and win the freedom of the fugitives, but they had all failed, some never returning. Others remembered a time when the trail had been well used and prayed earnestly for that to be the case again, which was what had opened the way for a new invasion to begin.

Leaves rustled among the trees high up behind Malak, and he turned, searching. He saw nothing out of the ordinary, just the thick canopy. Someone dropped suddenly down behind him, startling both himself and the horse, and he felt the sharp point of a blade against his lower back.

"Well, well if it's not the great and mighty warrior Malak. How is it? Tell me, how is it across the river in the land of shadows?" a female voice asked, "I could have taken your head while you crossed the river if you had been one of the evil ones," she continued and then sighed, "But, lo and behold, it is only you."

"Good to see you as well, my dear Nasar," Malak answered as he turned his horse to face the girl. He bowed slightly in greeting to Nasar, Guardian of the river crossing and of the village of Soteria.

She was a young warrior, dressed in the way of a wood dweller with loose-fitting trousers and a light green blouse. Around her thin waist, she wore a black belt and scabbard in which she sheathed her short sword. Soft black leather boots covered her feet. A short brown cloak attached over her breast with a golden brooch that marked her as a Bene Elohim draped over her shoulder. A quiver of arrows, the feathers brightly colored, extended above her back. She carried a long bow in one hand, which was her favorite weapon, although she could use the short sword efficiently as well.

Nasar wore her long, blonde hair free down her back, allowing the golden locks to hang to her waist, although she sometimes braided it in one long, decorative braid. She kept her hair from her eyes with a small purple headband. Nasar loved flowers and always had one tucked into the headband.

Malak dismounted, and taking her hand in his, bowed low before her, as she stood, flushed, her blue eyes sparkling in the sunshine.

"It has been a long time since I have been graced by your presence. I hope all has been well here in Soteria."

The horse stepped closer and nudged her in greeting as well.

She reached up and petted the stallion and bowed to Malak in return.

"All is well, but at times, I have wished to travel into the Shadow Realm again. My arrows have not tasted the blood of the evil ones for some time. Now, with your return, I know that the time is near. Let me ride with you on that great beast of yours back to the village. You can tell me why you have returned."

Malak mounted the mare and pulled her easily up behind him.

The path to the village followed an ancient trail that meandered almost aimlessly among the giant oak and hickory. The trail steadily climbed a low ridge until it emerged at the summit in a small meadow covered with multicolored flowers and lush, mountain grass, opening a vast, panoramic view of the deep forest in the valley below and the snow-covered high mountains to the west. Here, a soft breeze floated among the trees, spreading the mystic fragrance of the flowers. The scent was intoxicating to Malak, who breathed deeply, having been in the Land of Shadows with its ever-present stench of death and decay. The leaves fluttered merrily to the wind's caress, a few floating aimlessly across the meadow to land gracefully among the flowers.

In the valley below, thin trails of smoke rose from beneath the trees, marking the locations of the many homes and shops of the hidden village. Malak understood why the souls who inhabited such a peaceful place would want never to leave, but he knew that for final victory to be won, they would have to cross over the river into the Shadow Realm of the fugitives.

"Beautiful, isn't it?" commented Nasar.

The land's beauty and tranquility were breathtaking.

"They live in a place of such wonderment and peace. This causes them to hide out in their forest from the evils around them, content to live out their existence. Most do not seem to see the fugitives in the Shadow Realm who are lost without hope, although there are several who are praying that the time will come when the people of the Light will reach out across the river." Nasar stated as they watched the ribbons of smoke dissipate into the heavens above as the soft breeze rustled among the trees.

"Be strong, Nasar. Change is coming. The prayers are pushing the master's hand to accomplish His will in the realm. A true Apostolos Or has been found in the Shadow Realm, although he is now still unsure of himself. Events are beginning to usher in another move of our Lord," Malak turned to look into the deep blue eyes of the archer. "Does the woman, Sarah Garwood, still live in the village?"

"Yes, she lives alone, an older woman whose time is near, why?"

"Her prayers for change have been answered. As you know, the people of Soteria are distrustful of outsiders since they were driven here many years ago. Sarah will help the people accept those who are coming, especially since one of them is of her blood. The people respect her and will listen to what she has to say. We must be ready. I need to see Sarah and recruit those who will stand with us to protect the river crossing."

Nasar smiled, "There are several who will help us Malak. They just need to be pushed a little."

She slipped off the back of the horse and whistled, calling her horse, a spotted mare that trotted out from the dark shadows of the forest and neighed in greeting to Malak's horse, responded with a slight bow of his head.

"We'd best be on our way. Follow me to the village."

Nasar mounted her horse, and both Bene Elohim took the thin trail down the meadow and into the forest below.

Two stone guard towers just outside a cluster of wooden structures protected the village of Soteria. A wooden palisade connected the two towers after surrounding the entire village of thatched-roof homes and shops. The entrance to the village led through a wooden gate next to the closest tower after crossing a swift running stream on a covered bridge constructed of polished white stone with a wooden roof.

The village was situated in a bottomland meadow surrounded by low hills thickly forested with tall pines and even larger hardwoods. On the far side of the meadow, cattle grazed among scattered sheep and horses. Nearer the entrance road alongside the stream, well-tended vegetable gardens grew, protected by low wooden fences with hinged gates. Greenhouses filled with all types of herbs, flowers, and vegetables were also located within the fences.

A well-constructed and maintained irrigation system crisscrossed the vegetable patches separated by narrow, winding trails. Rows of corn over ten feet tall, each with two or three ears, grew next to low-running plants such as cantaloupe, cucumber, and watermelon. Other areas were covered with yellow squash and green zucchini, bright red tomatoes, and beans of all types and varieties.

Although secluded and unwilling to travel across the great river, the villagers were very protective of their own property. A dozen warriors armed with shields and swords as well as with the long bow formed a well-trained fighting unit led by the very capable Captain Murphy. The small band followed a well-regimented system of training, but because of Captain Murphy's unwillingness to cross the river into the Shadow Realm, they did not have experience in battle except for the occasional skirmish with roving bands of thieves who stumbled upon their hidden enclave.

A lone sentry in the stone round tower at the bridge spotted the two Bene Elohim as they rode out from the dense forest and emerged into the meadow and challenged them, the voice of a boy echoing across the valley. Two armed warriors emerged from behind the gate and stood beneath the bridge canopy, partially hidden in the shadows of the stone structure. Several men and women working in the vast sea of greenery that was the garden rose above the plants to look as well, several shielding their eyes from the glare of the afternoon sun. The boy in the tower announced that two Bene Elohim were approaching.

Malak commented on the soldiers on the bridge.

"They are a well-meaning and fiercely protective people. I have not been too successful in convincing them that when our Lord wished, they should cross the river into the Land of Shadows to help free the fugitives of their chains. Their leader, Captain Murphy is distrustful of all outsiders and does not wish to endanger his people by leading fugitives to the village. These people know the truth and have been given all that they need but wait to take action. They have said many times that they wish to do something, but they always put it off, saying that the warriors need more training or that they must plant more gardens first."

Nasar shook her head. "Maybe I am too impatient, but I have witnessed the horrors in the Shadow Realm."

Malak reached over to take the young archer's hand in his, "Don't worry. The time has now come when the people of Soteria may be stirred into action. The woman, Sarah, is the key. She is the widow of the first Captain of Soteria before your time. They had built a small town near Hedone many years ago, and the Light was spreading through the land slowly, but a time came when the armies of Krino besieged the town. The town held on for some time and was almost on the verge of victory. I was leading a detachment of Bene Elohim to assist them, but then they were deceived into opening their gates by a band that appeared to be children of the Light but were the enemy. The town was destroyed, and the people scattered. Many sought refuge in Hedone, others led by Murphy escaped across the river to this place."

"I never knew," commented Nasar sadly. "No wonder they are distrustful of strangers and do not wish to bring them in. You say that visitors are approaching. You have come on ahead to prepare the people?"

"Yes," Malak answered as the two approached the bridge. The villagers in the field gathered at the wooden gate next to the tower by the bridge. "And we only have a few days to do so. The band is but several days travel from the village."

The sentry leaned far out of the window in the tower above to get a better view of the new Bene Elohim.

"Well done, young Carman. Your eyes are stronger than the eagle." Nasar called her praise up to the young sentry.

"Thank you, Mistress Nasar. Can we climb to the falls again tomorrow? I'm only allowed to go if you go with me," the boy asked. He watched Malak suspiciously as the two Bene Elohim crossed the bridge, the hooves clattering on the wooden flooring.

"Possibly Carman, as soon as I am able," the archer smiled back at the boy as the two emerged from the bridge and dismounted in front of the gate guarded by the two soldiers of Soteria.

An older, bearded man, short of stature but strongly built, thick through the chest, with graying hair and a noticeable scar across his cheek, greeted them. A wounded spirit at times took a long time to heal, though Malak. Sometimes, the scar never heals at all.

"Greetings, Mistress Nasar," Murphy bowed slightly to the archer and then turned to Malak. "And who have you brought with you? A Bene Elohim?"

"This is Malak who has been traveling in the Shadow Realm. He wishes to speak to the elders of the village concerning urgent news."

Murphy immediately became apprehensive, "Urgent news? There is no urgency here in Soteria, which is exactly the way the elders wish it to be. The elders do not wish to hear of news from across the river."

"I wish to hear, Captain," an elderly woman's voice spoke from the crowd that had gathered beneath the shadows of the stone tower by the gate to look upon the new Bene Elohim.

Many had never seen another Bene Elohim other than Nasar, although the sight of his chain mail and broadsword had brought back buried memories in the minds of several of the older generations who had been children when the people had lived in the realm across the river.

Murphy turned as the woman, holding a cane to help her walk, stepped out from the band of villagers, "Madame Sarah, you know that the elders have stated very clearly that…"

"I don't care what the elders have said. It is time that we listen to our Lord and take a risk for change."

The elder walked past the captain who, although disagreeing with her statement, bowed his head in respect, as was the custom. Sarah was a short woman, even shorter with age because she walked slightly and stooped over. Long brown hair, streaked with gray and braided, crowned her head, and she had deep brown eyes. Her skin was bronzed from working in the sun, and although old, her brown eyes sparkled with life, showing her true strength.

The woman walked past the captain and over to where Malak stood, his massive presence dwarfing her. Nasar stepped to one side to let her pass.

Sarah Garwood was the oldest soul in Soteria and the widow of the late Captain Garwood, who had passed on to the next realm and his glorious reward years ago, shortly after the remnant had crossed the river and established their village among the great forest. The people respected her age, strength, and wisdom, and because of her position as wife of the first Captain, she was a member of the board of elders who ruled the village under Captain Murphy's leadership.

She reached a small trembling hand upward to touch Malak's face, looking deep into his dark eyes as distant memories came alive again, memories of great challenges and victories, and then, ultimately of deception and defeat.

"Madame Sarah of Garwood," Malak clasped her hand in both of his gloved hands and held it tightly, bowing down on one knee before her in respect for such a great warrior of the Light who continued to offer up prayers to the Lord of Heaven. He knew that his strength, in fact, the strength of all of his kind, rested on the shoulders of men and women such as this lady before him. "Do you remember, then, after all of these years?"

Sarah began to tremble as tears of both joy and sadness began to flow down her cheeks. For years, she had steadfastly prayed for the time when the way would be open for the people to destroy the darkness once again by the power of the Light.

"Yes, my dear Malak. I do remember. It is good to see you again. Your presence here in Soteria is proof that my prayers have been answered and change is coming. You can speak to the elders. If no one else is willing to assist you and young Nasar, at least you will have me at your side."

She straightened up, new strength in her spirit, a great smile on her face, "I think that I can still wield a sword in battle, even after all this time."

Malak laughed as he stood up. "That is good, my lady. With you at our side, all the Realm of Shadows will tremble with fear."

Sarah turned back to Murphy. "I know what we have said in the past, Captain, but times have changed." She touched the scar across his cheek, "It's time for you to allow your scars to heal as I have mine. Please, Captain, call the elders. Let us listen to Malak. The Light has brought him to us once more, which means that the time has finally come when we will once more break the hold of darkness over the Shadow Realm."

"Very well, Madame," Murphy surrendered and then turned to Nasar. "Come to my table for the afternoon meal. You must be hungry. After we eat, I will call the elders, and we will hear what you have to say."

The Light around the Captain's neck glowed stronger than it had done in years. Others noticed it, but Murphy did not. He had a wounded spirit that covered the Light with his pain from past failures and past mistakes. Sarah only smiled, knowing that his healing would come soon as well.

The entire village heard the news of the Bene Elohim called Malak even before the horses were fed and boarded in the stables near the wall at the edge of town. As in all small communities, news spread quickly; therefore, by the time the elders filed into the town hall for the meeting, the building was packed with all the inhabitants except for the sentries who manned the guard towers. Usually, the elders met in the small room at the end of the hall, but this time, the meeting was held for all to hear at Sarah's request.

The Spirit moved among the people and the hall glowed brightly with the combined lights that hung around the necks of all of the souls of Soteria. Both Malak and Nasar felt the power that originated from the lights of so many of the faithful as their spirits were individually stirred to action.

The time had come, an Apostolos Or had been found. Some were afraid of change, others had deep wounds that haunted them, but all knew that change was indeed coming.

However, there was one among them who secretly rejected the change. Although her light did shine as the others, the power came from another source. No one knew who she was, but both Malak and Nasar could faintly sense that something was not as it seemed as they passed through the corridor between the rows of wooden benches to the front of the meetinghouse. The enemy was present in the town.

Captain Murphy called to order, and Malak was allowed to tell the people of the Apostolos Or called Jonathan and his band, who were even now crossing the plains in search of the river crossing. As Nasar had warned before, the people were distrustful of strangers. The older villagers still remembered strongly how that they had been betrayed. Only Sarah knew Malak, although some could remember him as a child.

When Malak told of the two Knights of Kratos, one of the elders, a man called David of Soma, broke in, "We cannot allow them to cross the river. They are a terrible race of men who fought against us in the Light Wars. And now you ask us to open our gates and allow the likes of those animals to live among us. Do you know what they do with women, Malak? I have two daughters. We cannot risk it!"

Several in the audience nodded in agreement.

"Yes, David, I know who they are. I know what they did to your people in the past, but you discount the power of the Light. The Knights of Kratos are fugitives, just as you were. They have been deceived by the magic of Krino into believing that they no longer wear the chains of death. They believe that the only way in which to remain free of the chains is to follow Krino and do his bidding. They are men just as you are, but do not have the Light. The two that are coming know the Light and, therefore, should be allowed to cross."

A great hush came over the room as the Spirit spoke to each of the inhabitants individually. Malak and Nasar felt the presence of the Lord as He moved among the souls of Soteria. As hearts were touched, individual lights burned a little brighter as, one by one, and the people realized the truth in what Malak had spoken.

Sarah stood up then and spoke for the first time, "After my husband led many of you and your parents away from Hedone years ago to this haven from the evils of the Shadow Realm, I did not wish to ever cross the river and go back. As you know, a daughter was lost to us, taken by the Knights of Kratos as they stormed the town. We were betrayed by those who we thought were people of the Light, as we were, but it appears were in league with the Archons of the Realm. For several years, I mourned the loss of my child. My husband's wish was to return to the realm and again try to break the power that held the people captive, but because of my sorrow and fear, he did not. And then he passed from this realm into the next, and I was left alone with my scars, my wounded spirit still mourning. I lived in my past, remembering the old ways, the distant victories, the great possibilities, but forgetting the power of the Light that had made all that possible. When John passed on, I began again to feel the stir in my spirit and knew that I needed to break from the past and look to the future. I began to pray for a time when the people of the Light would again cross the river. I believe that my daughter may yet be alive, or maybe she has passed on as well. Maybe she has a family that is still in bondage. There may be relatives of yours there as well, and if we can do something to free them from the bonds of deception, then we should do so." Sarah paused a moment, and her expression grew softer. "The stories tell us of the Apostolos Or that will usher in a move of the Light in the realm. Malak has told us that the Apostolos Or is coming; therefore, we must follow our hearts and join with him. The Spirit is moving among us now. Do you feel Him?"

No one spoke as Sarah sat back down in her chair near the front of the meeting hall. Nasar glanced over at Malak who stood silently next to her. He was a great leader among her race, a legend to those like her that were younger and less experienced. Now he stood in her presence with her charge of souls.

He glanced down at her and smiled, speaking from his mind to hers, "Your village heeds the pull of the Spirit. You have done well, but I sense there is one among them that is not what he seems. I cannot locate the person, but the magic of the enemy is present. We must watch carefully and assist the people to find its source."

Nasar nodded her agreement, but before she could answer, Captain Murphy broke the silence as he stood, his chair scraping across the floor. "I, too, feel the Spirit and hear His voice. We will allow the travelers to cross the river if they can find the crossing, but we must be careful." He turned to face the two Bene Elohim, "I will lead the warriors to the crossing, but no further. If they are whom you say, and the Apostolos Or is among them, then they will know where the crossing is without our help. We will assist them if they are in danger, but only from our side of the river."

"Thank you, Captain. That will be a great service. We have several days before they arrive." Malak bowed to the leader of Soteria, and the meeting adjourned. The people filed out of the meeting hall with great expectancy, knowing that the time had come. Several had been praying for the day when an Apostolos Or would arrive. The strongman over the plains would have to be destroyed, and then the Light could once again pierce through the darkness and show those in bondage the way to freedom.

But one among them left with other thoughts. If an Apostolos Or was coming, she had to alert her master. Under the cover of darkness, she would ride to the portal and communicate with her master. She would have to be careful. The Light was growing stronger throughout the village now, and the presence of two Bene Elohim threatened to expose her. Her magic of deception was strong, but would she be able to keep her true motives hidden from both?

The woman watched as the villagers left the meetinghouse, backed around the corner of the building as the two Bene Elohim walked down the wooden steps to ensure they did not notice her, and then ran back to her cottage. It would take her a half-hour ride along the forest trail to the portal. From there, she could alert her master of what had just happened. She smiled as she wrapped herself in a cape, covering her head. She would get a great reward for the news. In fact, maybe her master would allow her to return to his castle.

She slipped out the door and ran alongside the palisade to the stables. Saddling a horse quietly, she waited until she was sure no one was nearby and then led the horse through the gate. The guard watched as she walked past.

She smiled up at him as he greeted her, "It will be dark soon, mistress Emily. Do be careful."

It was her habit to ride just before dark, but only the guards knew, never thinking anything about it.

"Don't worry, Eric, I'll be fine. I'll be back by then." She mounted the horse and galloped over the stone bridge and across the meadow to the trail to the river.

Once inside the forest, she turned the horse to one side and into the thick brush that, after a few feet, opened into another trace that led deeper into the wilderness. The trail widened, and her horse galloped toward the portal that lay hidden behind the great waterfalls. Only her magic could open the portal. The people of Soteria knew of the falls and often visited the place, never knowing what lay behind them. Emily had only opened the portal once before to ensure that she could. Her instructions had been very clear. She was to only use the portal if she had evidence that an Apostolos Or had been found.

CHAPTER THIRTY

It had been a long time since the young Carman had been to the waterfalls and after sitting up in the tower for most of the day; he was bored and wished to go again. Nasar had taken him and several other boys the last time, but she was too busy. There was a meeting going on in the town hall when he climbed down the ladder from the tower as his replacement waited below. There would be no harm, he thought. If he left quickly, he could explore the falls and be back home before nightfall.

He saddled a horse and slipped out of the gate. The forest trail to the falls led through thick stands of hemlock with a heavy understory. The trees formed a tunnel over the thin ribbon trail. The last time Carman had been there, he had noticed what appeared to be a cave behind the shimmering waterfalls but had not had the time to investigate.

He heard the crashing water long before he was within sight of the river and slowed the horse to a walk as the trail descended through a thicket of mountain laurel and stopped at a great pool where the villagers often swam.

The waterfalls plunged down from the rocky crags over a hundred feet high across the river from where the trail stopped. Sheets of blue-green water spilled over the lip of the cliff, falling in eternal, successive waves to splash into the pool below with incredible force. The water seethed and swirled along the far side of the pool, sending concentric rings across, continually stirring the water, the small waves reaching up to the banks at his feet. Even at this distance, the force of the falling water showered Carmen with a mist of cold water. The only way that he knew to reach the falls was to swim across the deep water to the opposite shore.

Carman dismounted and tied his horse to one of the low shrubs along the water's edge. He wanted to see how far the cave behind the waterfall extended into the mountain. Just as he prepared to dive into the pool, he noticed movement among the shadows under the heavy pine canopy above the rocky shoreline near the falls. At first, he thought it was a bear, but then he made out the shape of a horse and hooded rider. They were working their way slowly through the brush toward a cleft in the rock that led upward into the falls and disappeared behind the glistening water and the heavy mist.

Carman backed away from the shore to hide behind a clump of alder, the cold water lapping at his feet. Who could that be? There was no trail across the river, he thought. He knelt down and watched carefully as the rider emerged from the shadows and into the afternoon sun. Carman knew that he had to be careful. If his parents knew that he had slipped away to the falls by himself, he would be in big trouble.

The hooded figure dismounted at the trail leading up to the cave behind the water and removed the cape, revealing long black hair, but Carman could still not see the woman's face. She was a young woman and small. She glanced upward toward the thin trail that climbed the face of the cliff and tied her horse to a nearby tree. Taking a small pouch with her, she turned back toward Carman and looked carefully around as if she was worried about being seen.

That was strange, the boy thought. He sat perfectly still in the brush as the woman searched the shoreline, and when she turned to face him directly, he recognized her. Emily? Why was she here by herself? Probably the same reason that you are here. He whispered to himself.

She heaved the small bag over her shoulder and climbed up the narrow trail along the cliff wall to the cleft in the rock above. Carman silently slipped into the cool water and, diving under, swam across the pool to the opposite shore near the place where the water plunged from the cliffs above. Emily was just then reaching the ledge that led along the face of the cliff to the cave behind the veil of water. Carman could hear nothing but the crashing water nearby and didn't hear the horse approach.

He climbed out from the water and scrambled up the narrow trail behind the girl, watching carefully to ensure that Emily didn't notice him following her. Something wasn't right. He felt it in his spirit and wanted to know what the girl was doing.

She reached the edge of the falls, becoming just a shimmering, ghostly figure behind the mist, and turned to look back down the trail. Carman ducked quickly behind a broken ledge of red rock and watched her through a crack near the ground. A breeze was blowing, and he shivered from the cold water that continued to spray across him. She turned then and disappeared behind the water into the cave. Carman waited for a minute, then continued the climb up the trail until he, too, pulled himself up the last rock outcrop to the ledge behind the waterfall.

The ledge led behind the sheet of water into the mist and darkness beyond. The space between the rushing water and the slick wet walls was only a few feet, just enough room to walk safely through the water. Carman hesitated before entering the dark mist. What was the girl doing? Maybe she, too, was like himself and just wanted to explore, but something about the way she had looked around after dismounting from the horse made him believe that she was up to something sinister. His spirit felt an evil lurking in the shadows behind the mist.

"BE CAREFUL CARMEN. THINGS ARE NOT WHAT THEY APPEAR."

The boy entered the mist immediately behind the rushing water, the roar deafening, the water extremely cold, colder than the pool below. He crept carefully along the rock wall until the ledge widened and entered a large room with a shining rock floor and mirror like walls that reflected the image of the water as well as his own shadowy figure. He stopped, awed by the mystery before him.

The cave extended back approximately thirty feet to the reflective walls, but Emily was nowhere to be seen. There was nowhere to go. He stepped into the room to escape the rushing water, and immediately, the sound of the water receded. He reached his arm back to the sheet of water that continually crashed down from the ledge above the cave opening, but now the sound of the water was as if it was far off in the distance. How could that be?

He took another step into the strange cave, and the roar of rushing water disappeared entirely. All he heard now was his own breathing and the dripping of water from several ledges above along the cave wall. All around him, the walls reflected the shimmering water and himself so that it appeared there were several figures standing along the cave walls, all looking back at the boy. As he walked around the room, his reflections moved as well, all in unison. He jumped up and down, and the figures did the same. He twirled around, and the figures twirled around. He forgot himself in the moment and laughed, and the figures laughed along with him.

Then he heard a rock fall from somewhere against the back of the cave, and Carman immediately quieted and stepped back to the edge of the ledge where the sound of the water roared in the distance.

Where had Emily gone? Had she fallen from the ledge? Surely not. He would have seen her as he watched the ledge before climbing the rest of the way up.

A hissing noise echoed eerily through the darkened cave like water being poured on a fire. For the first time, Carmen noticed footprints on the rock surface where someone with wet feet had left their tracks on the dry rock. The prints led directly to the back wall of the cave and disappeared. He stepped back into the cave, following the footprints, cautiously watching the wall. There was no reflection on the wall at the point where the footprints disappeared, only darkness. Had that been there before?

He reached out a trembling hand to the wet granite wall, but there was no wall. His hand disappeared into a black void, and he jumped backward, pulling his hand free from the darkness. What was this place? The voice within warned him to be careful but did not tell him to leave. In fact, he had renewed courage and stepped closer to the strange blackness that loomed before him. He touched it with his finger, sending ripples outward along the surface like when a rock had been thrown in a pool of water.

Carman took a deep breath and stepped through the blackness and into another cave. He was now in a narrow corridor that led further back into the darkness of the mountain, and he heard the rushing water again. He turned back and jumped away. The waterfall fell immediately behind him, the crashing water spraying across his face. How could that be? The ledge was only a few feet wide, where moments before, he was over thirty feet away from the water.

"I beseech you Archon Krino to receive your servant's call." A female voice spoke from the end of the tunnel and Carmen turned quickly around.

A small fire lit up the room at the far end of the tunnel. Emily stood with her back to him, pouring a dark liquid over the fire, steam rising upward, filling the room with a red smoke that began to swirl around the woman, taking the shape of a man. Emily fell to her knees before the floating spirit, and Carmen immediately felt the presence of an evil unlike anything he had ever experienced. He gasped in horror as the red spirit disappeared in a puff of flame, and Emily turned to face him.

"Carman!"

The youth turned to flee, but strong hands grabbed him from behind and pulled him back into the cavern.

"You shouldn't have come here to this place, young Carman," a raspy voice hissed in his ear from behind, and two strong arms that held him around his waist lifted him up.

"Emily, help me." Carmen was confused. Someone else was in the cavern.

"Emily is gone now. She was a weak human, but necessary to use for my purpose. You should have stayed away. You have seen too much." The voice continued, and Carman was pushed out to the very edge of the ledge, the water roaring just inches from his face. Carman struggled to break free from the hairy arms that held him.

"What have you done to her?"

"Nothing," and the voice changed to that of a young girl, "I always liked you, dear boy, but you cannot be allowed to tell the others what you have seen."

What was going on? Carman turned his head to look behind and only saw a dark hooded shadow and golden eyes peering out from a faceless void.

"Who are you?" the boy asked. Fear welled up inside of him for a moment and then the Light around his neck glowed and he felt a surge of peace flow through his soul.

"Put the boy down!" the strong voice of a Bene Elohim echoed from beyond the portal, and Carmen was thrown hard into the cave of mirrors.

"Nasar?"

"Get out of here, Carman," the archer ordered. The boy scrambled to his feet and ran past her to the ledge outside the wall of rushing water.

Nasar drew the sword at her side, placing the bow across her back. She studied the walls of the ice cave carefully, her shrouded image reflecting her in glimmering lights of green and blue.

"What is it, Nasar? What happened to Emily?" Carman had re-entered the cave and now stood behind Nasar, a knife in his hand.

Nasar continued to search the walls for the portal that had vanished when Carman had been thrown free. "Emily was a shapeshifter Carman, an evil elf from the Shadow Realm. Stand back. I think I have found the portal."

She stepped cautiously toward the cave wall, her sword out in front of her, held in both hands. Shapeshifters were not very strong but very cunning, their greatest strength being able to change into any form around them. They could strike terror into the hearts of the souls of men because of their ability to become the most hideous monsters, but to a Bene Elohim, they were just a small woodland elf if they could be found. That was the trick, as Nasar well knew. This shapeshifter had been hidden well in the village as the girl Emily, unnoticed until this very day.

The entire wall shimmered as a solid sheet of blue green ice filled with the constantly flowing reflection of the waterfall as well as Carman and Nasar's distorted figures. But there was one place where the water didn't flow at the same rate as the reflections on either side of it.

"Hold the Light up, Carman. You have the power to see through the illusion of the mirrors. Concentrate on the wall directly in front of my sword."

Carman stepped forward and stared intently at the ice, holding the Light in front of him. For a moment, he only saw the water, but then as the Light glowed stronger, he saw the outline of a hooded elf holding a short sword standing at the portal to the inner cavern.

"She's there!" Carman pointed, and with a brilliant flash, the shapeshifter lunged away from the wall and attacked Nasar.

She parried the elf's blow with her sword and slashed down toward the shape shifter's heart, but the elf was quick and blocked her blade as well. The elf lunged toward the water to jump free, but Nasar blocked her path and drove her back against the wall.

"Stand in front of the portal, Carman, and do not fear. Whatever the shapeshifter appears to be to you, she is but a small woodland elf that you now see. She can't hurt you unless you fear her."

Carman stood before the portal, holding the knife nervously. He remembered the evil golden eyes that had stared into him from the blackness of a faceless void a few moments before but shook that memory away. Before him now stood a small elfin figure not four feet tall holding a short sword not much larger than his own knife.

The elf suddenly knelt against the ice and dropped her sword, crying, "Please! Mistress Nasar, don't kill me."

The elf changed back into Emily. Nasar stepped up to the girl and kicked the sword away, placing the point of her own sword against the elf's neck, forcing her head upward.

"What is your name?"

"I am Emily," the elf pleaded to Carman. "Carman, don't you recognize me? Don't let the Bene Elohim hurt me. You have known me all your life."

Carman stood by the portal, the Light of the Spirit strong in his soul. He saw through the deception and looked away from the girl. The image of the girl Emily disappeared, and the elf returned, herself a small creature with blond hair and blue eyes.

Nasar pushed the sword edge deeper, almost to the point of drawing blood. The elf winced and drew back her head.

"Again, what is your name?"

The elf sighed, "Jasmine."

"What is your purpose here?"

"He'll kill me if I tell. I can't tell you that!"

"I'll kill you if you don't tell," Nasar threatened, as she knelt before the trembling elf, placing the blade across her neck, "Right here and now, I'll kill you. Now again, what is your purpose here?"

"I was to wait for news that an Apostolos Or had been found and then let Archon Krino know."

"Did you succeed in your mission?"

"No, Carman came just as I made contact. Archon Krino knows that I called for him, but nothing else."

Nasar stood up, still holding the sword at the elf's neck, and looked toward the portal that had re-opened behind Carmen, revealing a long tunnel extending several hundred feet back into the cave to a room now glowing red with a swirling mist. In the middle of the room sat a pot on a round stone covered in the dying embers of the small fire that the elf had started.

Carman noticed the Bene Elohim staring past him and stepped to one side to look within the portal as well. Space seemed to be distorted within the tunnel before when Carman had first stepped through the portal door, but now there was only the tunnel. The mystical doorway had disappeared entirely. The swirling red smoke within the room circled the round stone with increasing speed, and suddenly, the embers exploded into a raging ball of flame that floated just inches above the rock. Carman backed away.

"Oh no! You have made the master angry!" Jasmine screeched shrilly. "Please, Nasar, let me go. We must get out of this place!"

Nasar stepped away from the elf as the red smoke gained substance, turning into the shape of a man who settled behind the fireball floating above the stone. Piercing yellow eyes glowed from the ghostly hooded face, first looking at Carman and then at Nasar.

"Bene Elohim!"

The yellow eyes burned brighter, and a sudden flash of fire from the earthen pot streaked outward toward the archer, who jumped to one side and blocked the fire with her sword, the impact knocking her back to the cave floor. What kind of power had she awakened?

The elf scrambled past Nasar, grabbed her sword, and leaped out into the water to escape, but she was not quick enough. A second bolt of flame shot outward from the tunnel just as she entered the water. Blue smoke marked her demise.

"What is it?" Carman shouted from across the cave over the roar of the waterfall. There were no longer any glistening walls or noiseless areas within the cave. When the portal disappeared, the cave had returned to normal.

Another streak of fire exploded outward, disappearing into the water with a hiss of steam. Nasar jumped back against the cave wall next to the opening. She heard the labored breathing of some type of entity and the crackling of the fire.

She sheathed her sword and strung her longbow. Notching an arrow, she turned quickly around the edge of the opening and fired her missile that streaked directly through the figure's face, embedding into the rock wall behind, the arrow momentarily splitting the hooded face between the two yellow eyes like water.

Another fireball shot outward from the cave and Nasar jumped back against the wall. She notched another arrow. That was dumb, she thought. The fire originates from the pot. If she broke the pot, then maybe she could destroy the phantom. And then she remembered what it was she was dealing with.

Carman hid against the wall of the cave near the ledge leading to safety, his knife still in his hand, although he trembled with fear. To reach the ledge, he would momentarily expose himself to the phantom. Nasar suddenly knew how to defeat the phantom.

"Carman, you must be strong and use the power of the Light within you to help me. I cannot destroy the evil within the tunnel by myself. Can you help me?"

"I think so," the boy answered as the Light around his neck brightened.

"We have encountered a shapeshifter that was trying to communicate through the portal with one of the Archons of the Shadow Realm. Her magic has opened a communication portal. There are many of them throughout the realm, and they are all fiercely protected, but if a child of the Light exposes one, they can be destroyed."

"What must I do?" the boy asked.

"Hold the Light in front of you and step out in front of the opening." The boy looked at her in amazement. "You must have faith in the Light of the World that lives within your spirit. The Light will protect you if you stand strong against the deception. You have exposed the evil in your village. Take this step of faith, and I can destroy the portal."

Carman stood silently for a moment. The Light glowed stronger as the boy studied what the Bene Elohim had told him, and then he took the Light in both hands and made a step of faith out into the middle of the cave directly in front of the opening. Immediately a giant fireball exploded from the depths of the cave that threatened to totally engulf the boy in its fiery embrace, but the Light shielded him from the blast.

Nasar stepped out to the opening just as the fireball flew past her and let loose her arrow, this time targeting the clay pot. The yellow eyes darted in surprise to look down at the earthen pot just as it shattered from the impact of the arrow, and the fire immediately disappeared, leaving only the dying embers of the fire started by the elf.

The ground around them shook as the phantom dissolved back into a red, swirling mist, and the walls began to cave in.

"Let's get out of here!" Nasar grabbed the boy Carman and jumped with him out into the rushing water, just as the cave collapsed behind them.

They fell a hundred feet along with the torrent of water, splashing down into the seething, foamy water in the pool. Nasar fought the downward force of the water, desperately pulling the boy up with her until they both emerged near the shore. She dragged him safely onto the sandy beach and then collapsed beside him.

"You said you wanted action." Malak looked down upon them both, mounted on his horse.

Nasar wiped the water from her face and laughed and then stood up, "It was a shape shifter as we suspected. Malak, the elf was trying to communicate with Krino. She may have gotten the message through, but I'm not sure."

"Then we must be prepared," Malak, answered and looked over to the young boy who rolled over to his knees, coughing and gasping for air. "You young Carman have done well today." The warrior saluted the boy and turned his horse back onto the trail.

Archon Krino roared in anger, flinging his goblet across the tent in a fit of rage. The guard outside the tent dared not ask for fear that the lord's anger would befall him.

"Fool!" Krino shouted.

The portal had opened, communication from the elf Jasmine had been disrupted, and his link with Soteria had been severed. But not before he had heard that an Apostolos Or was heading toward the village along with two knights of Kratos. He now knew where the traitors were heading, and he would be there waiting for them.

CHAPTER THIRTY-ONE

We traveled for several days across the rolling hills of the Plains of Hedone in the direction of the forested mountain slopes that were now shrouded in the morning fog, the highest peaks glistening in the early morning sun. We traveled by day, finding shelter each night, sometimes in secluded, wooded valleys, other times in darkened caves.

This morning, we entered an area that I knew well. Therefore, the captain allowed me to lead the group. I knew of another place to hide for the night near the cave of my fears from long ago. The closer we traveled toward the cave, the more apprehensive I became insecurity building within my spirit at the memory of past failures. The last time I had traveled through this country, I had been on foot, the chains a heavy burden around me. Since then, my life has been transformed. Now, I rode on a horse that I was beginning to trust. Three friends rode with me, and with each passing day, our friendship grew stronger as we learned from each other.

The scout, Peter, rode to one side, his eyes ever vigilant, as were those of his hawk who circled among the wispy pink clouds above. Heather rode next to Peter, and Patrick rode out of sight behind us, watching our back trail. Twice in the past two days, the hawk had alerted us of approaching horsemen, both detachments from Hedone.

Once, we had hidden quietly in a cave along a dry riverbed as a large body of Sahat rode by. We no longer feared them, but we did not wish to give away our position, for a large number of them could do us great harm.

All four of us felt the Spirit pushing us onward toward our destiny, and I noticed with each day we better understood the power of the Light within us. The three who rode with me looked to me as their leader because I had exposed them to the Light, but I still felt uncertain about being an Apostolos Or. The Captain had led men in battle, and the scout knew the ways of the realm and could see with a clarity that I had only dreamed of. And Heather understood the Light more than any of us.

She had been a slave of the Knights of Kratos, used for their pleasure, yet Peter and she had bonded to be the closest of friends during the past few weeks that we had traveled together. Peter had come to her as she sat by the fire several nights following our meeting at the monuments of life, and with deep regrets and tear-filled eyes, he apologized for the great wrong done to her by members of his race. He had never agreed with the way that his comrades treated the girls, but he had looked the other way. She forgave him that night and stood up and hugged him by the fire's light, kissing him gently on the cheek. The two had been inseparable ever since.

I looked at them as we rode across the purple sage, and my heart ached. I, too, had bonded with the soul of another. I thought of Lillian. I knew that she was alive; the Spirit within me had confirmed that. Through the power of the Light, I had seen her spirit, bound and gagged, reaching out to me as she was pulled away into the river. Now, I continued to stand upon the promise that I would return. That would have to do for now.

For the past several nights by our fire's light, Patrick began teaching me how to properly wield the short sword that he had given me. I had a lot to learn of such things, but Patrick was a patient teacher. He was an expert swordsman, and I barely had enough strength to hold the sword, but with each lesson, I improved. I was stronger and wiser in its use. Heather was also learning to use the weapon.

I still walked with a slight limp, and my leg ached at times when it rained. My wound was a reminder of where I had come from and where I never wanted to return.

Each night, Patrick and I sparred across the fire from where Heather and Peter sat next to each other. They encouraged me and laughed to my embarrassment when he would pin me to the ground each time. But the previous night I bested him in one match to the surprise of everyone, me most of all.

"You are a quick learner, Jonathan," the captain commended to the applause of the two spectators by the fire.

Krino pursued us relentlessly as we traveled toward the mysterious river crossing that only Patrick had seen. Each of us knew, by the Spirit within us, that we had to cross the river to a haven from our pursuers, but only Patrick knew the approximate location of the crossing.

My insecurities concerning my ability to lead others to expose the deception and spread the Light grew stronger as we neared the cave in the forest. In my mind, I replayed the murder of the girl and my inability to save her. At times, the vision of her disappearing in a blast of fire, the evil one staring directly through me with eyes of hate and contempt, haunted my dreams, but I had told no one. Hopefully, the battle raging within would be over when we crossed the river. So, we continued to ride. Did the others have their own battles to fight at the river crossing? The Spirit assured me that they did.

Peter interrupted my troubling thoughts as he waved for us to stop. Patrick rode out of sight behind us beyond a curtain of dark firs and scattered aspen. The elevation increased as we approached the mountains, and the timber changed, becoming more frequent across the flower-covered grasslands. The ground through this country was deep, with black soil supporting lush grass and wildflowers, and water was abundant in contrast to the arid land that we had crossed over the previous days.

The hawk had disappeared behind another dense clump of white-barked aspen ahead of us that grew around a small pond that glistened in the scattered sunlight.

"Does the trail travel past the pond ahead, Jonathan?" Peter asked.

"Yes, the northern branch does. I have traveled it several times. The fugitives of the forest have often used the area along the pond as a gathering place before their journey across the savanna to Hedone. At that point, the trail climbs through the forest and across a burned area to a small river across the first line of ridges. From there, I always traveled upstream. Patrick says that when we reach the river, we need to follow it downstream. I have never been any further in that direction, but I do remember a small trail that continued down the river."

The hawk suddenly veered sharply away and upward from the aspen grove as if something were chasing him. Peter pulled his crossbow from the scabbard.

"Stay here. The bird has seen something. I'll look before we proceed."

Peter walked his horse closer among the outer edges of the stand of trees as the bird circled above in ever decreasing rings assisting Peter to locate the source of its concern.

Heather and I watched intently, my hand on the hilt of the short sword that Patrick had given me. He had said that I was not ready for a man's weapon, the great broadsword, but should be able to handle the smaller weapon. He had been right, but the laughter around the fire that night didn't help my limited ego. I smiled sheepishly as I accepted, but now I could use the sword somewhat better because of the nightly training with the captain.

Heather sat quietly beside me, her green eyes alert. The constant traveling weakened her. She desperately needed a place in which to rest so that her spirit could help to overcome the ailment that held her flesh captive.

"You okay, Heather?"

"Yes, I'll be fine. You worry too much, Jonathan," she said, smiled at me, and then stared after Peter as he walked the horse further into the trees.

"He is a brave man, don't you think?" she asked.

"Yes, he is," I commented as we watched the scout dismount and creep further into the trees, now partially hidden by the thick white trunks and yellow leaves. Whoever had alerted the bird was just over a little rise that swelled up between the water and us.

"I wish that we could have met under different circumstances," she continued. You gave me life, and for that, I owe you, but Peter and I have bonded in such a wondrous way. We have become soul mates. Do you understand?"

I nodded. Yes, I thought with great pain within my soul, I understand fully.

The hawk suddenly dove back down with a piercing, high-pitched scream that warned of immediate danger. Peter looked up through the canopy just as a shrouded dark figure emerged from beneath the sand on an open place void of vegetation among a tumbling of sandstone boulders immediately in front of us. A second jumped down from the trees in front of Peter.

It was a trap.

Somehow, they knew where we were traveling and had waited for us. Heather screamed a warning, but it was too late. Another warrior attacked Peter through the trees in a swirl of fallen leaves, as the one before me attacked with a great sword.

He was a bearded warrior with bright red hair extended to his shoulders and braided as was the custom of the soldiers of Hedone, a race not human, or so it was believed. Hedone had an army of humans similar to the knights of Kratos, but a group of red-haired warriors also guarded the city from a distant realm shrouded in mystery.

The soldier lunged his sword toward me, and I drew my sword just in time to dodge his attack, but the blow knocked me from my horse. I fell hard upon the ground as the horse ran off, and the soldier stepped over me, the two-edged broadsword high over his head as he prepared to finish me with one massive blow. My sword lay in the grass just out of reach.

The clash of arms resounded through the trees as Peter fought the other two warriors, but all I saw was the fierce warrior standing over me with blood-red hair and a painted face, the sun shining brightly behind him. He swung his sword, and I managed to roll over in time so that the sword tore at my tunic but missed my head by inches. I tried to scramble to my feet, but the man kicked me down again and then pinned me to the ground with his foot to my chest. He flipped the sword over, determined to impale me through the heart.

I struggled to free myself, but his strength was incredible. My sword lay on the ground just a few inches from my outstretched hand.

"Lord, help me!" I managed to gasp, and suddenly, the Light around my neck shot forward like liquid, temporarily blinding my assailant, and he backed away.

I regained my footing but still did not have a weapon. Where had the sword gone?

The Light went dim as the warrior swung the sword blindly before him with one hand, rubbing his eyes with the other. Then he regained his sight as I finally saw my weapon. He stepped forward with an upraised sword to attack but gasped in surprise and pain as I stood before him. The great sword fell from weakened hands that clutched his stomach as his chain mail bulged outward, the links separated by the bloody end of a sword. The warrior fell forward dead at my feet.

Heather stood in front of me then, the bloody sword in her hand. She had saved my life.

"Hurry, we have to help Peter!" she breathed.

I recovered my sword and ran for my horse, but Peter needed no help. One of the red-headed warriors lay at his feet, and the second suddenly dropped his sword and ran off through the trees. He was not of the strange race but a human, his chains of death interwoven with his armor. He mounted a horse hidden nearby to escape.

Peter grabbed for his crossbow, but the man was out of sight on the open prairie before he could get off a shot. Heather and I ran up to Peter as he emerged from the trees, breathing heavily. It looked as if he had been wounded slightly across the shoulder.

"Are you okay?" I asked.

"Yes, but we must leave. There must be more around here. The patrols of Hedone always travel in groups of twelve or more. I pray that Patrick is safe."

We collected our horses and mounted them, riding away from the aspen grove, searching intently for Patrick, who should have ridden through the distant forest of fir trees by now. Peter lifted his arm, and the hawk landed on his gloved hand. He placed the bird on the perch behind him and gave him a small treat.

"You have done well, my friend," he said, stroking the bird's neck.

"Maybe we should go back?" I questioned.

"Wait!" Peter pointed toward the dark green line of timber. "I think I see him emerging from the trees. See the small cloud of dust. He is riding fast."

I followed the direction of his gaze and saw the tiny wisp of dust and the dark shape of a horse and rider galloping across the grass.

"How far is it to the trail into the forest?" Peter asked.

"Not far at all. It's just on the other side of the pond. We can ride past the aspen where the water extends into the grassland."

"Is there another way?"

"Not for many more miles. The forest is too thick for the horses except on the trail. It's the only way until we pass the burned area. Then the timber is huge and open and several trails down to the river."

"Then most likely their friends," he pointed to the dead warrior nearby, "are at the trailhead or close by."

Peter stood up in his stirrups to look intently across the grassland behind the captain. "There is a great dust cloud across the far ridge."

I also saw the cloud hanging low over the horizon, but something about the cloud didn't seem right. It looked to be dust from a large group of mounted men, but then again, the dust was lighter, with streaks of gray and black mixed in. Then it occurred to me: It wasn't dust at all. It was smoke!

A great fire gained strength across the parched grass. The wind blew, strengthening the emerging flames and pushing them relentlessly forward. I noticed the orange glitter of fire in the low grass, leaping upward with greater strength. The flames continued to spread in a line across the grassland at the edge of the scattered trees, as if someone was methodically setting the fire.

We all searched, and as before, Peter was first to see the dark silhouette of a man running along, the fire spreading behind him.

"Look! Someone is setting the fire!" he pointed as Patrick rode up to us, the horse heaving and sweaty from the ride.

"It is Krino himself, Peter!" Patrick answered, his horse beneath him breathing hard. He turned and saw the dead warrior nearby.

"We were attacked," I answered his unspoken question.

"Then there are others before us. He is setting the fire to run us toward them or trap us against the forest and the flames. Somehow, Krino knew exactly where we were going." Patrick shook his head and turned to look back at the approaching fire.

A strong wind blew in ahead of the smoke, an unnatural wind possibly caused by the fire or maybe even Krino himself. The tall grass bent under its assault, and the trees swayed back and forth as the wind grew stronger. The fire also responded to the wind and suddenly burst into a solid wall of flame and smoke. The fire danced over the tall grass, licking forward with greater intensity and consuming everything in its path like a living, breathing monster, a billowing cloud of grayish smoke angling ahead and partially covering the sun, turning it into a pale orange ball. White ash floated down over us. A deafening roar billowed around us as the beast raced across the grassland, driven by the wind, lusting for everything alive before it.

The soldier who had run before from Peter's sword galloped through the flames, trying to escape, but the horse threw him and continued, running past us. The soldier stood up just as the main wall of fire engulfed him, knocking him back to the ground. He screamed as the fire consumed him, leaving a smoking, blackened corpse standing stiff like a statue behind.

The fire pushed directly toward us. The heat dried my face even though the fire was still several hundred yards away, as our panicked horses retreated away from the inferno and toward the grove of aspen.

If one of us fell from our horse, it would mean death. Our only hope was out running the fire. Firebrands rained down over and around us, ejected from the jaws of death behind as two arms of fire reached out and around us to cut off our retreat. The embers started spot fires ahead of us, one landing on my shoulder, burning a hole through my shirt before I could knock it away from me.

The children of the beast immediately spread into their separate fires that threatened to block our path. The assault of blinding, choking smoke engulfed us. The air itself turned a red glow as oxygen was sucked back into the flames.

The heat was incredible. Scorching shots of pain pelted my back as the flames overtook my horse. The others rode in front of me like ghosts in the thick smoke. I felt that I was going to die.

Peter pointed out of the smoke and yelled at me, but I did not hear him because of the deafening monster's scream as it poised for one final thrust of its outreached arms to engulf me. I looked toward the direction he pointed, a break in the smoke where blue sky peeked through.

A pond glistened under the bright sun, a welcome safety zone that could protect us, but armed soldiers of Hedone stood in the water for their safety, blocking our path.

An arrow embedded itself in the pack just behind me with a thud and a second shattered on impact with the captain's shield fastened to the front flank of his horse. Patrick turned away from the pond, and I followed his lead and saw the mountain trail at the edge of the forest through another break in the smoke. I motioned to the others to follow me, and we all jumped through the approaching flames as the firestorm raced past us and across the pond, completely covering the men and horses that had taken refuge there. A horse leaped through the fire behind me, badly burned and wild with fear and pain.

The forest at this point had an open understory with plenty of shade that kept the fuel moist and more difficult to burn than the dry grass out on the prairie. Momentarily, we were outside the fire's path, and the roar of the front began to subside as the fire continued past us, driven by the strong wind. Small fingers of flames fanned out and entered the forest in front of us, where the vegetation was dense with plenty of fuel. Soon, the fingers found the dried leaves and dead branches along the forest floor and stirred by the wind, and the steep slope of the rising mountain grew into another wall of flame, birthing a new monster that started a race up the mountain before us.

"There is a burned-out area across the ridge. It is our only chance!" I shouted and pointed up the trail.

Heather took the trail first, with Peter and Patrick close behind. I followed last, with the injured horse running alongside. Again, the race for life commenced as we pushed our mounts up the trail, the fire gathering new momentum below us.

At first, the fire reached out alongside our path, pushed by the wind diagonally across the face of the slope, and we could keep ahead of its out-reach claws. However, our horses grew tired, and the terrain steepened, the trail covered with rocks. The flames gained on us toward the top of the ridge, the flaming front running parallel with us.

Again, the intense heat burned through my clothing, and the dense smoke billowed over me. My eyes burned, and it was tough to breathe as poisonous gasses from the fire that threatened to choke me replaced the oxygen.

Heather disappeared over the crest of the ridge above me, and Patrick reached the summit. He turned his horse to one side of the trail, yelling for us and waving. The great head of the monster exploded across the ridge top several hundred yards from me down the ridgeline in a final gasp of expended energy and heat, but more fire raced up the slope behind me.

Peter reached the summit just behind Patrick. The acrid smoke burned my eyes, blurring my vision, and I saw just one ghostly horseman in the thick smoke above me, waving me up. The last few feet of the trail turned extraordinarily steep and rocky, causing my horse to stumble. She fell to her side, throwing me out in front of her as she rolled back down the trail below toward the onrushing fire.

My hands and arms were covered in blood from the abrasions caused by the jagged rocks, but I felt no pain. I scrambled up, trying to crawl the last few feet to the summit in the blinding smoke. My horse screamed in pain behind me as the monster consumed her in its fiery wrath. Thousands of glowing red embers showered me in the darkness of the smoke, pelting me with piercing darts of pure heat.

I frantically scrambled over the rocky trail, trying to stay low because some breathable air was near the ground, but I had lost my way. I no longer saw the trail, couldn't catch the summit, and didn't know how to escape the oncoming wall of fire behind me.

A gloved hand reached through the smoke and grabbed me by my outreached arm, pulling me over the summit just ahead of the main fire, which exploded upward above me as I rolled to safety on the blackened earth on the lee side of the ridge. Patrick had saved me from the fire.

CHAPTER THIRTY-TWO

I lay in the burned area from the previous year as the smoke continued to bellow upward from the other side of the ridge far into the heavens above, an eerie red glow covering the sun. The fire itself finally reached the end of its line of victims. The blaze died at the ridge top with no fuel left to burn in the blackened forest.

The four of us lay there for several minutes, panting, struggling for fresh air, our energy gone. Our hearts pounded with fear, excitement, and praise because we realized we had all survived. My arms and hands were cut and bruised from the fall, and we all had received minor burns, but we were alive!

The horses continued to run down the slope below us. I grieved the loss of my horse. I had also lost my pack and everything I owned except for the sword and, more importantly, the Light tied around my neck. I held it in my hand, and it glowed with a soft light. I felt healing virtues strengthening and encouraging me.

"Now, what do we do?" I asked nobody, and we all began to laugh, releasing the tension of our harrowing race.

Peter stood up, and the hawk rushed downward through the lingering smoke and landed on Peter's outstretched hand.

"We need to find the horses. Hopefully, they can still make it to the river. Krino started the fire to trap us, but he failed. Now, he must wait for the fire to cool before he can follow us, which gives us time to get ahead of him," Patrick said as he stood up and brushed the black soot from his pants.

I helped Heather to her feet, and we began to walk through the burned hillside covered with blackened logs and twisted snags. It was a tortured landscape of past failures and defeats, persecution, and strife. But scattered, fragile green sprouts of a new forest regenerated through the ashes, fertilized by death, a new beginning of life and possibilities that did not know the past but reached the future.

"LIKE YOU MUST DO."

The four of us had just gone through our battle through the fires of life and had come through victorious. We had escaped the flames and now stood stronger because of it. I knew that I had to face the fears and insecurities of my past and renew my spirit. First, we must reach the river crossing.

The horses stood by a small stream alongside a thin trail at the base of the burned area. They drank from the stream as we found them and, miraculously, did not appear to be burned but were worn down from the race up the mountain. We refreshed ourselves with the cold, fresh water and filled our canteens. We were all filthy, our eyes still reddened by the smoke, the acrid smell a permanent part of our clothing. We would have loved to jump in the water, wash the dirt and soot away, and cleanse the smell of smoke from our clothing, but we did not have the time.

Across the mountain, the fire continued to crawl. Small fingers slithered over the summit in green areas like red snakes. On the other side of the mountain, the fire burned intensely, towering walls of flame exploding upward at the summit, birthing more snakes that spread slowly down our side of the mountain below the area that had burned the year before. But we no longer feared the persecution from the fire because we had found a safe zone the fire could not cross.

"It will be some time before anyone can safely cross the mountain trail now," I said hopefully.

Patrick chuckled, "Krino is most likely throwing one fit about now. There are two elements that he dislikes: water and fire. He uses fire to destroy his victims, but it also has the power to destroy him. He'll wait for the fire to burn out before he crosses the mountain completely, and it will take time for his men to realize that we escaped."

How far to the great river?" Heather asked.

"I think possibly one day's journey and then a few hours to the crossing."

"And then what?" I felt the answer deep within but still asked.

"Have faith, my young friend. You are the Apostolos Or. You will know what to do when the time comes," Patrick reassured and clasped my hand, looking into my eyes. "I thought you were a goner back there."

"So did I. Thank you for pulling me out." I shook my head with relief.

"You did the same for me when you gave me the light," He released my hand and reached for the reins of his horse.

How could he be so sure? How could he know I would know what to do when the time came? I was aware that I had to face something at the crossing. It was that unknown that scared me.

Patrick broke into my reverie. "You and Heather share her horse. If we take it slow, the horses should be fine. We have a day to try and reach the river. We'll continue through the night along the river's edge and hopefully find it in the morning. But we must watch closely so as not to pass it at night."

Anticipating my question, Patrick continued, "I remember a large white stone next to the river on a sandy shore below high red cliffs. We can travel along the shore the entire way, but be careful. The current will immediately pull you in if you touch the water anywhere but the crossing. I remember seeing several soldiers sucked into its depths. They just disappeared."

"Is the crossing a ford then? Or a bridge?" I asked.

"I don't know for sure. The legends you spoke of, Jonathan, legends you heard long ago, are true. As I told you before, I only remember seeing the crossing as a young boy. But during the Light Wars, I fought against the children of the Light. They had a city near Hedone. I was a youth in the army, burning with hatred of the Light. In a great battle, we destroyed the city and pursued a remnant across the plains to the crossing. They crossed without any problems, but the water destroyed everyone except me when we attempted to cross. I was knocked unconscious and was found the next day by another troop of knights."

"What is on the other side?" Heather asked.

I knew the answer to this one, "Peace and safety, Heather. The Light has led us this far. I'm sure that we can make it safely across the water. Then we will be able to rest."

Did I believe that?

I helped her mount and then pulled myself up on the horse in front of her, to the horse's disapproval. We rode off, Patrick in the lead and Peter behind us. As before, the hawk flew over us.

We continued to ride the rest of the day, taking frequent rests. The horses were worn down, and Heather and I were exhausted. Patrick and Peter were used to the hardships of constant travel, but we were not. My entire body ached, and with each step of the horse, my back muscles convulsed in pain. I tried to reposition myself to ease the continued throbbing pain through my back and side but could not.

Finally, resigned to the pain, I slumped over. Somehow, we continued into the night. The trail followed the small river through an open stand of hemlock and pine. As the darkness crept over us, our lights shined, lighting the path before us.

Once, I looked over my shoulder and saw the red glow dancing against the dark sky along the now-distant ridge as the fire burned through the night. Then, the trail dropped deeper into the trees, and we were surrounded by the thick forest of ghostly trees just outside the circle of light around us.

I fell asleep in the saddle, the shooting pain in my side caused by the continuous rocking of the horse fading into a dull ache. Sometime later in the night, I suddenly awoke when the horse stopped. I had no idea how long I had slept. Heather moaned behind me and stirred, and I heard Patrick out in front of us on the darkened trail. The distant sounds of rushing water echoed against the cliffs next to the trail, a contrast to the musical bubbling of the stream beside me.

"The river is close. We can rest for a while and wait for Peter to catch up. The crossing should be a close distance downstream."

I just nodded, too exhausted to comment, and slipped from the saddle to the ground, my legs numbed by the hard ride of the past day and night. Heather slumped forward, holding the horse's mane. I carefully lifted her from the saddle as she wrapped her arms around my neck. I placed her in the soft dirt and thick layer of needles below a hemlock near the stream.

"How is she?" Patrick asked.

We had all come to love the girl and worried that her time may be near.

"I don't know. Hopefully, when we cross the river, we can get help for her. The Light is strong within her, but her physical body is weak."

I knelt beside Heather. Patrick knelt by the water as well and drank from its rejuvenating coldness. I clutched the Light around my neck, praying she would cross the river. The Light grew, illuminating a greater circle around us, joining with the Light around her neck and Patrick's, who had moved closer. We had been through so much. We had been running for our lives for several weeks ever since accepting the power of the Light within. We were exhausted, and I feared what would happen if the evil one caught up to us. Where was Malak? Why had he left us out in the wilderness to go through this alone?

"YOU ARE NOT ALONE, JONATHAN. I WILL NEVER LEAVE YOU OR FORSAKE YOU."

"We'll be alright, Jonathan. Just a short distance, and we will cross the river where Krino cannot reach us." Patrick stood up and stretched.

I looked up into the shadows at the edge of the circle of light. His face was only partially visible in the glow.

"How can you be so sure, Patrick? You keep saying that I am the Apostolos Or, that I will have to face my fears and past at the crossing and that I will prevail. But how do you know? You don't know the fear that I feel! I hear the roaring of the river out there in the darkness. The sound itself makes me tremble. How can I overcome it?"

At first, he didn't say a word. He just stood above me, his face hidden in the darkness as the Light around my neck withdrew and dimmed with my statements of disbelief. He rubbed his tired eyes, pulled back the curly locks of hair from his face, and sighed. Patrick was over thirty years my senior. He had fought the Light most of his life and knew the ways of leadership and battle. He was a strong warrior and would make a bold child of the Light. What was I compared to this warrior who stood above me? Why couldn't our Lord have chosen him to be the Apostolos Or? I was just a pitiful fugitive now freed of the chains who had spent his entire life as a coward, unlike Patrick, who had fought for what he believed in even if it had been wrong.

Patrick knelt back down in front of me, his Light illuminating my heart in my weakness. I saw his face and realized he had rubbed his eyes because he had been crying. He looked directly into my eyes, and my spirit leaped within me.

"Jonathan, I know you will succeed because if you do not, my entire life will have been a total waste. When the Light removed my chains, my Lord told me I had one last battle to fight and would succeed. As a child, I was chosen to be the Apostolos Or, but because of my father, I rejected the call. That was no excuse, but it is the one that I held to all of these years. It is too late, but I will fight the good fight to ensure the mantle has passed into your hands. You will succeed if only to fulfill the destiny of my life. I, too, must face the crossing before us."

He stood up and walked to his horse. The Light around me strengthened. I could not let the man down.

Heather awoke below me and murmured, "Have we crossed the river?" Her strength had increased, and she sat up.

"No, but we are close. Patrick thinks that we can make it in a few hours. We have stopped to rest and let Peter catch up to us. How are you, Heather?"

"I feel much better than before I fell asleep. But I'm hungry."

I brought her water, dried meat, and fruit and sat beside her as she ate. She drank the fresh water, allowing it to run down her face and neck. The water was fresh and cool and further strengthened our spirits. When she finished, I helped her up. At first, she wavered, then stood firm.

"Oh my, the riding has affected my legs. They are numb," She laughed lightly.

"Both of you have done well. Today, even I have felt the effects of our journey," Patrick patted his back. "We'll rest a bit. The morning is near. With the light of the day, we should be able to find the crossing easily."

Patrick found a place to sit near the stream, and I returned to the place by my horse as Heather continued to stretch her sore muscles. I was suddenly exhausted again. It was cool in the moist forest near the stream. A few leaves floated out of the darkness to land on my leg. Autumn was upon us, and soon, the early winter snows would cover the deep forest with a mantle of pure white.

I dared not breathe for fear that he would hear me. I lay in the darkened cave again, hiding among a tumbled mess of my past failures and present insecurities. It was cold, and I was frightened. A shadow of a man stood at the entrance to the cave, hooded, only twin red eyes glaring out from the dark phantom's formless face. He stepped into the cave and pulled the hood from his head.

"Please help me!" a girl, bloody and naked at his feet, pleaded, reaching a frail, small hand out to me before she vanished in a sudden burst of fire.

The phantom laughed and revealed his face, the scarred face of the leader of the Sahat who had once ridiculed me as I lay in the cave of my fears, helpless and shamed.

"You will forever remember the things that you have seen this night," the phantom told me and then disappeared. I began to cry.

I awoke suddenly, someone's hand on my shoulder. I struggled back away from the hand, looking wildly around me, and then calmed when I realized that Heather had knelt before me, Patrick at her side.

"Jonathan, what is it?"

I shook my head, the vivid memory of the girl exploding in flames before me sketched in the recesses of my mind. "It was just a dream, I guess. Don't worry, I'm okay." I sat up and looked at my friends, their faces lined with concern.

"It was so real," I explained groggily.

"I was in a cave, and the scarred Sahat stood before me. A girl, a lost soul, was taken before my eyes, just like hundreds before her, and I did nothing. I could do nothing to help her."

Patrick knelt before me, "That was Krino himself. Jonathan, he has marked you. He must be close and has entered your dreams, as mine. We must not despair but hold to the Light strongly because His power is great."

There was a rustling in the darkness, and Peter emerged from the shadows beneath the hemlock. A pale glow grew from the east, promising a new day. Peter dismounted with a wave to us and knelt before speaking and drinking from the stream next to his horse.

"Any sign, my friend?" Patrick asked when Peter had finished.

"I waited until they finally crossed through the fire and picked up our trail. I covered our tracks and diverted them. It will take them a few hours to figure out the true way," he smiled.

"How many are there?" Patrick asked as I stood up.

"I counted thirty knights of Kratos and a dozen from Hedone, but Krino was not among them. And thank our Lord, they do not have the Harag with them."

"Harag?" I asked, "Are you referring to the Sahat?"

"No," Patrick answered. They are a fierce race of man-eaters who answer to only Krino and the other Archons of the realm. I have only seen them once. He uses them to search for traitors or to combat the Bene Elohim directly. We thought he may have loosed them from the castle to follow us."

"Do you think that since Krino was not with them, he knows of another way to the crossing?" Peter questioned. Yet how would he know that we were headed there?"

"He knows more than we think, Peter. We must hurry but be wary lest he knows another route."

"Can you ride again, Heather?" Peter asked, his voice tinged with worry.

"Yes. I feel much better than before. Thank you, Peter," Heather said and smiled up at him. "The crossing is close, and we should go."

Patrick mounted his horse and looked down at us, "Peter, keep a watch behind us, but remain close." He paused a moment, looking at each of us. His eyes showed his worry, yet they sparkled with an inner conviction that everything would work out. He gazed directly into my eyes as he spoke. "Whatever happens, whatever you see, you must remain focused on the task before us. Krino will do anything to prevent us from crossing the river. But we must, at all cost, including our lives, overcome for you, Jonathan, to cross safely." He glanced over at Peter, who nodded his head in agreement.

It took a moment to realize what Patrick meant by that statement. I shook my head when I fully understood the reality of his words: "No, Patrick, we all must travel over the river together."

Patrick placed his gloved hand on my shoulder. "Don't worry, son. We'll all see each other on the other side." He reassured me, gathered the reins, and turned his horse toward the river.

We mounted up with renewed strength and continued our way, my worry for my friends strong. They were prepared to give their lives for me to cross the river. I would not let that happen.

After a while, the great river sparkled in the early morning light out ahead of us between the giant trees that lined the trail. We rode out of the wooded forest and onto a wide sandy beach. The river roared nearby, the power of the crashing water spraying a mist over us.

"Remember, keep a safe distance from the water and watch closely for the stone pillar," the captain cautioned over the deafening roar.

I had never seen a river that possessed such power within its banks. How could we ever cross such power? I wondered. A warm, orange glow ascended from the rolling hills across the river, a new day finally beginning. Slivers of light penetrated the broken canopy of the forest and washed across the open beach, highlighting the dark, frothy water. There appeared to be no rocks in the river, yet the water flowed in constant turmoil, crashing and swirling with great force in an area where the water should have been calm and serene. Peter emerged from the trees a few moments later, his horse sweating and heaving from a challenging ride through the forest. Patrick turned his horse to meet him.

"I don't know how they did it, Patrick, but they are less than an hour behind us, maybe even less."

"That is not possible?"

"I know, unless Krino has magic we have not seen before."

Patrick looked down the beach toward the hidden crossing. "We need to hurry then. With daylight, they can ride hard through the trail, and our horses are spent."

We tried to hasten our escape, but the horses could not go any faster. They had been through too much, ridden too far without proper rest. We would be lucky if they made it to the crossing at all.

CHAPTER THIRTY-THREE

White sand and scattered rocks covered the beach over one hundred feet wide. A few alders grew along the shore. A heavily timbered slope of pine and scattered aspen slanted sharply up among rocky ledges and deep canyons that climbed upward to a sandstone rim void of trees to our side. As we followed the river, the slope grew steeper until a broken wall of red rock formed an impenetrable barrier except where narrow side canyons, covered in broken rock, opened in the solid walls. Scattered clumps of pines held tenaciously to ledges across the face of the great cliff. High above on the rim, dark pines glowed in the early morning light. We were close. The crossing had to be nearby.

The hawk circled low over the tree-lined bluff above us, shrieked a warning, and climbed higher toward the clouds above the cliff. The glint of metal sparkled briefly in the sun's light along the upper ledges, and a darkened missile streaked through the pale morning light. With a sudden jolt and a scream of pain, the hawk flipped over and fell to the sandy beach before us. His body struggled in a last desperate attempt to stand and then collapsed on its side near the water's edge.

All eyes were on the cliff wall, and Peter dashed forward. Patrick drew his crossbow. Peter leaped and reached the bird as it fluttered one last time. Patrick, Heather and I watched as he knelt to touch the beloved creature with an ungloved hand. He pulled the arrow from the body and stood, looking toward the cliffs. The hawk was dead, and we all suddenly felt exposed. He had been our eyes, alerted us when the enemy was near, and saved our lives on several occasions, but now he was gone. Peter's eyes glistened as he remounted and returned to where we waited.

"Kratos," he said with disgust and broke the fatal arrow, throwing it to the sand below.

"They have found a way to the river ahead of us but are still high up the cliff," Patrick stated as he looked intently along the upper rim, his horse prancing nervously, smelling the blood on the broken arrow at his feet. "We must find the crossing before those ahead reach the shore."

"But how will we know what is before us without the bird?" Heather asked, her voice trembling with fear. We were trapped, it appeared, and then a stirring deep within voiced a truth in my spirit.

"Heather, we'll make it," I said and looked at Peter, who was now visibly shaken by the loss of his long-time companion. "Peter, the bird was a close companion, and I am sorry for your loss, but we have become new creations by the Light that lives within us. The old ways have passed away. We must rid ourselves of the old traditions and learn to follow the Light within us to lead our way."

Then I glimpsed the white polished stone ahead of us by the water as the sun's rays finally moved across the lower canyons and flooded the river and shoreline with welcome light. The stone glistened brightly, a lighthouse leading us to the crossing.

"Look!" I shouted, "I see the crossing!"

With excitement, we spurred our horses forward. Just then, a troop of Sahat burst out of the forest behind us with a great shout. I looked over my shoulder to see dark soldiers on the white beaches. Heather screamed in my ear and pointed up to the cliffs above. The red walls were dotted with dozens of dark figures climbing down along the broken ledges to try to intercept us before we reached the crossing. We were so close but so terribly far. I leaned forward, Heather holding me tight as the glistening stone grew more prominent in front of us by the turbulent, rushing water.

The granite rock jutted out over the river, and the waters were calm underneath in contrast to the turbulent chaos on the other side. Here, the water was crystal clear, with a bottom covered in small pebbles of all the colors of the rainbow. Trout swam lazily in the shadows under the rock. Several gnarled oaks grew out of crevices along the shoreline where the rock first lunged outward.

Malak stood next to one of the oaks with Nasar at his side. They had been watching the crossing for several days, waiting patiently. They could have crossed the river but knew that the souls would have to find the strength to cross the turbulent waters within their spirit.

Soteria had supplied six of its best archers and one particularly large swordsman, Nathaniel. With his broad sword, he could beat all the souls of Soteria. Malak had sparred with him just the day before and was impressed by his knowledge of the weapon. When the offensive began, he would make a formidable warrior in the Shadow Realm.

The warriors had set up camp in the forest, hidden from view of the cliffs across the river. They were eating a small breakfast as the first glow of another day emerged over the mountains.

Nasar was the first to see it, a hawk circling high above the cliffs across the river. She tapped Malak on the shoulder and pointed to the bird floating on the currents of the wind.

"Beautiful, isn't it."

Malak glanced up. He nodded.

"They are near," he stated.

"How do you know?" the archer asked as she replaced her gloves. There was a chill in the air.

"I have seen the bird several times before. He belongs to the scout, Peter, who has found the Light and now travels with the chosen one. Watch closely for them. I will go back and alert the Soterians to prepare. Hopefully, they have seen their pursuers, but I don't think so. I feel the evil presence. Krino is close by."

Malak backed down the rock slowly and melted into the forest's shadows. A few minutes later, he emerged from the trail and walked to the edge of the rock outcrop. The warrior Nathaniel and Captain Murphy stood at the shoreline as the six archers climbed the large trees along the shore to their pre-designated perches. From their vantage point, they could defend the crossing and assist the fugitives if they were pursued.

Nasar climbed down to the shore to where the others were waiting. She prepared her bow as they searched the opposite shore and the cliffs above them. Nathaniel pointed up high on the cliffs, seeing movement along the face of the red walls overlooking the crossing.

He turned to Murphy, "Captain, someone is high up on the cliff."

Murphy also searched the area and noticed a dark figure climbing down the cliff beneath several twisted pine trees.

"Mistress Nasar, do you see the movement near the top of the cliff?"

Bene Elohim looked up in the direction pointed out to them as the Captain continued, "There, by the broken rock next to the twin pines. A man climbs through the trees, and above him on the rim is a dark horseman hidden in the forest's shadows."

"It is Krino!" exclaimed Malak, "Nasar, he has set a trap for them. They are riding right into his lap."

"What can we do, Malak?" Nasar asked with alarm.

"I can't communicate with them from this side of the river. If they don't show up soon, we'll be no help to them."

Just then, an archer dressed entirely in black and wearing a long overcoat that blew back with the wind emerged from the cleft in the rock and stood in the early morning light. He drew back his longbow, and with one shot, the hawk spiraled out of the sky and fell to the sandy beach near the crossing.

"He's killed the hawk," Malak commented and then pointed, "There they are! Prepare your men, Captain Murphy, and keep your archers hidden from the sniper above. Their bows can protect the crossing, but can they reach the canyon's rim?"

"I don't think so, Malak."

Malak walked to the very edge of the water, careful to remain hidden in the alders along the bank. He saw several figures climbing the cliff, but the lone sniper was lost in the shadows.

"Malak, others are behind them now," Nasar could see the opposite shore from the edge of the rock, "They are beginning to run now toward the crossing!"

They were running into a trap, Malak knew, and although he and Nasar could not help them until they entered the portal to cross the river, maybe the archers of Soteria could.

We rode as hard as we could to escape the soldiers behind. I leaned forward, spurring our horse on, afraid to look back again. The shouts of the enemy chased me out of the early morning mist.

Patrick rode beside Peter and me against the cliffs, their dark tunics blowing back into the wind, Patrick's long hair swirling over his face, unbraided. I wished to be a warrior of determination and great calm, as they were, but still, I feared we would be trapped here at the door to safety.

"HAVE FAITH JONATHAN. TRUST IN THE LIGHT AND TAKE ONE STEP INTO THE TURMOIL OF YOUR LIFE AND WATCH AS ALL BECOMES PEACE."

I glanced over at the stormy water to my right. How could anything peaceful come from that?

"Nasar, can you take out that sniper? We are very vulnerable to his longbow." Malak asked.

"I believe so. At least I can keep him busy, but we can do nothing until they touch the portal," the archer answered as she strung her bow and pulled one of her arrows from the quiver.

She notched the arrow, holding the bow down in front of her. Nasar could handle the short sword better than most, but her true weapon was the elaborately carved longbow with her multicolored arrows. She left the others and crept back up to the rocky outcrop.

Opposite her position, higher up on the cliff, a dark figure darted from one ledge to the shadows of another tree, but not before she caught a glimpse of movement. The upper half of the canyon was flooded with the rising sun's light. Her position at the bottom of the gorge was shrouded in the mountain's shadows, which was presently to her advantage, but soon, the entire valley would be washed in the growing light.

"Very good," Malak nodded and turned to Captain Murphy. "Murphy, we cannot assist until one of them enters the portal, but your archers can. As soon as the horsemen are within range, lob a few volleys into them. Hopefully, it will break up their charge and give our fugitives more time. As soon as one of them enters, we can attack across the ford to cover their retreat. I don't think Krino knows that we are here. Hopefully, we will surprise him."

Murphy hesitated initially, which was his nature, but it was becoming too clear. From his vantage point, he saw the figures scrambling down the cliffs at the crossing ahead of the souls running for safety with a whole troop of knights closing from the rear. They were trapped and would be cut off from the crossing unless he and his men came to their rescue. With a final resolve, he knew that he could not watch as souls like himself were slaughtered. He understood that he would have to join in the fight.

"Very well, Malak. We will stand with you. Nathaniel will bring up the horses. We will mount and wait in the pines. When they reach the water, we will attack to defend the crossing."

Murphy then signaled the archers and pointed to the approaching horsemen. In another minute, they would be within range of his archers hidden in the trees.

We continued to ride, but my horse was broken. She heaved beneath me, sweating profusely, and wavered about a hundred feet from the polished stone that marked the crossing. I kicked at her in panic but to no avail. She turned suddenly and fell over to her side, throwing Heather and me across the sand near the river's shore. Heather rolled and almost fell into the crashing water, but somehow, I reached for her and pulled her back before I, too, fell head-first into the deep sand. The horse lay near, panting heavily with labored breathing, gasping for air and thrashing wildly.

The stone stood in the sand at the water's edge only a few feet before me. For a moment, I lay stunned from the fall and then heard a shout above. Peter reached a firm hand and pulled me up.

Thrusting a sword in my hand, he shouted in my ear, "Our way is blocked!" and pointed to the crossing.

Several soldiers jumped down from the broken rock at the base of the cliff before us. All our struggles, pain, joy, and hopes now lay dashed before us. I had escaped the maze of life, survived the pit of pride, outraced the fires of persecution, and persevered through the wilderness of despair, and now, yards away from the hope of safety, my way was blocked. Patrick said we would all face our fears at the crossing, but we had to fight to get there.

"PUSH YOUR WAY TO THE WATER. TAKE A STEP OF FAITH INTO THE WATER AND THEN WATCH WHAT HAPPENS. YOU ARE THE APOSTOLOS OR. YOU MUST FACE YOUR FEARS AND OVERCOME THEM, AND THEN MY SPIRIT WILL BE FREE TO FLOOD THE SHADOW REALM."

Mounting his horse, Malak turned in time to see the Apostolos Or and the girl fall. The two knights could have made it to the water. They should have continued as the Spirit urged them to so that help would come, but they did not. They both dismounted to stand along with the others. Now, their way was blocked. The Spirit spoke then, and Malak could see the Light around Jonathan suddenly flare with understanding.

"Be ready, men." He drew his broad sword, and the horse prancing about kicked up the loose dirt in anticipation.

"We must enter the water!" I shouted.

I did not understand how we could cross the turbulent river, but I knew that if just one of us could reach the portal, our salvation would be ensured.

But there were now six warriors standing before us at the crossing and over thirty more riding down upon us from behind.

"We have no choice. If we die, at least we leave this realm as free men!" Patrick shouted back over the water rage and rushed the closest warrior.

The captain could handle the broadsword better than most men. All his life, he had used this ability against the Light, but now he fought for the Light with a passion that came from a spirit that wished to overcome past defeats with renewed victories. He had once been chosen as the Apostolos Or, but something had gone wrong. Now, he knew it was time to redeem himself and ensure the true Apostolos Or reached safety. He was given the chance to overcome the darkness that held the captives of the Plains of Sin in bondage. His time had come, his battle won.

Patrick slashed down and across the first soldier's chest, blood showering his face, knocking the man back into the water, where he instantly disappeared in its turbulent embrace. A second stepped to intercept him, and a third jumped down from the rocks, swinging an axe.

And then I joined the fight. I blocked the blow from a red-headed soldier and pushed Heather past me into the crossing as she screamed in terror, demons of her past life swirling in the mists around her. As she fell into the water, a portal opened before her, revealing a glistening white trail that led across the water to the opposite shore.

"Run!" I shouted to her as another soldier swung his mighty axe over me.

I dodged the blow and fell backward into the water as well; dark images of the cave and people burning in front of me flashed through my mind, of Lillian, her spirit bound and gagged, being dragged away. *Did you leave her?* I scrambled to get up, and the images disappeared.

"Now!" Malak shouted when he spotted the girl fall into the water and spurred his horse forward. Captain Murphy and the warrior Nathaniel were at his side.

The archers let loose a full salvo of arrows that sliced over the water in a graceful arch, plummeting down and across the charging knights and catching them by surprise. Four were struck, and one horse flipped over, throwing his rider into the water. A second salvo of six arrows immediately followed, effectively scattering the riders who veered off to the protective cover of broken rocks and scattered timber.

Peter slashed across in front of him, catching his assailant just under the chin and cutting the jugular. The man immediately dropped his weapon and grabbed for his throat. He was dying, and he knew it, the realization of it washing across his face and eyes in panic. He fell to his knees and forward into the sand at Peter's feet.

The scout turned quickly to face the oncoming charge of horsemen. He had one shot with the crossbow, and then they would be upon him. Heather had reached safety, but Jonathan and Patrick were fighting desperately to open the way to the portal. It would end here, he thought. But peace within his spirit assured him that his soul would be well no matter what happened.

Peter raised the bow to take aim at the first Sahat when, to his surprise, the horse dropped to its knees, head down, throwing the rider into the water. Several other horses ran past him. Someone had fired a volley of arrows into the charging horsemen, breaking up the attack. The warriors in the back, seeing several die from an unknown assailant, found refuge among the rocks. Peter turned and ran to the crossing. Maybe they had hope after all. Someone across the river was helping them.

When Malak gave the order, Nasar pulled back the bowstring and patiently searched the cliffs for a sign of the dark archer who had slain the hawk. He was hidden well. She could see soldiers climbing down the trail to join the fight below and an unknown horseman who held back under the shadows of the twin pines, but the archer eluded her.

His name was Logan, a silent killer who traveled across the land doing the bidding of his master. He was not human but was created to look like one, although he was a soulless creature that loved only death. He could kill with a knife or poison, bow or sword. He had crafted his longbow as all archers in the realm did, and with each kill, he notched the bow in blood. There were thirty-six notches; today, he hoped to gain a few more. Let the brave but foolish warriors battle to their death below. He would kill silently from high among the rocks and ledges.

After killing the hawk, which gave him particular pleasure, on orders from Krino, he immediately climbed across the face of the cliff to a point where he could better see the crossing below. A small aperture was behind a rocky outcrop beneath a twisted, scrubby pine that offered cover and shade from the morning sun that glared across the canyon. The battle raged below him. A young woman ran across the portal.

She made a perfect target. She would be first, he thought, killed just as she felt that she was safe. Then he would take the boy if the soldiers didn't finish him first.

He notched the poisoned arrow, which would kill almost instantly, and leaned out to aim at the retreating girl. He calculated that his arrow would strike just below the back of the neck. What a shame, he thought. She had such beautiful, long, blonde hair.

Nasar spotted a flicker of movement about midway along the face of the cliff beneath a twisted pine that had grown almost miraculously out of a small pit of soil that collected within the crack between the rocks. The archer had located a target and was leaning out. He pulled back the string, holding the end of the arrow against his cheek as he aimed. Nasar let loose her arrow before he could fire his. She held steady for a few seconds as she watched her arrow almost float upward across the chasm while instinctively reaching for a second arrow.

Logan suddenly caught movement from a rock across the river out of the corner of his eye just as he released his arrow, which caused him to move ever so slightly, but just enough for the arrow to swerve a bit to the right and disappear harmlessly into the water behind the running girl. Three mounted warriors passed her as he ducked away. Where had they come from?

He reached for another arrow when he heard the unmistakable whish of an arrow as the missile raced just inches past his neck and slammed into the rock wall behind him, shattering on impact. Someone was shooting back!

The horseman hidden in the trees above noticed the archer across the river and the warriors riding across the crossing. Bene Elohim! The man swore and turned his horse away from the rim. If Bene Elohim were present, he would have to descend the cliff himself. He thought they were no match for him, and the traitors would never cross the river to safety. Like others before, they would die within sight of the crossing. There was a quick way down that only his magic could make. He vanished within a cloud of red smoke.

Nasar couldn't tell if she had hit her target, but she knew that he could know where her arrow originated if he was alive. She backed across the face of the rock, keeping a constant watch at the point where he had ducked away from the missile. If she didn't kill him, at least she had saved the girl. She focused all her energy and concentration on the aperture on the rock beneath the pine and began to pull out of the shadows, the outline of a man crouched beneath the tree. He was there, she could tell, but she could not see him well enough to get a good shot.

I fought desperately, trying to work my way through to the crossing, but I was further from freedom than before. Peter joined our side, and we were surrounded. Heather ran away from us across the portal. At least she was safe. I faltered, the sword heavy in my arm, the warm, slick blood of the soldiers that lay at our feet covering my face and arms, my sword soaking through my clothing.

Patrick shouted encouragement to me as we stood back-to-back. The enemy was wary of our blades, but more were arriving, and I knew that it would only be a few more seconds before we would all fall before their superior numbers.

"Jonathan, you must make it across, or it is all in vain!" Patrick shouted to me, and I remembered our conversation the night before. He had one more battle to fight. What had he meant by that? Did he know somehow where his destiny lay?

I broke through and ran across the blood-soaked sand, covered in the bodies of the wounded and dying, toward the crossing. A swordsman suddenly jumped down from the rocks and blocked my path. He swung the great sword down, and I turned to block the blow, but Peter took the full force of the attack by parrying with his blade and dove into the warrior, both falling across the bodies at their feet.

I reached the safety of the river, crying because I knew that my two friends were sacrificing their lives so that I might live. They believed entirely that I was the Apostolos Or, but in my own heart, I was still unsure. Dear Lord, why have they trusted me so much that they would do such a thing?

I turned to see Patrick crumble under the thrust of an axe across his shoulder. He dropped his sword as he fell backward, his left arm hanging limp at his side. Another warrior leaped forward and stood over him, raising his sword to impale the stricken Captain through the chest.

"No!" I screamed. I would not allow them to die for me. As horsemen galloped past me, I bolted out of the portal, knocking me to my knees.

Peter struggled to help his friend as well but couldn't reach him. He, too, fell beneath the onslaught of the enemy as an axe struck him from behind, tearing through his chainmail and ripping a gaping wound across his side. He fell to the ground. Through the swirling haze of semi-consciousness, he saw Jonathan fall to his knees as horsemen lunged out from the portal and dashed past him, and then all was black.

CHAPTER THIRTY-FOUR

I glanced through the dust of battle at Peter, who I had thought was dead, and realized that he had somehow recovered from his wounds and was regaining strength. Patrick lay before me, crawling toward the portal, pulling himself with his one good arm, leaving a dark trail of blood behind him. The three horsemen from across the river fought our assailants off, pushing them back against the cliffs from where they had come.

The way was clear for me to enter the portal again, but I could not leave my friends behind. I did not know two of the horsemen, but Malak I recognized, brandishing a two-edged claymore, slashing down and around him, knocking all who dared oppose him beneath the horse's hooves. His purple cape flowed down over the horse's flanks, and his long, black hair blew free in the wind, for he wore no helmet, only the purple band that kept his hair from his eyes. I crawled over to Patrick just as Peter reached the stricken warrior.

"Is he dead?" I asked.

Patrick finally had fallen face first in the sand, his energy spent, his life's blood draining from the wound, across the sand and into the water.

"No, but he will be soon if we can't get help for him."

I reached to help pick him up and realized that his left arm had been completely torn from his shoulder, only the silk shirt he wore under his armor holding it to him. I pushed against the open wound to slow the blood flow, and we carefully lifted him between us. We turned to the crossing, the sounds of battle growing farther behind us.

Across the water, I saw a group of archers, children, and women standing in the morning mist, shadowy figures floating in the fog. Were they real? Many waved for us to cross, and several of the archers left the shore and began running across the portal toward us.

Heather emerged from the portal before us suddenly.

She stared at us in horror. We were all covered in blood, Patrick most of all.

"Heather, we must get Patrick across the water. Our only hope is across the river."

The raging battle continued to recede down the shoreline, but I did not look back. Help had finally arrived, and the way to safety was open before us.

Nasar crouched next to the rock, intently searching the crevice for any sign of the dark archer. Because of the underbrush, she could no longer see the battle below her at the crossing. Her entire attention focused on where she had last seen the archer. He had not moved, but she could not see behind the crevice that was his hiding place to make a shot.

She climbed higher over the rock overhang, hoping for a more advantageous location to see her opponent, when, to her surprise, she noticed the fleeting glimpse of an approaching missile as it streaked through the air toward her and slammed into the rock over her shoulder, shattering from the impact. She ducked away and rolled over behind the ledge, puzzled because the arrow had come from a direction different from where she had calculated her opponent to be. Was there another sniper? Or had he moved, and she had missed it?

Your senses have dulled, she thought to herself. She peered back out around the ledge in time to see several small rocks rolling down the cliff wall and briefly saw a shadow dive behind another tree. She quickly fired her weapon, knowing she did not have a good shot, but she wanted to return the favor. The arrow embedded itself into the tree.

"I can do this all day, my friend," she spoke across the void of space below her.

She notched another arrow and backed around the far side of the rock, jumping down to the shoreline. She climbed the limbs of a giant oak she had used many times before to see across the river. She scrambled through the massive limbs until she found a safe perch hidden in the thick foliage with a small opening for a clean shot. The arrow was visible in the tree, and the end of his longbow extended beyond the tree by a few inches. Nasar pulled back her bow, placing the end of the arrow next to her cheek, her right thumb just below her eye, sighting in on the area just above where the end of the bow could be seen and waiting.

He peered out from behind the tree a moment later, and she fired. Holding the bow outstretched in front of her, she quickly snatched another arrow from the quiver with her right hand and reloaded, firing a second arrow that followed close behind the first. The first missile struck the sniper's bow, tearing it away from him and causing him to be more exposed. The second struck him through the left shoulder, above the heart, with a sickening thud, the force of the impact knocking him back against the rocks.

Logan stared across the river in surprise. He felt no pain and did not bleed but knew that the arrow of a Bene Elohim was fatal to his kind. He staggered briefly on the ledge, searching for his opponent, but Nasar remained hidden. Then he stumbled and plummeted down along the cliff, hitting several ledges on his way down, his body flipping over before falling face down in the sand at the crossing.

Nasar scanned the beach below her, noticing the four fugitives helping each other toward the open portal. One was hurt and could not walk, so the others carried him as they stepped over the dead bodies on the beach. Their way appeared clear, and then a dark horseman materialized out of the red rock through a hidden tunnel that opened and immediately closed. With one step, the horse blocked the passage.

Nasar immediately fired at the strange being, but the arrow passed entirely through the horseman, embedding in the soft sand at his feet. Several Soteria archers running across the portal were flung back as a wall of flame shot forward from the horseman's outstretched hand.

"Malak, we have a problem," Nasar spoke, and immediately, Malak turned his mount to face the crossing.

"What is it?" shouted Murphy.

"Krino! Murphy holds the line. The Sahat is beaten." Malak ordered and galloped back toward the crossing.

He knew that he did not have the power to defeat Krino in battle; only the Apostolos Or had the power to do so, but he had to attack to somehow force Jonathan to believe in the Light within him. He had to think that he was indeed the Apostolos Or. Malak charged his horse past the four, slashing with his sword. Krino parried the blow with a bolt of fire that reflected off the blade and landed among the trees, starting a fire in the dry grass. Malak turned the horse sharply and attacked again, "Jonathan, remember you are the Apostolos Or. This is the challenge you must face."

Another flash of orange exploded with showers of gold, and Malak fell backward from his horse, momentarily stunned.

Nasar jumped down from her perch and drew her sword, running through the portal past the fallen archers who lay unconscious. She thrust her sword at the horse's flank, but Krino knocked her back into the turbulent water and immediately kicked her out onto the sandy beach, unconscious.

Krino pulled back the hood that had covered his face as the black horse pranced in front of the portal.

It happened so quickly before me. Two Bene Elohim lay nearby, and I looked up into the fiery red eyes of the death horse above me. The fear of a lifetime of running from creatures such as this one welled up within me and clawed at my spirit with deadly tentacles, paralyzing my soul.

The man had dark eyes and a scar across the cheek, partially hidden by a short beard. He was rather handsome with strong features and curly black hair. He wore a long cape fastened in front with a silver brooch decorated with the head of a red dragon.

"Krino!" Peter shouted and stepped forward, but I was too fearful to do a thing.

Heather screamed, and a violent wind slammed into Peter, knocking him back against the polished stone, where he crumbled down, dropping his sword. Patrick slumped down at Heather's side, and I froze, fear suffocating my spirit. Before me stood the man I had seen back in the cave when I first found the Light. Was he my challenge? How could I defeat this monster?

"YOU MUST DEFEAT HIM. HE HOLDS POWER OVER THE REALM OF KRATOS. HIS POWER MUST BE BROKEN FOR THE LIGHT TO FLOW AGAIN."

CHAPTER THIRTY-FIVE

"How?" I said out loud, and Krino waved his hand over me. I immediately stood high on a mountaintop overlooking the entire Shadow Realm, from the great forests to the hills of Halom. The spirals and glistening walls of the great city of Hedone dominated the central plains. I turned and saw the river crossing far below.

Patrick, Peter, and Heather stood, totally covered in chains. The Bene Elohim Malak stood tied to a tree, bloody and beaten, his cape at his feet. All around him were Sahat and hideous, hairy creatures holding clubs. What had happened to me?

I looked down and saw the chains of death around my body! How could this be? The Light had freed me.

Krino appeared before me along with a dozen of the dreaded Sahat. Fear gripped my soul.

"You are going to die," a raspy, hollowed voice spoke from the recesses of my mind.

The Sahat sat motionless on their black steeds, surrounding me. Their faces lay hidden by dark hoods, only the twin red beams of light that were their eyes glowing from the blackness. I shuddered and looked away.

"You have been a fool, Jonathan. Do you think that I would allow you to be free of your chains? You are a coward." He laughed. "They say that you are an Apostolos Or. That is preposterous. You are a fugitive covered in chains. You are nothing. Remember that night long ago, you hid in a cave."

I looked down at the ground.

"Remember!" he shouted, and I quickly looked up.

How could I ever forget?

"You watched from a tree while the dark ones destroyed three people, and you did nothing. You ran away from the woman that you say you loved. Do you think she is alive, Jonathan? Or maybe she has been made a harlot for the Sahat's pleasure."

What he was saying was true. I was a coward. How could I be an Apostolos Or?

He walked the horse around me as I stood silent before him.

"You watched from the tree as those three souls were killed on the plains. You thought you saw their salvation, but you saw their eternal damnation."

"THAT'S A LIE, REMEMBER THE FOURTH MAN."

I could not hear the voice within me.

"I gave you a chance when the nomads found you. Remember the night when you saw the hooded riders? They were sent to tell Connelly that you could be a member of their clan. They were your only hope, and you turned away. Not only are you a coward, but you are stupid."

He stood before me again. I was helpless and frightened, my strength ebbing away, my spirit weak. I had been running for so long, fighting for my life, and it had led only to this.

"You foolish, stupid boy," he continued, "You think that something as foolish as the Light that you wear around your neck can free you of your chains of death?"

"THE LIGHT IS WITHIN YOU NOW, JONATHAN. IT HAS DONE EXACTLY THAT."

The voice was a whisper, but my spirit was held captive by fear and unbelief.

"Do you realize what you have done? No, of course not, because you are stupid, you are a coward. Your spirit has been weak. You have allowed the flesh to place the chains around your soul. You have done it, not me. See, they are still around you. Because you missed the census and broke the covenant with the nomads, they have grown, and now you are helpless. Your time has come, Jonathan. You can no longer run, but first, I want you to witness what you have done to those that you call your friends."

He turned and pointed to the river crossing before me.

Several Sahat dismounted and forced Peter and Patrick to their knees.

"Those two were free of their chains before you led them astray with your stupidity. They had a good life. They were real men, brave men. Unlike you, they fought for what they believed in. Have you ever done that, Jonathan? No, of course not. You are a coward. How can you be the Apostolos Or?"

"LIES. YOU HAVE THE POWER."

The voice was stronger now, but I was not. He was right.

"Because of you, they will now die. Can you stop it? Will you fight for their lives?" He laughed as I watched, doing nothing.

"They have both committed treason, and you will watch their sentencing."

I watched in horror. What had I done? I heard the leader of the Sahat address the two captives.

"THIS IS AN ILLUSION"

It looked so real.

"Because of your treachery, the High Master has sentenced you to death immediately."

Two Sahat impaled them with long spears through the chest. I began to cry.

"Oh, shut up, you worm," Krino ordered.

I looked back up at this face but could not look him directly in the eyes. Was it that he could not look directly into mine? That was strange.

"YOU HAVE POWER OVER HIM"

But how? What could I do? I had lost; my friends were killed because of me.

"And Jonathan, remember Heather, the poor fugitive like yourself. She, too, found refuge in the nomad camp and could have been freed of her chains, but you deceived her with your false stories of hope. Now, her time has come. Look what you have done."

Heather stood by the river, not the beautiful girl with flowers in her hair, but a frail, tormented girl covered in chains. The Sahat taunted her as she pleaded for life, like Gloria in the cave. They ripped the chains from her and stripped her naked. The four of them surrounded her then and pushed her down to the sand on her back, and I turned away, hearing her screams and the laughter of the Sahat. Oh God, what have I done?

"IT'S NOT REAL!"

Did I dare believe that? It seemed real. The screams were real. The pain of the chains around me was real. The foul breath of the horses was real.

"You see, Jonathan, you have been living in an illusion. You are not free of your chains. I hold reign over this land. I decide whose chains are removed. Your kind is pitiful. They are stupid. You have lived a terrible life because of your cowardice. You don't even believe yourself that you are the Apostolos Or."

I looked up into his eyes at that statement, and he looked away.

I thought he was afraid of me. He couldn't look me in the eye. My spirit regained strength. His horse shied just a bit, but Krino didn't notice.

"You do not deserve your chains to be removed from you."

"THAT IS THE FIRST THING THAT HE SAID THAT IS TRUTH, BUT IT DOES NOT MATTER. I HAVE MADE YOU WORTHY"

The voice grew stronger, as did my spirit, and Krino continued, "Your faith in the Light is a lie, and now your time has come. Jonathan, I am the only way for you to live in this realm. I didn't want it to be this way. If you turn to me now, I can undo the things you have seen here and remove your chains and those of your friends. What do you have to say?"

I stood there for a moment, pondering what he had said and what I had seen, and then I remembered what Patrick had said.

"Overcome your fear with faith."

Other words welled up within my spirit.

"YOU HAVE OVERCOME BY THE BLOOD OF THE LAMB AND THE WORDS OF YOUR TESTIMONY."

Suddenly, the truth rose within me as well. I was not afraid of Krino; I was scared of failure. How could I fail with the Light of the World within me to guide me?

"YOU CAN'T. YOU MAY MAKE MISTAKES, BUT YOU WILL NEVER FAIL."

This is all an illusion. It's a lie, I thought to myself. Immediately, the tentacles of fear that had bound my soul melted away. The lamb on the mountain, the Lamb of God, had removed my chains of death. I did not deserve the chains to be removed. That part of Krino's statement was genuine, but it didn't matter. When I reached out in faith to grasp the Light, my chains were removed, not by anything I had done, but only by my faith in the Light to remove them. The lamb had taken the chains for me so I would not have to.

"Krino, if you have the power to kill me, then go ahead and do it because I will not go into a covenant with you." My voice grew bolder and surer with each word. The images around me began to waver and shift, some melting back into the shadows around us.

"I have overcome you by the blood of the Lamb of God. Yes, I have failed in the past. Yes, I was a coward, but now the Light changes me, not by anything I have done. I also overcome you by the word of my testimony; therefore, I boldly speak the truth to you today that I have been freed of the chains of death, and you no longer have control over my life. I ran in fear of your kind for most of my life and will no longer do so. Now I live by faith!"

Immediately, a bright white light exploded around us, and I stood again on the sandy beach facing Krino, my sword raised, its blade pointed directly at Krino's heart.

"Be gone from this place, Krino! I claim the territory you have ruled over for Christendom and all the fugitives roaming the plains. I am the Apostolos Or, which gives me the power to do so."

His horse suddenly reared up in panic as the earth around us shook, and the turbulent waves of the river reached outward and engulfed the horse and rider. The flashing lights of a rainbow showered the beach. The river seemed alive with silver phantoms that swirled violently around him, pulling him deeper into the crashing waves. Krino lunged forward from his horse with stretched hands, his eyes red like the Sahat's. The horse disappeared beneath the water with a scream as Krino jumped free of the water. I stepped backward from him, no longer fearful, as the Shadow Archon fell at my feet.

"You miserable fugitive, you will not defeat me," he screamed defiantly.

"I don't have to. The Lamb of God already has," I answered and turned my back on him. He was no longer relevant.

"No!" Krino screamed as the water surrounded him. He disappeared into the murky waters, which immediately became calm.

A great and powerful wind erupted from the forest across the river and blew across the land. The remaining knights of Kratos dropped their weapons and rode away, those who had lost their horses running on foot. The wind spread across the forest, bending the trees beneath its power. It swirled around every tree, cave, and hiding place, awakening the sleeping fugitives and spreading hope. It continued to spread across the plains, swirling through the fugitive camps, rattling the chains, screaming to the souls of men that freedom was near if they would believe. The wind covered the entire land once ruled by Krino until every fugitive heard its call to freedom and felt its cool embrace.

The wind bypassed Hedone as the guards manning the great towers and walls looked upward, hearing the wind but not feeling it. It swirled around the city because it had no power there and continued to the great keep of the Dark One. It circled the gates until it found the castle section ruled over by Krino. The soldiers watched in horror as an unseen force exploded the iron gates leading into Krino's keep. The wind pushed through the myriad of corridors until it reached Krino's throne room, where the throne itself exploded with one final burst of energy.

The Dark One screamed in anguish because he felt the concussion as one of his Archons of the Shadow Realm had fallen.

Malak stood next to me at the portal. Another Bene Elohim, a young woman, stood beside him.

"You did well, Jonathan," he praised me.

"What did I do?" I was still shocked by everything that had happened.

"By your faith and the prayers of many others, you have broken the hold that the strongman had over the land of the fugitives. Now the Light can spread through the land once ruled by Krino, and the fugitives that wish to be freed from their chains can be so," he answered, placing a hand on my shoulder.

I looked up into his eyes, his long, curly hair blowing in the wind across his face. He pulled back the untamed locks and tucked them into the headband.

"Whose prayers, Malak? I am only one lonely fugitive who wishes to be free. How could I have broken the power of the strongman?"

"The prayers of those in front of you," he told me and pointed across the river to where a group of people stood: women, children, warriors, and an elderly woman walking with a cane in front of them. Recognition jumped in my spirit, even though I had never seen her.

"Your spirit knows her, Jonathan. Her name is Sarah, and she is your grandmother."

I could not believe it. I had been an orphan all my life. I did not ever remember my parents. How could this be?

"They have long prayed for a leader to come. You are that leader. Your destiny is to prepare the way for the Light to enter the land, not only this land but Halom and Hedone as well."

I thought of Lillian. Yes, now I would return and save her.

"You searched so hard for the Light and found it because Sarah constantly prayed that her children, anyone alive from her family, would find the Light. You see, her prayers are the real reason that you are here."

He then looked at each of us, Patrick, who leaned heavily on the scout Peter and Heather standing nearby. The four of us had traveled for weeks to reach this place. We had grown in the faith together, bonded together in true friendship. We depended on each other, and we finally made it. Our way was open to a new life, a new destiny, and a new mission.

Malak stepped up to Patrick, who stood straighter before him, although weak.

"I remember you now, Malak," he whispered. "You were with me when my father beat me, when he abused my mother when he finally killed her."

"Yes."

"I was to be the Apostolos Or, but I walked away from you. I scorned everything related to my father."

"Yes, I was there to lead you to the Light but could not force you. Patrick, that is behind you now. You have done your duty. The Apostolos Or has been found, and the way has been open. You have fought your battle well. You are truly a brave warrior."

Malak clasped Patrick's one good hand in his and then stepped back and saluted the captain.

"Jonathan, we must get Patrick across. We must get him help," Heather pleaded.

"Place him on my horse," the Knight of Soteria called Nathaniel offered.

"No, I will walk across the portal," the captain spoke.

He was very weak from loss of blood, and I suddenly knew with great pain in my heart that his time was near. He had led us through the wilderness. He had taught me how to fight with the sword and command the horse I feared. He instructed me on how to overcome my fears and how to lead men by his example. He had believed in me when I did not believe in myself. He had pulled me from the fire and given up his safety at the crossing by turning back when Heather and I had fallen. And now he stood before me, leaning against his old friend, his life slowly draining from him.

"But Patrick," I pleaded. "You are weak. Let the horse take you across. Maybe the people in the village can help you."

Patrick held his hand, took mine, and looked deep into my eyes, "I have fought my last battle, Jonathan. All is well with my soul. I have overcome. When I accepted the Light, my Lord showed me the crossing. He reminded me of my calling and told me that I was to lead you to the crossing where you would face the strongman. My life has not been in vain because you are the true Apostolos Or. You have won freedom for the fugitives. Carry on with your mission. Mine is complete. I cross over the river to a new realm." He smiled at me, then, through his pain.

"Take my broadsword, Jonathan. You have earned the chance to wield it. It belonged to my father. I used it for evil until these past few weeks. Now, you use it to free the people. I leave this with you." He smiled as he handed me the sword, "I think you can handle a true man's weapon now, just maybe."

He turned to Peter. "Help me across," he ordered, and the two knights of Kratos, now knights of Christendom, walked through the portal, leaving Heather and me standing on the sandy shore.

A few moments later, the captain slumped over, and his friend carried him to the opposite shore. We followed behind as the portal closed at our passing.

Sadness welled up within me, but then I realized that he was going to another realm, and one day, we would travel there as well, to a place where the battles of life would be no more. I had a destiny that pulled me forward.

"I AM THE LIGHT OF THE WORLD. SPREAD THE LIGHT AND WATCH THE CHAINS OF DEATH FALL AWAY AND THE SOULS OF SHADOW REALM ENTER INTO A NEW LIFE."

I took Heather's hand, thinking of Lillian. Her time would come, and I would also lead her across the river. This I knew. We walked across the portal and to the opposite shore. Peter placed Patrick down by a tree as the villagers gathered around them. I watched as a brilliant flash of light covered the captain's body, and he vanished into the next realm, into the presence of the Lord, the Savior of men's souls.

We continued across the portal, the two Bene Elohim at our side as the villagers waited. The elderly woman dropped to her knees at the water's edge in prayer as I approached her. I was beaten and bloody, but I had never felt stronger in my life. I knew now that I was indeed the Apostolos Or.

I had begun this journey searching for the truth. I had finally found it.

Made in the USA
Columbia, SC
23 September 2024